On the Road Again

The Society of Women Writers WA

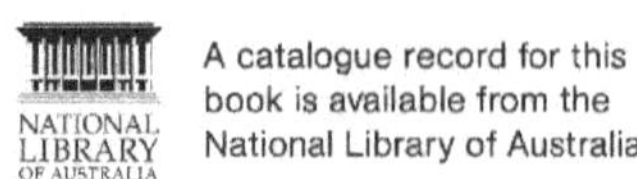

ISBN-13: 978-1-923174-20-7

Linellen Press
265 Boomerang Road
Oldbury, Western Australia
www.linellenpress.com.au

Dedication

In memory of our Patron,
Ruth Reid AM, CitWA.

Acknowledgments

The Society of Women Writers WA would like to acknowledge the following members for their collective efforts in bringing members' writing to publication: the Selection panel – Jan Altmann, Helen Iles, Sue Colyer, and Shirley Rowland – the anthology Receiving Officer and book and cover designer Helen Iles, and proofreader Maria Bonar. We thank each of you for bringing *On the Road Again* to fruition.

Contents

Saint Michael's Cave

The Rock of Gibraltar is more like a mountain than a rock, but there must be rock somewhere inside because it is still standing after millions of years of being pounded by enormous seas and gale-force winds. Over three hundred metres high it guards the only entrance to the Mediterranean Sea from the Atlantic Ocean. It is British but is within plain sight of Spain, and not too far from Morocco.

Legend claims that it is one of the two Pillars of Hercules; the other is in northern Africa. These were created when Hercules broke in half the mountain that connected Africa and Europe and created what is now the Strait of Gibraltar. It was also presumed by the ancient Greeks that the huge cave near the summit was an entrance to Hades. The name derives from the Spanish equivalent of a Moorish military commander who invaded it in the eighth century.

Our bus slowly and noisily laboured its way up a long, steep, winding road perilously close to the edge of a precipice. Several passengers felt the effects of vertigo and hid their faces behind their hands, or behind the seats in front of them. On stepping out of the bus into the sunlight we found ourselves confronted by a woodland where monkeys chattered and swung from the trees. They demanded food, but the guide told us that feeding them was strictly prohibited by local laws. He also explained that the wire mesh containing them was there for a good reason. They were not friendly towards humans. Besides humans, these Barbary macaques are the only free-living primates in Europe. The name refers to the Barbary Coast of Northwest Africa, from whence they came. Another legend suggests that beneath the enormous cave at the summit of the rock is an underground tunnel, some 24 kilometres long, through which they arrived.

So human-like are these monkeys that Galen, a Greco/Roman physician from the second century AD dissected one, presuming its internal structure to be the same as that of a human. He was not far wrong. We now know that we share about 95% of our DNA with such primates. We also have some residual DNA from our Neanderthal forbears, who inhabited Gibraltar around 50,000 years ago. It appears that the caves continued to be used by homo sapiens well after that. Stone tools, ancient hearths and animal bones dating back 40,000 years have been found in deposits left in some of the caves.

In geological terms, St Michaeel's cave was formed by rainwater slowly seeping and dripping, like thoughts from another world, through limestone rock and turning into a weak carbonic acid, which over thousands of years dissolved the rock. By this process, tiny cracks in The Rock's geological fault grew into long passages and large caverns. A veritable forest of stalactites and stalagmites were formed by an accumulation of dissolved rock within the dripping water. An easy way to remember the difference between stalactites and stalagmites is that the 'tites' hang on tightly to the ceiling, and the 'mites' might one day reach up to the ceiling.

Geological terms, however, are not enough when it comes to describing these mysterious places. Naturally cold and dark, caves are full of strange and eerie presences, including fearsome cave bears. They were used in a variety of ways in the distant past, as these ancient tools and bones testify. They are places of darkness and danger, but also shelter and safety, as these ancient pre-humans found. As places of refuge and mystery caves were also used for spiritual ceremonies and burials. Thus, they were seen as having supernatural and religious powers.

The cave on Gibraltar is known as The Cathedral, or St Michael's Cave, since it is similar to a grotto in Italy where Saint Michael is said to have appeared. It is not surprising that we modern humans also experience both fear and fascination as well as spiritual visitations in such places, since we still carry traces of ancient DNA.

The word 'cave' comes from the Latin root "cavus" meaning "hollow." It names an absence, an empty space waiting to be filled with mysterious meanings. Caves were once consecrated to the gods and were often thought to contain an entry to the underworld, as St Michael's once was. To Homer, they were the pathways of the Immortals. They are, after all, an interior space, an opening in the earth, an inside world, so this is understandable.

To enter a cave is to meet our Jungian shadow side: our fears, those parts of ourselves that fear too much light, the dark places of the soul. This is probably why some people cannot bring themselves to enter. To enter a cave is to enter another world, a world outside of normal time and space; but it is also to enter one's own inner world. It is like an inward spiral.

Caves are sometimes compared to cathedrals, and this one certainly felt like a cathedral, full of stained-glass windows and a thousand glowing candles. The floor took on the appearance of a blue lake with red and gold water cascading into it. A sense of total immersion seemed to bring together a world beyond and a world within. Perhaps, as the ancient peoples believed, caves are a portal to some higher reality, a journey from darkness to light. They offer an escape from reality, but by excluding the outside world of reality they encourage us to explore inner realities. Barriers are broken down, and the inside world becomes available. Daylight recedes, but in this case, it is replaced by otherworldly light. The cave becomes a world between worlds, a place where darkness turns into celestial light.

Like Alladin's cave, the cave of Saint Michael is a magical place, but we did not require a magic lamp to enter it. Aladdin's Cave was full of gold, silver, and jewel-bearing trees; and so is Saint Michael's. The outside light was suddenly replaced by otherworldly lights of blue, red, gold and green. They streamed and poured from the ceiling like coloured rain. The walls sparkled like crystalised Christmas trees. The stalactites and stalagmites glittered and glistened as we were immersed in this 'otherness'. It was a new reality – a reality somewhere beyond time and space – a reality between the physical and spiritual worlds – a reality that could be described as cosmic. We stood on solid rock but, for a few moments, the coloured rain became a torrent, the rock turned to water, and I floated in a world of pure light and colour.

There are no dimensions in a cave. The surrounding space is all around and constantly shifting. The height of the ceiling and the distance between the walls is not set. It holds a different reality where everything is possible and everyday reality can slip away. In the cave of the nymphs in Homer's Odyssey, there are two entrances: one for descending and one for ascending. There is a world above and one below – one past and one future.

Keats thought that we all need some time in a cave. Inside a cave, nothing is quite real. Everything is possible, but at the same time, the experience cannot last. Maybe this is just because the right words for that experience do not seem to exist. They remain somewhere in the limestone grooves and the coloured crystals because they do not want to enter human consciousness. Maybe the constant dripping of water in and through the rock and the magic of the crystals keep them alive. Plato suggested that the cave is the way to the ultimate reality, but then T.S. Eliot is also correct when he states that 'humankind cannot bear very much reality'.

Jan Altmann

St Michael's Cave

The Silk Road

The wake-up call came at 4:00 a.m. It was still dark. From our hotel at the resort of Sharm El Sheikh on The Red Sea in Egypt, we had to take a short flight into Jordan. From a small airport near Petra, we were taken to meet the guide who would walk us through a hot, dusty gorge to see the magnificent sights of Petra's architecture and to tell us something of its history.

The ruins of Petra, date back to 9,000 B.C. They are stunning to look at, and they provide extensive insights into the lives of the many peoples who have lived there. It was a long walk; the stone cliffs on both sides were imposing and rose to great heights. In these pink- and purple-coloured walls, also at considerable heights, were hollowed-out caves where people once lived. Modern-day tourists can only gaze in wonder at the strength and ingenuity of the people who built this city of stone.

Weary tourists were offered 'taxi rides' on the backs of colourfully adorned camels. These lumbering 'ships of the desert' with plenty of 'attitude' were dressed up in tassels and colourful saddles that looked like richly woven Persian carpets. Their drivers were mostly members of nearby Bedouin tribes. The Bedouins have been nomadic, desert people for several thousand years, and their camels are so highly valued that they are often considered a 'gift from God'.

The population of Petra was once so large that in the fourth century B.C. it became the capital city of the Kingdom of Nabataea. Under Nabataean rule, Petra prospered and became a centre of the spice trade that involved such far-flung realms as

China, Egypt, Greece, and India. With this prosperity, the city's population flourished and reached an estimated 30,000.

As well as showing the history of the local people, the ruins of Petra also highlight the pervasive influence of Greek architecture in ancient times. The city was built on a terrace, traversed from east to west by the Wadi Musa (the Valley of Moses). It is one of the places where, according to tradition, the Israelite leader Moses struck a rock and water gushed forth. The valley is enclosed by sandstone cliffs veined with shades of red and purple varying to pale yellow, and for this reason, Petra was called by the 19th-century English biblical scholar John William Burgon a "rose-red city half as old as Time."

Empires by the Nabatean Arabs, the architecture of Petra, as well as other cities in the region, often reflected the work of Greek architects. In fact, the name of the ancient city itself is the word for 'stone' in Greek. Its stunning Corinthian-styled columns create a dramatic entrance to the main building which is the tomb of one of its kings. It is frequently referred to as The Treasury because of the riches that it once housed. It is still thought by some to contain hidden treasurers.

The huge buildings and sculptures were made from carving directly into the rock face. The main building is two stories high with three portals and six columns on each level. The columns are surmounted by intricately carved Corinthian capitols. There is also a huge crypt underneath. It is the only building known to have been constructed from the top down. There are still slots and cavities in the surrounding stone which would have supported the scaffolding needed for the architects and artisans to carve out these features.

In a desert landscape where rainfall is unreliable, and water is precious, the Nabateans developed ingenious methods of dealing with this problem. The gorge in which Petra is situated afforded a natural watercourse to capture the rainwater from the sometimes-torrential storms that did occur. This water was stored in vast underground cisterns, and it provided enough for daily living and even for a few gardens to flourish.

The Nabataeans worshipped Arabic gods and goddesses during pre-Islamic times and also deified several of their kings, all of whom are among the figures carved into the rocks. Their chief god was Habul, the Syrian god of the moon. There were also several powerful female deities including the 'mighty' Allat, the goddess of fertility. There must also have been a knowledge of other religions of the time, as indicated by the Moses story and by the Greek-styled architecture.

Petra

Petra gained its prosperity and prestige from being an important trading centre on The Silk Road. Established when the Han Dynasty in China officially opened trade with the West in 130 B.C., the Silk Road routes remained in use until A.D. 1453, when the Ottoman Empire boycotted trade with China and closed them. The name is derived from the highly lucrative trade in the silk textiles that were produced almost exclusively in China.

It started in Shanghai on the east coast of China and travelled all the way across China, Mongolia, Persia, and India. It crossed mountains, deserts and the steppes of Central Asia and continued on to the Mediterranean. It ended in Venice on the east coast of Italy bordered by the Adriatic Sea. Islamic and Byzantine architecture can still be seen in Venice today.

There were Silk Road routes, not one single road. Many side roads branched off, travelling southwards down into India and up into what is now Germany. Some routes were not roads at all, but sea voyages crossing the Caspian and the Mediterranean Seas. There were also many trading centres along the way.

The Silk Road played a significant role in the exchange of goods, ideas, and cultures between the East and the West. It was a vital link between civilisations, and it helped to shape the world we live in today. In fact, The Silk Road is probably the first widespread example of trading in luxury goods. It was possible to buy and sell not just silk, but also spices, porcelain, jewellery (especially silver) and perfumes. Consumer culture was beginning its long and prosperous history. In a short time, Chinese silk became sought-after in Rome, Egypt, and Greece. Other lucrative commodities from the East included tea, dyes, perfumes, and porcelain. Honey, wine and gold, as well as paper and gunpowder, also became popular and probably altered the trajectory of world history.

When the Nabataeans were defeated by the Romans in 106 CE, Petra became part of the Roman province of Arabia but continued to flourish until changing trade routes caused its gradual decline. After an earthquake damaged the city in 551, significant habitation seems to have ceased. The Islamic invasion occurred in the 7th century, and a Crusader outpost is evidence of activity there in the 12th century. After the Crusades, the city was unknown to the Western world until it was rediscovered by a Swiss traveller in 1812.

The journey along the Silk Road was a long and arduous one. There were harsh deserts and rugged mountain ranges to cross. Along the route, there were many dangers. Bandits, sandstorms, and extreme temperatures were just a few of the hazards that the caravans had to face. Camels were perfectly suited to the task of transporting goods across these harsh terrains. The caravans were made up of many camels, each carrying a heavy load of goods. The journey could take months, and the caravan would stop at various points along the way to rest and resupply. Camels played a crucial role in moving goods and people across these vast distances.

Despite the dangers, the trade along the Silk Road was incredibly profitable. The merchants who braved the journey were able to make a great deal of money from the sale of their goods.

One of the best-known Westerners to make this journey was Marco Polo, a Venetian merchant explorer and adventurer who wrote about his travels along the Silk Road between 1271 and 1295. In 1271, aged just 17, Marco accompanied his father and uncle on what was the elder men's second journey to East Asia, visiting the court of the Mongol leader Kublai Khan in China. Kublai Khan was the grandson of Genghis Khan, and he ruled what was then the largest empire on earth from the city now known as Beijing. Marco met the great Khan and having learnt the local language, must have made quite an impression because he was appointed a permanent and roving envoy in the Mongol Ruler's service from 1275 to 1292. The Polos eventually returned home to Venice in 1295 and Marco served Venice as a sea captain in its war with Genoa. He was wounded and captured by the Genoese but was eventually released and returned to Venice where he married and had three daughters. On his deathbed in 1324 he claimed that he had not described even half of the wonders he had seen.

Part of the Silk Road still exists as a paved highway connecting Pakistan and parts of China. The old road has given inspiration for a plan for a trans-Asian highway, and a railway counterpart of the road has been proposed by the UN Economic and Social Commission for Asia and the Pacific. Trade between countries on its route is still strong, but trucks and trains will not replace the magic and the colour of the former traders, their camels and their and their goods. Whenever I wear my wrap made from camel wool I think of my trip to Petra and the noble beasts who made human habitation in the desert a possibility.

Jan Altmann

Payment for Services Rendered

Julia was an excellent travel agent.

She gave her customers a travel plan that gave them adventures, fun, romance and memories.

Her office was filled with letters of gratitude and gifts from places around the world. Her colleagues sought her advice and her expertise. She worked tirelessly for her customers; often well into the night, so she had no qualms about the extra amounts of money she made from them.

She had learnt, over the years, where she could add a slight increase in costs, which the happy customers readily paid, and that she paid into a separate bank account. *Her* bank account. It wasn't much but it was what she thought she was worth. The company she had worked with for twenty years had begrudgingly increased her salary, but only when following Union Rules. They had never sent her on the 'find out all about it' expeditions that they sent the new, young, and pretty staff members to, all expenses paid by the Cruise Lines or the Adventure Tours. No, she stayed behind while staff members were on one junket after another, but she gave the customers exactly what they wanted. She enabled them to create memories, and they were grateful for it. Their cards and letters told her so. She made sure they were grateful, and that gratitude went into her bank account. Indeed, over the years, it had swelled to a considerable sum.

At fifty-four, she was about to spend it. All of it. She had started with a target amount of money to achieve and she had realised that target. So now she set about booking her leave, her well-earned holidays, and along with that she booked her trip.

She was going around the world on the *Three Queens*, the Cruise Liners named after the British Royal Family. She would be away for six months so that would mean she'd be expected back somewhere before Christmas. But, of course, she wasn't coming back.

No, she planned on finding a country she would enjoy living in, one without an extradition policy because, after all this hard work– twenty years of it – she certainly wasn't about to retire to a prison cell.

Oh, the pleasure she had when the tickets came through. The staff had asked her where she was going for six months since she'd never taken more than two weeks' holiday at a time before. So, she invented an old grandmother living in, oh where was it now, oh Ireland, and how she was going to see her through until the end. Staff were touched by her selflessness; they commented on how it was so like her … so generous of her.

They were even planning on a send-off afternoon tea, with cake and all the trimmings. She thought she'd like that; even felt she deserved it for all the times she'd rescued the newer staff from their gaffs and bungles. Trusty Julia, they had called her. Now it was her turn to smile at the inappropriateness of the name they'd given her.

Her last day at work came and went, and she took the bus home weighed down with flowers and cake. She opened the door to her small, cramped apartment. The sight of the two suitcases filled with new clothes standing waiting for her in the hallway almost took her breath away. In fact, it *did* take her breath away as she closed the front door. She clutched her chest. The pain was so intense that her eyes grew like saucers.

In her anxiety, she couldn't find the handbag she had dropped. She needed to get the phone out. She had an emergency App on her phone, but before she could get to her bag to retrieve her phone, her legs gave way and she fell.

No one would have opened her flat for six months were it not for the peculiar odour coming from it. The police were called and, when they pushed open the front door, they found two new suitcases and one woman on the passageway floor. Near her body was a handbag filled with a swag of holiday tickets, credit and debit cards, alongside a small fortune in cash, all tidily held together with rubber bands.

As one constable said to the other, holding a mask over his face, "She was about to have the holiday of a lifetime, wasn't she!"

Lynley Barnett

The Power of Travel

I have often contemplated the power of travel: what it does to those the traveller moves amongst; what changes it makes to the traveller themselves, some changes profound, some just temporary.

Initially, the traveller prepares for the journey. There is the fun, the excitement, the creating of plans, the emergency measures taken; the home safety to be remembered. There is the weather, the seasons, the must-take-with-me items, the in-case articles, the preventative medicines, and the current medications. And then there is the paperwork: passports, visas, permissions to go here or there. And don't forget the headscarf that will be needed in many countries. There are so many customs to be aware of, and all of this before the traveller has even left his or her hometown. So, packed and ready, with all contingency plans made, the traveller sets off.

The journey is half the fun, or half the trouble if the seats are cramped and the room to move decidedly too small. And the meals that are served … are they great or eaten because there is nothing else? Still, the excitement carries the day. You, the traveller, are going somewhere.

Imagine if it is somewhere you have never been before. The images you create in your mind. You may have read plenty about this country or this town, but the reality will never match your expectations. There is always something different. The pictures do not do it justice, or the pictures must have been taken on a fine day when the town was at its best, and that must have been a long time ago.

Disappointed? No, not really, even when it does not live up to expectations, it is still the thrill of seeing it as it really is. And then there are the people. This is what you will always remember. The people. Those whom you meet, those who share their stories with you, those who help you when you are lost or just need somewhere to eat, and they take you to a place where the food is memorable. How they live their lives, so different to yours, so interesting. The homes they live in. Not like back in your town or city. And if you are lucky enough to be invited into one such home, how you are in awe of the different way they live. Perhaps you have heard the stories about their lifestyle, but now you are seeing it. And you marvel at it. And you visit a school for little ones and they sing for you. Why? Because they want you to enjoy being in their country; they want to show you that they are so proud of it. And you leave feeling like you have been given a gift.

Then there is the gift given to you by a gesture – someone pays for your bus fare because you didn't know you had to buy a token to get on the bus. You only had money. Or the invitation to sit on their rug as they watched the outdoor concert you found by following the sound of music. And they want to share their picnic with you, people they have never met before. The kindness of strangers.

The openness of the big, burly stranger who invites you to his mansion because he loves the country you come from. The invitation is open-ended; whenever you can come, he will make you welcome.

You wonder if the heart-full feeling you have can get any better. And it does. A whole busload of people look for you because you got lost in the maze of streets in the town until someone spots you going endlessly up and down the foreign streets, unable to get your bearings. Do they mind that you have made them late? No. They are just happy they found you. And you are profoundly grateful that they did.

Then there are those who direct you to a small and beautiful shop or a place right off the beaten track where you will see something different – something they know you will like, a painting on a wall in a café, or a church with exquisite windows. And all of this is travel.

Then there are the little fireplaces that warm your legs while you drink a hot chocolate on a cold day, mittens around a steaming mugful. And it's just to die for. And while everyone else is doing the same thing you get included in a total stranger's conversation – they recognised the traveller in you.

You go into the tiny but exquisite dress shop with a window at the front and a door behind which the owner sews her Haute Couture clothing. You wish you could stay long enough to order some of her wares. Nothing like this exists in your hometown. But she willingly shows you clothes, even though you have interrupted her day. You know she has enjoyed the break. Her smile tells you; it is as large as a mother with a new baby.

You visit religious churches and buildings and they are all works of art in themselves. The religion they practice may be the same as your own, or wildly different, but the glorious buildings they use for their religious celebrations are awe-inspiring. And these are memories that you will keep forever. The site where the Mother of God was reported to have visited three children is the most peaceful place in the entire world. That, you do not have back home.

And then, as you cross an open square, you see a small hand begging. The child is no more than four years of age. So you buy her the most nourishing sandwich in the square and her little eyes light up with pleasure as she has breakfast. And you know she has to take money home, so you put something in her pocket for Mum or Dad. You have to accept that this is their life, you cannot change that any more than you could change the group of people you see living under the shelter of an overhead bridge. But you acknowledge that this is something you also see back home. So, in this way, some countries are similar, their governments are also slow to act on helping their homeless.

And, just as suddenly, you begin to understand. These people teach you. They have their sadnesses, their stories, their families, their differences; similar to what you might encounter back home. But they also live in a different environment which you experience with a degree of awe, and they have a culture to show you that changes your thinking and expands your knowledge.

And you realise that this is travel. Finding the things about others that you share in common and learning about the aspects of living that you do not share. And you are left with the wonder of how much you do not know, and how you could travel for years learning a little more with each trip. And you wish for the time in years to accomplish this.

Lynley Barnett

The Traveller

It had always been a dream of hers, to travel.

Oh, to visit distant places, to see different people, to try their food, to see their customs, and to engage with people she had only ever read about. Her eyes lit up with the joy her thoughts brought her.

She smiled at her fantasies of the Himalayas and the people who lived in Nepal. Not rich or wealthy like so many Western countries, but who seemed to be so rich in their culture and their people. How they worked so hard and made so much of the little they had. Weather-beaten skins and faces that never told their age, their lives centred around their families.

Her thoughts floated to other family-oriented countries. She thought of the people who lived on islands in the Pacific and how they were always portrayed as happy people. They loved their food and their rugby, and they seemed to create festivities for all sorts of reasons.

If the crops grew well, or a beautiful baby was born, they celebrated. How they enjoyed themselves, the fun they created. She knew of the Fijian's love of singing and how their churches rang out with religious songs.

She also knew that their culture was patriarchal. Property was passed down through the men in the family. As she thought about that, she wondered how many other cultures were like that. She knew that the Polynesians loved their food and their ovens in the ground. But she wasn't sure that they used many spices, and she wondered why. Did their countries not grow spices?

And her mind slipped into thinking about the countries that

did use spices in their food. Indian cultures, their love of spice, the aromas they could create when cooking. She could almost smell the hot curries she had tried in the past. Indeed, she had tasted many a curry from the Curry House in her small town.

But she had never been to India, nor would she ever go to the Pacific, nor would she ever watch a game of rugby again.

She had wanted to feel snow too; well, you can't play Rugby in the snow, can you? But just once, she would have liked to watch the snowdrops fall, to watch the snow mount up until you could make snowballs and engage in playfulness with children and adults while making a snowman. She chuckled as she thought of the carrot they always used for the snowman's nose, then sighed – she had never decorated a snowman.

That was never going to be a possibility for her.

She lay in her bed and let her mind wander like a magic carpet from country to country. She often opened her large Atlas and spent hours imagining what it would be like to ask to go to another country and actually be taken there!

To be immersed in their activities, to try their food and to wear their clothes. Her mind's eye saw the photos of the gold jewellery that the Jewellers' shops displayed in some of the Asian countries. So beautiful. But then her face clouded over, not for her an arm full of golden bracelets, or the glorious golden hooped earrings.

But she brightened as she thought how wonderful it must be to be driven across the desert, watching a sunset over hills of sand, then to crowd into a tent and sit cross-legged while sharing food with your fellow travellers. Now that would be her idea of heaven. She would learn, she really would, how to scoop up food with the flatbreads they served, no knives and forks, just clever use of the breads they made. She longed to touch the silks the women wore and to find how they kept them all in place while they worked. She often thought she would be hopeless at that;

the silk would just slither off her, she felt sure of it.

Her mind darted here and there. She wondered what it would be like to sit in a Paris coffee shop while having her breakfast and be so Parisian reading the newspapers while she drank her coffee so slowly. And then she thought, *but I can't even speak French, let alone read it.* And the ghost of a smile played across her face.

She had read quite a lot of history over the years and could be quite creative when she thought of the Roman days, the Roman people, although she imagined that they were now very like the Parisians, beautifully dressed, with exquisite bags and accessories. She liked their food, the pastas and the meatballs, but she knew nothing in the world compared with French cooking.

The sauces, the meats, the flavours. Oh, how magical it would be to sit in a Michelin Restaurant and just order whatever took your fancy. To have a chef who would cook everything just the way you liked it. And serve it to you himself. Why were chefs always men? Now she knew that, in today's world, that wasn't so any more, but she was kind of stuck in yesteryear thinking. Her imagination always conjured up male chefs. *Oh, girl,* she said to herself, *you are showing your age.*

She lay for a little while, her mind almost empty. She had travelled far and wide today; she had used her imagination to its limit, even without the Atlas or her library of history books for help.

And so, she let her mind see the sea, and the small boat that took her out onto the calm waters and let her drift. She had the blue sky for company, and the stillness only broken by the gentle lap-lap of the water against the hull of the boat. She snuggled into her pillows and let the imagined sun's rays warm her as she closed her eyes.

Today was a beautiful day. She had travelled all around the globe, created lovely thoughts, seen caring people, and watched customs that made her smile, and now she was tired.

She let sleep take her as the nursing staff by her bedside tucked her blankets in and quietly tiptoed out of her hospital room to leave her to take her rest.

Lynley Barnett

Early Years

I was born and raised in northern climes
dark wintry days, long summer nights
post-war fifties fashions, dull grey, brown
bomb-damaged buildings like crooked teeth

remnant blackout curtains behind the door
gas lighting, coal fires, old ration books
an overcrowded Glasgow tenement with
four kids to a bed, top to tail, never lonely

Saturday matinees, Roy Rogers & Trigger
teddy boys strut in crepe-soled shoes
Rock Around the Clock, jive
Little Richard & Elvis, skiffle groups

housing schemes birthed
tenements demolished
vertical villages   disrupted

swinging sixties, a burst of psychedelic colour
Mary Quant's miniskirts & PVC coats
Beatles, Rolling Stones, mods & rockers
Lulu, Cilla & Dusty Springfield eyes

if you're goin' to San Francisco
be sure to wear some flowers in your hair
hippies, smoke, Bacardi and coke
the answer was blowin' in the wind

what was the question?

Maria Bonar

Eastfield, Cumbernauld

we visit my sister's grave
I wish she could see
her daughters today
the flowers of her life
in full bloom

in the nearby meadow
a pollen-laden bumblebee
blunders past my ear
lands on the tallest thistle
silhouetted against the blue sky

my nieces lead me uphill to see
Arria, steel mermaid rising
arms outstretched
from her fingertips, twin arcs
of water flowing, merging as one

ten metres high
a shining colossus
dominating the landscape
the *Angel of the Nauld*
rising from the past into the future

Maria Bonar

Heavenly

galactic rose
gravitational pull
opposites attract

heart nebula
swooping wings
cupid's arrow lands

necklace nebula
string of diamonds
Lucy in the sky

jewel box
cluster of gems
wedding banns

rosette nebula
stellar nursery
starbursts

Maria Bonar

Kinross

At dawn the stag appears on
the misty hill near Loch Leven
I watch silently from my
window until he bolts

I fancy I hear the prayers
of a captive queen
echoing down the years from
the ruined castle on the loch

later, I wander through
the lavender fields
amethyst gems
sparking with raindrops

their fragrance holds the
memory of summer days
bumblebees and soft-scented
sheets birling in the breeze

Maria Bonar

Memories

When we were young
five of us hitchhiked
to Loch Lomond
one rainy weekend

three dressed fashionably
fringed skirts dripping
denim jackets soaked
they went home next day

you and I carried on in our
hooded anoraks and boots
tramping country lanes
found a tiny youth hostel

Inverbeg, on the hilltop
overlooking the loch
elderly caretaker couple
like grandparents

wood stove, kettle on the hob
long haired guitarist,
nightly singalong
answers blowing in the wind

a glorious time
until the money ran out
only an apple each and
wedge of cheese left

were lucky enough
that day, to hitch a ride
all the way home
in a chauffeured Rolls Royce

later, we crossed the world together
before taking separate paths
new brides, new cities
you in Malawi, me in Melbourne

fifty years have passed
fat airmail letters
emails, rare visits
over many miles and many moves

now you rise in the night
wander by the Loch, your
tired husband takes your hand
walks with you in the dark

you forget names, people, the past
remnant memories no longer
include your children
too many words lost in the mist.

Maria Bonar

Prehistoric

Rock art adorns the caves
of Altamira and Lascaux
drawn with ochres
red and brown and black

fleeing from the lethal arrows
of the hunter's supple bow
horses, bison, reindeer, boar,
outrun the fierce attack

created in the firelight's
dancing yellow glow
species long extinct survive
forever in the dark.

Maria Bonar

Siberia

The wolf limps over the frosty
ground beneath the silver birches
once proud leader, now dying
vanquished from the pack
the unfamiliar scent of coffee
halts him.

The shepherd steps from
the shadows
rifle pointed at his old enemy
hesitates, reappraising the
bloodied remnant of his
wily and elusive foe.

He shoots in pity, not victory
drags the carcass to the barn
a legacy of the wild
the meat for his sheepdogs
the pelt to make fine
winter caps for his sons.

Maria Bonar

The Anthropocene 2084

after painting Number 1 by Jackson Pollock, 1949

Those fertile fields are gone
as the planet warms and fails
drought and withered stalks
dead snails, sand, ash, grit

she kneels upon the arid field
seeks signs of emerging life
no seedlings sprouting green
remnants of a dessicated frog

faded sun-moth wings with
traces of orange-bronze glory
windblown shell of a fragile egg
scattered yellow breasted feathers

her memories of the slow
flowing river, the golden crop
flash in her inner eye, like
Wordsworth's dancing daffodils

hidden in an ancient cave
at the far end of the station
her remaining sheep
a dwindling store of hay

a struggling vegetable patch
close to the back door
canned and bottled bounty
preserved in the pantry

her rainwater tank empty these
long months. Rank bore water
from deep in the dusty earth
her family's only salvation.

https://www.moca.org/collection/work/number-1

Maria Bonar

No More Trips

Trip 1.

It should have been a routine trip to the vet for a scale and polish. George had started howling his head off in the car, as usual. He knew exactly where we were going and was protesting unreservedly. You feel like the biggest bitch.

We arrive at the vet's. George doesn't want to get out of the car. He glues himself to the seat and gains twenty-five kilos when you try and lift him. There's undeniable fear in his eyes as you carry him through the door. He is scared rigid and therefore manages to poo all over the vet's floor. He's trembling and trying to escape, trampling poo everywhere. A reassuring cuddle will have to wait.

It's going to be a bitch to clean.

Trip 2.

You receive an unexpected phone call. The vet needs to see you before George's anaesthesia wears off. The receptionist cannot confirm why, so your mind becomes bombarded with every kind of worst scenario. One of these scenarios turns out to be correct. They have found a highly suspicious tonsil tumour whilst cleaning his teeth.

You're trembling, barely able to think or focus. Tears and snot are dripping down your face and your throat is threatening to close shut.

Do you not wake him up? It would be kinder, wouldn't it?

After a million questions peppered repeatedly, the vet is completely non-committal.

Momentarily, you want to hold him by his shirt collar and scream 'Tell me what to do!'

With no clear or easy answer, you elect to have the lump removed.

For the first time, you don't feel like the biggest bitch.

Trip 3.

You get a call to say that George has come through his operation. Next day, another call to pick him up. You arrive there and listen to him bark for nearly two hours while every dog and owner get seen before you. The temptation to rip him out of his cage is overwhelming. You want to be a rescue squad bitch.

They finally bring him out of captivity. He is so excited. Despite looking damningly at you, his tail is wagging wildly and appreciatively.

You take him home. Hand-feed him sardines. Scratch his ears. Overindulge him in home comforts.

There is life in this old dog yet.

Erica Bowman

Dedicated to gorgeous George and all who loved him.

A Morning Walk in Chang Mai

A Haibun

I walk through twisted streets interrupted by ancient monuments once revered in humility, now surrounded by foreign tourists who can't get enough of borrowed nostalgia.

In quiet moments
The past reveals itself authentic.
Beauty in old bricks.

Coloured umbrellas shade the travellers from the harshness of afternoon sun. Refreshed by cool drinks sold alongside souvenir reminders of a brief encounter with a reincarnated religion. Snapshots taken will assuage any guilt when Buddha's portrait is hung as a holiday reminder.

Prayers are offered
Candles burned illuminate
Mortal sins of disregard.

I offer my own silent prayer of thankfulness for a simple life.

Aileen Boyer

Between the lines

A trick of light
A flicker of eye
A quick escape
Between the lines
Another world
Another life
Another journey
Read the signs
Take a left
Take a right
Take a turn
See what shines
Quick return before shadow fall
Quick recap, a thought recall
Quick, quick, get it all!
A story born. No guidelines,
Just a quick escape to naught
Brought together all it brought
And the moral of this errant tale
Is that writing always will prevail.

Aileen Boyer

Doorway to Elsewhere

Hummingbird, hummingbird,
Sitting on the fence,
Will I or won't I
Be put to the test?
Options fly free
Above sea and shore
And I sit and ponder
Because I want more.
Will I remain here
In no time or space
And through the doorway to elsewhere
Find my own grace
Or as planes fly over
And boats sail on
Will I try join them
Find another home?
The grass is always greener
On the other side
But the sea no longer echoes
The incoming tide.

The doorway to elsewhere
Will always remain
An outlet for dreaming
Whilst I am contained
Here on the fence
In no time or space
And through the doorway to elsewhere
I will seek my own grace.

Aileen Boyer

Finding Leonard Cohen

In the lost bookshop in Chiang Mai
I found Leonard Cohen
Perched on a shelf, between Plath and Hughes, his Book of Longing calling to me
"Consider your dreams before it is too late. Storing regrets is a pointless objective. They become so heavy they silence you. So sing instead. Sing like a nightingale. Sing like you mean it and I will dance you to the end of love."

Aileen Boyer

It's a Start

Mount Agung hides behind a misty stratus.

After hundreds of years of watching over the island in quiet sleep, I take note of what Mr Google says: It came alive in 1843, shocking and surprising the inhabitants of Bali with angry eruptions throughout the years until 2019.

I'm sitting on the beach at Nusa Dua, being served lychee iced tea, my new favourite drink, and soaking in the sun.

After more than two years of COVID isolation from the rest of the world, I feel alive and free. However, I am reminded that things have changed. Hotel staff and a few tourists are still wearing masks, like stage players or shadow puppets in a modern version of Wayang topeng theatre. Agung, hiding on the horizon, is also a reminder that nothing is stable.

It's a sobering thought that I quickly dismiss from my overactive brain and straying thoughts, taking a big sip of my tea to drown out the sour taste of the past.

Clouds are dissipating in the heat of the day and now I can see the peak of that ominous mountain, logging its presence into my consciousness.

My eyes are heavy, and I can feel myself drifting into a well-needed sleep after today's journey from Perth.

My friend Jo, from Sydney, will be joining me later this afternoon. I haven't seen Jo in person for over three years. COVID not only cut travel internationally but also domestically in Western Australia, keeping us safe but confined in Fortress WA.

It's ironic that now borders have opened, and COVID is rife in WA, but here in Bali, there are only a handful of cases, so it's safer to meet up here than at home.

I let myself relax, slipping into the land of nod. It's so good to feel this newfound release, this freedom. Back home, I was so wired, I could have easily erupted. This holiday is my lifesaver.

I see the clouds swirl around Agung through half-closed eyes. The sea seems to be swelling as the clouds gather and grow darker. I'm covered in sweat.

In my head, I picture the Tsunami warnings and evacuation plans that are scattered throughout the resort. I'm trying to remember the pathway I must take in an emergency.

The waves break loudly on the shore, crashing my thoughts and I'm sure I can hear shouting in the background. I panic, swallowing air as my throat constricts.

I feel a hand shake my upper arm. My eyes pop open in fright. I blink a few times, adjusting to the light as I gather my bearings. I look up and see Jo smiling at me.

It's going to be a while before I can truly relax again. I smile back at her. It's a start.

Aileen Boyer

West End

The Bayseeker Bus trundles the solitary road.
The island unfolds her naked beauty,
invites me to lay aside
my melancholic, winter-dampened soul,
allow her to heal my annual bout of sun-deprived woe.
Dare I accept her unconditional gift,
enter, wholeheartedly, her open hands
that beckon towards a new gradation?
To accept, I must let go and set adrift
familiar fear, risk the awesome unknown.

Perched, stone-like, I gaze on rolling scenes,
tempted to resist her bewitching smile that beguiles
the dismal gloom that clings and twines
steadfastly through my veins.
A doom, though fearful, has cast its spell,
woven a sheaf of plaited knots around my grief.

Confused, unsure, I reach West End.

My suppressed mutton bird soul
soars high above the limestone cliffs.
In sun-soaked sky, an eager eye
searches among cowering ice plants
as they shiver and shake and appreciate
the magic of this August day.

I survey the tranquil, ancient landscape
and, with quick precision,
choose where I will burrow and make my nest.

A languorous lizard slides silently in sleek abandon,
entices me, persuades me, to pause awhile.
Perhaps this is where my weary spirit will abide?
Weave a path through clumps of budding flora,
establish my claim to share this sacred place?

With each gentle rise of simmering sea
a dolphin rides an emerging wave.
Frolics, plays, dares to join in her carefree day.
I lean forward, ready to dive;
a gliding osprey catches my eye.
Once more my spiralling spirit reaches upward to the sky.

All too soon 'tis time to leave,
retrace my path, set face to home.
I sigh not. Confusion, doubt, gratefully spent.

As each lengthening stride
casts a shadow, separates me and my gliding osprey,
I pray a silent breath of thanks
for the brief time I flew and slithered and rode the waves.
Sure now my wounded spirit can survive
to re-emerge and soar and glide
with life's sonorous rhythm. Move on.

Helped by a new-found friend,
this healing place they call West End.

Elizabeth Brennan

April in Paris

On Monday, 4 April 1997, we were at London's Waterloo station, boarding the Eurostar for Paris. It was only a few days since we left Perth on April Fools' Day, an appropriate date for two grey nomads to head off, carrying backpacks, to spend five months exploring Europe and Great Britain.

We had a pleasant trip via the Chunnel, but the train moved too fast for us to see much of the French countryside. The weather in Paris was beautiful, and from our room, we had a view across a sea of rooftops to the Eiffel Tower in the distance.

The next day, after breakfasting on French bread, jam and coffee, we went to the Champs Elysees and walked up through the Tuileries Garden to the Louvre. There wasn't time to join the long queue waiting to go inside, but I had hopes of going back some other day. After a bus ride to the Chatelet, an old tower north of the Ile de la Cite, we bought *jambon et fromage* rolls for lunch and ate them in the gardens. In the afternoon, we caught a bus to the south of the Seine, where, finding a public phone, we rang the family back in Australia. No mobile phones back then. The next stop was the Eiffel Tower, but we weren't up to climbing it, just enjoyed the gardens, took photos and bought a luscious ice cream before wending our way home via bus and Metro.

On Wednesday, we went to Ile de la Cite to visit the famous Notre Dame Cathedral, where the stained glass of its enormous stone rose windows cast a rainbow of colour over the beautiful old carved panels inside. I am so glad it could be restored to its former glory after that catastrophic fire. From there we walked across to the left bank, where I was disappointed not to encounter anyone who looked like they were carrying on the area's bohemian art traditions. Perhaps we were in the wrong area. We walked for miles, stopping to photograph several impressive old buildings, including the Pantheon, ending up at the Luxembourg Gardens, where we enjoyed delicious cones of sorbet.

Paris would need at least a month's visit to do it justice. It certainly seemed to live up to its reputation as a beautiful and romantic city. Perhaps as a result of the Revolution and France's early republicanism, places that were originally royal palaces and gardens have been preserved as public areas. There are several long vistas of parkland stretching through the city, unlike London, where the historic sites seem to have been crowded out by modern commercial buildings. I was most impressed by the sculptures scattered throughout these spaces. Though much of it is nineteenth century, there are also many older works.

Paris seemed a much more 'user-friendly' city than London did at that time. Due to fear of IRA bombings, they had removed all the seats, even from the train stations. In St James Park in London there were a few public seats and chairs for hire. In Paris, seats were everywhere – and free. Perhaps we went to the wrong places in London, but I had the impression that Parisians make use of their extensive and beautiful gardens much more freely than Londoners do theirs.

On Thursday, we went to St Denis' Basilica, where the old French kings are buried, then, to satisfy Rob's love of anything on rails, we caught the only tram in the inner metropolitan part of Paris to Bobigny, where, for some reason, I haven't been able to discover, the train station is named after Pablo Picasso.

Then it was back to our digs to pack and get an early night, as we had to be up by 5 a.m. the next morning to catch the train to

Bayeux, where I wanted to see the tapestry and Rob hoped to tour the WWII Normandy landing sites.

Lynne Cairns

Florence in May

We arrived in Florence on the first of May, just one month since we flew out of Perth to spend a few days in London before heading to Paris to start our European train journey odyssey. Four days were never going to be a long enough stay in that beautiful city, but with the rest of Europe, Ireland and the UK to see in just five months, we had to travel on, through Brittany and Normandy, south through Spain, and along the Mediterranean Sea to Italy.

We arrived at Florence about lunchtime, and found a hotel, an 'Albergo', in Via Faenza. After settling in, we went out and wandered around admiring the famous buildings and checking out the street stalls. After a delicious dinner, we went to bed fairly early.

Next morning, we caught a bus up to the youth hostel, Villa Camerata, to try to book into the hostel in Rome but couldn't do that until Sunday. It was lovely and peaceful up there, with views all round of the vine-covered hillsides, so we stayed a while to enjoy the beautiful gardens before returning to the city. After lunch, we walked around finding the places we hoped to visit next day. We saw the Palazzo Vecchio and the Uffizi, then walked across the Ponte Vecchio and back over another bridge.

On Saturday morning, I visited the laundromat while my husband joined a long queue to see the Duomo. With the laundry done, I joined him there. The interior of this great domed landmark is really awe-inspiring, and the singing of a choir added to the impact. Next were San Lorenzo and the Medici Chapels. I was thrilled to see Michelangelo's sculptures in the 'New' Sacristy, and was fascinated by the marble and semi-precious stone inlays in the Chapel of the Princes.

We lunched on rolls, ham and tomatoes from a market, before touring the Baptistery with its marvellous mosaics, including a huge Jesus on the ceiling, and intricate images above the women's gallery. Next was the Uffizi. Once again there was a long queue, but we finally got in. There were Greek and Roman sculptures and the wonderful original paintings of Botticelli, Michelangelo, Titian, Giorgione and Caravaggio. Pleasantly tired after an enjoyable day, we had a cold dinner in our room and went to bed early.

We would have loved to stay in this grand city much longer, but still had Switzerland, Germany, Austria, Belgium, Holland, Ireland and the UK to see before heading home, so we needed to check train times, visit a bank and take a last look at Florence. A tourist bus took us outside the city, over the bridge and up to the Piazza Michelangelo, with its wonderful view across the city. Then back, past lovely villas, gardens and vineyards to town, before returning to Villa Camerata to book the hostel in Rome. Back at the hotel, we wrote letters and cards home, before a final walk around the streets, packing and an early night.

Lynne Cairns

Nullarbor

The Song of a Homesick Sandgroper

This land of ours stretches far and wide
It's a long, long way to the other side
and I've been travelling far from home
away from the people I call my own

They say it's a long road that has no turning
but I'm tired of this place and my heart is yearning
to be back on the long straight road again
Across that treeless plain

It's a long shortcut from the east to the west
Back to the place that I love best
It's a long shortcut back to my hometown
but it's quicker than the long way round

Lynne Cairns

Red Dirt Travelling

Like a roughly ploughed field a hundred metres wide, it stretched out before us into the distance, the worst road I've ever seen. All other so-called 'horror stretches' have paled into insignificance in comparison. My husband wasn't with me, so may sometimes have wondered, over many years of outback travel, at my laid-back approach.

It was August 1964 when my parents, my brother and I, together with a loopy cocker spaniel named Gloppy, bumped over what I believe was euphemistically called the Great Northern Highway, in an EH Holden station wagon. This was back in the days before iron ore mining opened up the northwest of Western Australia. The railhead was still at Meekatharra, and truckloads of stock were brought down the 'highway' from outlying stations to be transported to Perth. The ground was flat and the earth packed hard on either side, so when the truckies found one part of the road too dug up, they simply moved over to make another track.

That was when the car really started to become part of the Australian way of life. Previously, many people had lived quite happily without one. My parents had owned a Rugby back in the early 1930s, but the Depression and finally Dad's blindness had separated them from the car-owning part of the population, though Mum had enjoyed a camping trip to the eastern states with my older brother in his Singer sedan in the 1950s.

My younger brother, Barney, had a new EH Holden named Mandy, and wanted to take our parents for a trip up north during his annual holidays. I've always felt guilty about leaving my new husband behind, but it was only a couple of weeks and Barney needed a relief driver, so off we went. Mum, Dad, Barney, Gloppy and me.

We had camped in the bush before. Mum and Dad as young people on the goldfields, and all of us while Dad built our houses at Scarborough and Mt Helena in the Darling Ranges, so we were prepared to rough it. All we took was a tarpaulin to make a kind of awning, a card table, a couple of folding chairs and two folding banana lounges.

Mum and Dad slept in the station wagon, with Barney and me outside on the folding lounges. It was lovely to sleep out under the stars, although one of the folding lounges had a tendency to buck you off, if you weren't careful.

Back then, except for short stretches through some towns, the bitumen stopped not far north of Perth. But there was very little traffic on the road once you got away from the big towns, and you could camp practically anywhere, light a little campfire, cook your dinner and sit back and enjoy the beautiful starlit night.

We drove up the coast to Geraldton, then on to Shark Bay. After buying supplies at the little town of Denham, we crossed the peninsula and camped at Monkey Mia. It was a lovely, unspoiled place where there was nothing but the beach, the sea and a water tank. The next stop was Carnarvon, where we bought essentials and fruit.

After a mishap south of Onslow, we limped into Onslow with a bent stub axle and had to wait a couple of days for the repairs. Onslow's caravan park was a pretty basic place right on the water's edge.

Back on the road, we drove north to Roebourne. The present-day highways, built to service iron ore towns yet to be established, didn't exist, so we took the Roebourne to Wittenoom Road that passed through Millstream station, a lovely green oasis in the dry red country. Then we stopped for a swim at beautiful Python Pool before continuing on towards Wittenoom. The asbestos mines were still working and the town was yet to become a place to be avoided.

There was little traffic on the road, but just outside the town, a taxi sped past sending a rock flying up to shatter Mandy's windscreen. After removing the shattered glass, we drove into town, only to be told that it would take a week to get a replacement. Next day, we decided there was nothing for it but to push on eastward to Roy Hill Station, to cut the road that ran from Nullagine in the north to Meekatharra, hoping to get the windscreen fixed there.

Well, south of Roy Hill is where you came in. Imagine travelling over that ploughed-up dirt road in an ordinary two-wheel-drive vehicle, with no windscreen. Mum and I donned plastic shower caps to keep the flying grit out of our hair and we finally got to Meeka, but were again told it would take days to get a new windscreen. Barney had to get back to Perth for work, so we decided to soldier on. Nothing could be worse than we'd already got through and despite the problems, it was a very memorable experience.

Lynne Cairns

Riding The Hogwarts Train

We rode the Hogwarts train, long before it would be seen thundering through clouds of smoke and steam, across the movie screen. It was the year that Harry Potter first appeared, when movies would have been at most, a fragile, flickering dream in his author/mother's brain.

And we hadn't to perform some magic trick, and take a scary run through solid brick, to reach that hidden platform. We just caught a Muggle train to Glasgow, hired a car, a Cinquecento, then took our time to drive, beside Loch Lomond and Loch Fyne, to Inverary.

From there we had to go, via Glen Nevis and Glen Coe, to Fort William, where we hopped aboard the train, before it chugged out of the station, passing lovely Highland scenes, to the place that you have seen the train to Hogwarts cross that viaduct on the screen.

From the viaduct you look down on Loch Shiel's peaceful shore, and Glenfinnan's little town with a monument that marks the site where Bonnie Prince Charlie's flag was raised, calling the Jacobites to follow him to sad Culloden Moor.

Next, we passed above Loch Eilt, a lovely place where tiny isles are clad with remnants of the pines, that forested the land in ancient times. You've seen one isle before, I'm sure. It's where they buried Dumbledore.

We saw more lovely, lonely places before we reached the mainland shore where sea lochs stretch their long arms out, to reach the open seas. Then we headed north along the coast, glimpsing the Hebrides before we finished our Highland stravaig at Mallaig.

Lynne Cairns

The Old Roads

The blacktop scribes its way across this ancient land,
tracing new patterns on the russet earth,
and though I don't begrudge the outback folk
their smoother, faster ride,
sometimes I find it hard to hide
my longing for the old roads, the dirt roads, the red roads,
the little gravel side roads
that led to who knows where.
Where we could find a quiet spot
with starlit nights and wildflower-scented air

Lynne Cairns

Lucy's Painting

The storm was rolling in above the rooftops as Lucy unpacked her paints. She glanced out of the window with a little frown of consternation and attended to her task with more urgency.

First, she laid out the tubes of acrylic colour on the kitchen table, plus a clear, quick drying medium and her paint-stained palette. Next, Lucy filled a jar with clean water, got out several different sized brushes and a couple of cleaning rags. Last of all, she placed the clean canvas on the easel. The rest of her art materials remained in their wooden box. She was ready.

Broad brush strokes of cerulean blue covered the top of the canvas. Lucy applied layer on layer, using the medium to good effect, creating a sky with immeasurable depth. A fine brush and titanium white saw wispy clouds float against the expanse of blue. The faintest touch of crimson made the clouds dance across the canvas in delight.

About a third of the way down, Lucy changed the water and her colours. Now she used French ultramarine blue, along with a transparent pthalo turquoise and a light cobalt turquoise to create her ocean. Carefully placed strokes of green-black suggested deeper waters in the middle stretch through to the horizon. Lucy reached for her fine brush again, this time dipped in pearl titanium, to outline the edge of the waves lapping the shore. Pale gold stippled the ocean's surface, reflecting the sun's light back up to the sky.

Next came the sand. Lucy applied layers of transparent yellow, carefully blended with opaque cadmium yellow to give it substance, and a little more titanium white for subtle contrasts. Lucy considered the raw sienna but decided against it. Perhaps some shells and starfish? She looked out the window. There wasn't time for that kind of detail.

With each brush stroke, the sky through the window darkened, leaching all colour from the world as the storm expressed its power. Rain pelted the earth, banging Lucy's roof and windows with ferocious determination. A flash of lightning lit the world for a moment with brilliant white light, then Lucy's kitchen faded to shades of grey and black. She shut her eyes, momentarily blinded. When she opened them again, her painting was glowing, incandescent in the darkness.

Lucy stepped back and looked at her work. Just two more things and she was done. An umbrella appeared on the beach – a cheerful orange with a burnt sienna handle dug into the sand. Lastly, a towel was carefully placed beneath the umbrella, striped with cobalt blue and white. All that was missing was a person to enjoy it.

The kitchen was deep in shadow when Lucy took off her oversized painting shirt. She hung it carefully over the back of a chair. Clad in a bikini, she popped on a broad-brimmed sun hat and picked up her book. With a last glance at the storm angrily lashing the world through her window, Lucy stepped into the painting.

When Lucy's husband arrived home later that evening, the house was dark. A light shining under the kitchen door drew him to it. The light was bright enough for him to see Lucy's shirt hanging over a chair, but the room was empty. As he stood before the easel, gazing at Lucy's luminous painting of a woman sitting under a beach umbrella looking toward the ocean, he wondered where his wife was.

Gillian Carter

Kuala Lumpur - London - Paris

At the international airport
check-in was on the go
all was a buzz
a trip overseas
Kuala Lumpur, London, Paris
ACTIV RECREATION group was on the move
I and five other volunteers
with thirteen intellectually challenged clients

All the paperwork medication correct and finished
through check-in tickets in hand onto the plane
Kuala Lumpur first stop
hot and humid
all shopped until we dropped
two nights then on to London we go
Central Hyde Park was where we stayed
double-decker buses
the underground tube – taxis
walked the streets of London
shopping for all, many a bargain found

Weather was warm and easy to please
Musicals – Madame Tussaud – Palaces- Castles
touring the countryside, Bath, Salisbury, Windsor
Bath, the Olympic torch ran a fleeting glimpse
pubs and cafes, food galore
UK ten days in total fun had by all

Then to the EUROSTAR – train
Paris our next call
days were bright well into the night
Eiffel Tower, Seine River cruise
historic buildings galore
bridges- thirty-two in all
Paris is a must for all
architectural delight
awesome sights
photo shoots and more

Euro Disneyland an adventure, loved by all
we shopped some more
tried escargot – snails
those who were game
not every one's delicacy
We loved our trip overseas
volunteers and clients with ACTIV RECREATION
enriched by the experience
embracing the encounter with exuberance
then home to rest and relax
until our next adventure

Faye Teale-Clavi

A Venetian Farce

My finger paused over the *Book Now* button on the screen of the online hotel booking service. I hesitated, not because the room price was $140 reduced, nor that the hotel was only 120 metres from the train station (Venezia Santa Lucia), but because of two words – *shared bathroom*. With trepidation, I pressed the button to finalise the booking.

On arrival in Venice, having found that the walk from the station was only 120m as promised, we checked into the hotel. So far so good. Our room was on the second floor, up a narrow, steep staircase, with two landings per flight to the floor above. The ever-expanding bags gained weight with every step. A little out of breath, we stood outside Room 200. A turn of the key. The door opened part way, partially obstructed by a bed. It was a tight squeeze to enter this converted broom cupboard. A remnant from the hotel's previous life as a mansion in another era. We climbed over and around two single beds with barely enough room to put bags on the floor. My trepidation about this booking returned. A cautious, brief orientation located the *shared bathroom* just 10 paces along the corridor to the right; most convenient for any night-time visits. Maybe all would be well. On that first night, a previous guest left the bathroom floor wet and the toilet soiled. Somehow, we coped, minimising contact with any bathroom surface.

The second afternoon, after walking the winding crowded alleys and lanes of Venice, we returned early at 3 pm, anticipating a clean *baino* at that time of day. It was clean, so we enjoyed showers before venturing out again for a Venetian pasta dinner.

Feeling much refreshed, and in high spirits, we set off to enjoy the bustling evening atmosphere along the canals. We also wanted to find our route to Tronchetto bus station, for the early start the next morning.

After the pleasant Venetian evening with some delicious pasta, a little red wine, and immersed in the Venetian atmosphere, we sauntered through the hustle of tourists and locals, to arrive back outside our room at about 9 pm. We stepped from the stairway, just in time to see a fleeting figure in night clothes dash from an adjacent room into the *shared bathroom.* A short while later, with packing for our early start the next day almost finished, it was time for the final ablutions of the day. With towel and tooth brush in hand, I found the bathroom door closed and locked.

I returned to the Room 200 and waited. A short time later, a door opened and closed somewhere in the corridor. I hurried out with towel and toothbrush in hand again. The bathroom door was still locked closed. There was a sound of water running from within. I returned to my room and waited. I fiddled with last-minute items for packing to keep occupied. Door sounds again. Out I rushed to see a different woman trying the bathroom door handle, only to walk away with a shrug of her shoulders. The door remained closed and locked. No response to our knocking. So, back to my room to wait, less patiently. A minute waiting for the bathroom can seem like an hour after several glasses of wine!

Twice more the door routine took place. In desperation, at about 10 pm, I knocked loudly on the bathroom door, shouting in my best Australian vernacular '*Come on, mate! People are waiting to use the loo*!' Silence. A long pause. The door finally opened, releasing a cloud of steam, body wash and pink fluffy robe. Scurrying feet made a hasty retreat to the room opposite. With toothbrush and towel in hand – again, I hurried to the bathroom, but was brought to a halt at the door. The floor was flooded, three to four centimeters lapping at the edge of the bathroom door, and the sink blocked to overflowing.

One can only tolerate so much after waiting an hour for access to a *shared bathroom.* I stamped down the stairs to Reception to complain about the condition of the bathroom. The night receptionist was polite, '*I can do nothing at this time of night*'. I insisted he come with me to inspect the bathroom. At the door, I had to hold him back from wading into the flooded room. '*I can put up an-out of-order sign*', he said as he turned to go downstairs to his night desk.

As he stepped onto the stairway, I asked if there was another *toilette* that we could use. He pointed around the corner to another bathroom. Oh! the relief, but embarrassment at not realising other facilities were available just around the corner. Then I discovered *son* (or perhaps *daughter*) of the broom closet. A bathroom so small that when sitting, one's knees invaded the shower stall, while the left shoulder pressed against the wash basin. Relief overcame agitation. Then amusement replaced embarrassment as the saga of the bathroom morphed into a farce worthy of Italian comedy.

Ah, bella Italia!

Footnote. I have always wondered where all the water on the floor went, as the bathroom had drained dry by morning! A rough estimate of the area of the floor suggests that about 100-200 litres of water covered the floor that night!

Sue Colyer

Worst Holiday

I cannot recommend going on holiday if you happen to be inexperienced parents with a baby son of six weeks old, especially if the infant cries from colic half the night. But my husband's firm presented him with an old jalopy, and he wanted to run it in. I needed a change of environment, as my nerves were frazzled, so we set off with the optimism of youth. We loaded the car with baby outfits, numerous towelling nappies stored in a metal baby bath, and a pail to soak them in. Disposable nappies hadn't been invented in 1959.

The movement of the car and the strains of Mozart lulled our child to sleep; apart from my husband's love of classical music, research had revealed music helped to develop a child's brain. With this in mind, we exposed our infant to a variety of stimuli, hoping he'd turn out to be a genius. My husband had recently passed his driving test after ten lessons which resulted in a bumpy ride as the car kept stalling. We passed through the New Forest, where I observed, from the car window, wild ponies roaming freely in the forest while my husband's eyes were fixed on the windy road ahead. We began to relax, looking forward to a peaceful week away from our crowded London suburb.

When we reached the crest of a hump-back bridge, we slowed down, and the car came to a standstill; it refused to start because the engine had died. Behind us, traffic had banked up, causing irate drivers to sound their horns. On a Sunday, there were many cars heading for the sea, so we had caused a major hold-up. I left the car holding my baby, who was screaming with hunger, but I couldn't breast feed him in front of a line of traffic. My husband, who followed me, knocked on the door of a nearby farmhouse; when the owner learned of our predicament, she offered us her hospitality. He then phoned the A.A., and when they eventually arrived, he accompanied them as they towed the car away, complete with our luggage, to the nearest garage.

I managed to feed the baby in the privacy of the woman's bedroom, but the nappies were still in the car. The kind woman tore up some old sheets and fed me with wholesome homemade soup. At first, I sat on the verandah, inhaled the smell of summer flowers, and then wandered around with the baby, saying, 'Look at the cute little chicks and piglets.'

In his book Baby and Child Care, which I considered my bible, Dr. Spock said, 'Talk to your child even though he can't understand you; he'll experience the rhythm of language.'

At sunset, my husband returned with the repaired car to drive us to our destination.

The guest house in Bournemouth was shabby, with a double bed covered with a faded quilt; the baby slept beside us in his carry-cot; no en-suite in those days, just a shared bathroom. How lucky I'd brought the baby bath because, for me, bathing was a ritual, a time to splash and play with our offspring. We met the woman who occupied the adjacent room when she knocked on the door. She looked around thirty and had staring eyes. She told us she suffered from mental illness, so after that information, we were reluctant to leave the baby alone in the room as there was no lock on the door. She took a fancy to my sympathetic husband and kept knocking on our door so she could ask him for advice, and then she would forge her way into our room on the pretext of wanting to look at the baby. In the middle of the night, she went downstairs and played the piano, and in the early hours, we could hear her pacing around her room, talking to herself and rustling paper; we hardly slept in case she set the place alight. We couldn't wait to get home.

I think our baby enjoyed the holiday because we gave him our undivided attention during the day. He was so exhausted that he slept at night and seemed more settled. On reflection, it wasn't the worst holiday ever because we were happy with each other and had bonded with our son.

Pat Curtis

Couch Trip

Horizontal rain morse codes across the window
heralds a no-show of things to be done.
Even the fire will soon demand a refill
but I am curled too tight to move.
Eyes heavy with memory fragments fall into place

and I'm lost in the shapes and colours of language
patterns of skylines, the brazen dazzle of sun
lost in a confusion of cloud and soft silent rain

in cobbled laneways, museums and forests
the age and the wonder, the green flood of spring
a tapestry of postcards, a blue glass of champagne

Lost in a maze, in search of a landmark
The crash of an ocean, lost gardens and beaches
The chatter of youth, their laughter coloured beads of talk.

Geraldine Day

Birdsong on Barrington

Cocooned in a blanket, hands warming on a mug of hot coffee, I wait for the show to begin.

The Great Creator raises his baton, sweeps it across the sky and rolls back the curtain of night.

A smudge of coral appears on mountain rims like the start of a watercolour painting. Mauve and gold seep into the sky. The bright crescent moon lingers, reluctant to exit.

Now, a gentle breeze shakes the blue and grey gums, wake its inhabitants. Tiny waves race across the lake and shake clumps of reeds. Mother duck appears with a flotilla of ducklings, and Moorhens strut in annoyance.

A new day's music starts with a dawn chorus from the Creator; the dawn chorus composed by the expert would enthral Mozart, Beethoven, Wagner, and Tchaikovsky.

It begins, whistles soft as flutes. Tweets and trills violins at their best. A tinkle of bell sounds floats down the Barrington Tops, accompanied by the bass and drums of ducks and black cockatoos. The crescendo of skylark, robin, and rufus whistler. Magpies chortle, and kookaburras call for others to join in. The finale is the wedge-tailed eagle, king of the mountains, his piercing *kee-kee* the symbols. Then, just as it began, the music fades, and a brilliant blue replaces the coral and mauve, as the sun smiles down on us. A grey kangaroo hops across the grass, leaving impressions in the heavy dew.

The only cost to this brilliant performance was my attention.

Exhilarated, empty coffee mug in hand, I return to the motorhome and breakfast.

June Earle

Going Fishing

Cricket clicks and bird whistles mingle with the slosh-slosh of waves circling reeds. In a quiet valley, an excuse for a road disappears into the river – tranquillity evaporates. A vehicle approaches, splutters, coughs, and bumps along the track to halt alongside a craft moored at the water's edge.

Weighed down with trappings strapped to the roof rack, the old car slumps in the sand – a middle-aged couple emerge.

'What a place. Perfect. You are in for a fantastic time.' He gulps air, thumping his chest like a has-been Tarzan. Eyes raised heavenwards, she sighs, clearly unenthusiastic about what lies ahead.

'I am sure I will, dear. Did you bring the hamper and flask of hot water?' she queries.

'Sod that, where did I put the bait? ... Right, got everything. Into the boat you go, I will push off.'

'I can't get my feet wet – these are new shoes.'

'For goodness' sake. You are supposed to wear old gear.'

'You didn't say. I am also wearing a new hat ... do you like it?'

'I'm sure the fish will be impressed. Now sit down. I will row out to the middle – they are bound to be out there – if not we will head further up the river.'

'This seat is uncomfortable. Does this wee boat come with cushions?'

'No. Sit on my jacket.' From beneath his seat, he produces a battered tackle box. 'Here is a selection of flies for you to try on your line.'

'FLIES!! I spend most of my time trying to eradicate them. Haven't you got a piece of chicken? A fly is so small, I am sure the fish would prefer chicken.'

'Stupid woman! It is not THAT kind of fly. Never mind I will bait your hook. Cast out as far as you can and wait for the first nibble.'

Giving him a weak smile, she asks, 'Will that be long, sweetheart?''

Silently, he counts to ten. 'Patience, woman, patience!'

Leaning forward, she pats his knee. 'Is that what you displayed over the flat tyre this morning?'

He ignores her and lights his pipe. 'You must admit out here time stands still. What more could a man ask for?'

He thinks of the one that got away last time – she of the dress she admired in a local boutique.

The sun silvers the water and deepens the blue of the sky. Minutes tick by. He chews on his male dummy content in the aroma of sweet tobacco. She fidgets and shakes the line bored with the lack of action.

'Darling?'

'You've got a bite?' He tugs her line.

'No, I need to go to the little girl's room.'

'WHAT! Right now?'

She reels in. 'Yes, dear. I am not equipped with a handy gadget like yours. Besides, we can spread the blanket on the shore, and I will make us a nice hot cup of tea. I made cucumber sandwiches special for today – I know you will enjoy them. My friends at the bridge club say my cucumber sandwiches are delicious. I cut the crusts off and made them into bite-size triangles.'

'Damn it, woman! I came to fish, not eat blasted sandwiches.' Knuckles white upon the oars, he heads towards the bank – she hums a nautical tune.

Later in the day, she visits her neighbour, who is surprised to see her.

'Hello, Caroline, I thought you would be back later this afternoon. Did you catch any fish? Let me put the kettle on and you can tell me all about it.'

'I caught two horrible wet slimy things, bug-eyed with sharp teeth. I shall have nightmares tonight.'

Cups and saucers clink; a dainty plate of cake and biscuits is placed on the table.

'How did David fare?'

'Well ...' In between sips of tea and mouthfuls of cake, she explains how the day unfolded. 'He didn't catch a thing. Spent most of the day baiting my hook and untangling the line. We got stuck on a sandbar and while trying to retrieve my hat with an oar, he fell overboard. Then I accidentally caught my hook in his bag of worms and tossed it overboard – that did it. Bless him, he did not utter one obscenity – just turned a ghastly shade of purple.'

The neighbour chuckles. 'Sounds like a fun day – better luck next time.'

Caroline shrugs. 'Not for me. I hate their eyes and awful teeth – Yuk!'

'Really? Why on earth did you go then?' Another cup of tea is poured as Caroline helps herself to a slice of fruitcake.

'David has been at me for ages about the wonders of fishing and how I must try it. So, I thought if I made things difficult ... in the nicest way of course. On the way home, he grinded gears so many times I thought he would do the gearbox in. He suggested, in the nicest way of course, that I really was not suited to this kind of outing. He is going to ask your Jim to go out with him next weekend.'

'Terrific. That gets me out of going to play golf. I cannot see the point of hitting a little white ball then walking forever to hit it again. I am going to try your feminine wiles.'

The sun begins to sink in a pink glow. Caroline stands up to leave. 'I must get home and cook tea – my catch of the day.'

They laugh.

'How about taking in a movie on the weekend if David is taking Jim out in the boat?'

Caroline smiles. 'Good idea. What's playing?'

'A thriller called *Jaws.*'

June Earle

Jack's Waterhole – Gibb River Road

Savage beasts there may not be in this huge and diverse country, but that takes no account of the dangerous or venomous ones. My most memorable critter slid under the wall and into our room at Jack's Water Hole at midnight.

It had taken most of that day to cover 225ks, and we decided it was worthwhile paying $170 for a donga, rather than camp in a distant field with no facilities. It was one of four in a row along the front of the homestead, and had two narrow spring beds, a table between, and one fold-up chair in a corner. No space for anything else. The only recognition that this was wild Oz was the fact that the corrugated iron walls (almost) met the floor, probably to keep critters out, or allow water to pass through when the river, the Durack, rose. The door latched with a bolt, operable from either side through a hole. No ceilings, so we were fair game to anything that chose to fly in or climb up and over.

We ate dinner with the family – no other guests – and by 8.30 everybody was ready for bed. Also, electricity was supplied by a generator, and the sooner everybody went to bed the longer the fuel lasted – something to be considered when replacement means a day or two on the road to fetch more.

As usual, I passed out within 2.4 minutes. Actually, it may have been 4.2 minutes in the uneasiness of knowing only a 2-way bolt lay between me and Whatever, Whoever, lurked Out There!

Sometime during the night, I had to go to the toilet. No point in being nervous - it had to be done and no way was I going to step from the concrete ramp that led to our room into the great blackness out there. Let me guide you through the route I had to take. No lights, remember, and no moon that night either.

Torch in hand, I ratcheted open the bolt, stepped warily along the outside walkway, and, aware of the said blackness to my right, marched through a kind of atrium area, through a large living/dining area – no doors anywhere, and walls ending 18 inches above the floor – along another outside walkway, down a passage between the two "sheds" where the family slept, around a corner and into the communal ablution block. Very quietly, so I wouldn't wake our hosts, their little boy and the grandparents. All without incident.

Plod, plod, plod, back again, bolted the door, felt thirsty, used torch to find my water bottle on the floor at the end of the bed … and saw a snake, small, thin and dark in colour, winding towards me and my bed. I leapt onto the bed, grabbed my little backpack off the floor, shone the torch again as the snake slithered under my bed.

"BJ!"

"BJ!!"

"Wha'?"

"There's a snake! Do something!"

But by the time he lurched over from facing the wall to facing the room, untangled himself from his bedclothes and peered at the floor, the snake had disappeared under my bed.

"Where? What am I supposed to do?"

"I don't know, but I can't sleep with a snake."

He stared at me for 1.2 seconds. "It's probably a tree snake – it won't hurt you." Turned his back to me and snuggled down again.

I waved the torch around for a couple of minutes, trying to find the snake, eyed the lump in the other bed, considered several options – mostly loud and violent – and finally decided he was right. The snake was probably just passing through and had not been lying in wait for me to get up. Besides, what could he do? Finally, I placed the torch in bed beside me, slid it under my doona, tucked it tightly around my neck, and spent the next half hour or so on full alert, expecting the snake to track across my face, or at the least, to feel pressure on the bedclothes.

I did go to sleep again, but it was an uneasy night, disturbed twice by dingoes howling very close and a gentle "flap-flap-flap" over my head several times. It couldn't have been a bird, maybe a large moth?

Next morning, I was enchanted to see a tiny bat hanging by its feet from a long piece of wire above BJ's head! Several uncharitable thoughts crossed my mind, and since telling this story to a few people, I've been offered several much less charitable suggestions as to what I should have done about his reaction to my snake!!

In the newspaper, about a month after our return was a report:

" 52-year-old man is in critical condition in hospital after being bitten by a 50cm brown snake near Kununurra. Bites from Death Adders are rare at this time of year but their venom is three times more dangerous than that of the tiger snake, twice their size."

No wonder the family turned pale when I told them about my snake next morning at breakfast.

Pat Fletcher

Husky Ride – Norway, March 2023

We could hear the dogs the moment we stepped down from the coach. Lyn and I had signed up for a Husky Sled Ride from Kirkenes (pron. Shickeness), well into the Arctic Circle and only 8ks from the Russian border. Pristine whiteness stretched out beyond the snow-covered roofs and trees, and we were glad of our thick coats and snow boots. Temperature: -5°C.

We were all ushered into a changing shed and given down-filled snow overalls and gloves. Question: do we need to wear our winter coats as well? A: That depends …. No help at all!

I couldn't haul the overalls over my jacket, nor get my boots down the legs. Off with the boots – no mean feat as they first had to be unlaced then edged off, and I couldn't quite reach them. With all others rapidly heading out from the shed, I was getting desperate and asked the young man to help. He yanked off the boots, told me to shove my legs down the leg holes; hauled the suit up so I could insert my arms, and zipped me up. Later, he also helped me to undress.

A short walk to where the dogs were leaping and straining against the reins, all the while barking hysterically, wild with excitement. Let no one who hasn't seen these dogs, bred for sledding and racing, tell me they are exploited.

Lyn and I were last to board our sleds, which are built for two, one behind the other. They are quite narrow, fashioned from wood planks, with animal skins lining the seats – no springs, no cushioning. Two to a sled, she was seated in front of a man we had chummed up with on the ship, and I climbed in to sit between the legs of a lady I didn't know. Nothing like a bit of close togetherness to help you lose your inhibitions, and as a padded armchair, she was very comfortable.

Brakes released, a shout from our musher, and we were off: 0 to 20 in five seconds. Almost immediately, my glasses fogged up and I took them off to wipe them. Big mistake. They slipped out of my grasp and over the side of the sled. Likewise, one of the gloves, which I had removed to deal with the specs. Later, people asked if I'd called out to our musher, but I was too busy trying to stay balanced as the sled hit bumps and swayed around the bends.

Pam, sitting behind me, kept fiddling with her snow mittens in front of my face, effectively blindfolding me. And she must have had trouble seeing over my beanie because I felt her push down on my head several times.

Exhilarating?

Yes, I suppose so. My impressions are of a wondrous expanse of white, dotted with spindly, leafless trees, rather like our desert where red earth stretches from horizon to horizon.

When I told the young man about my accident, he had a look at the area where it happened, but they were nowhere to be seen. I wore my prescription sunnies for the rest of the holiday – "incognito" as one man put it – and binned the other glove.

Pat Fletcher

Photos: courtesy of Lyn Tolliday

Patagonia: Edge of the World

South America was never on my list of places to visit. Images came to mind of Machu Picchu, Iguazu Falls, Carnival in Rio, and tourists like a plague of locusts converging to see and snap photos. Not my scene. Until I saw photographs of the spectacular mountain peaks of Torres del Paine National Park in Patagonia. My research revealed that Patagonia is a region just over one million square kilometres in size, encompassing the southern parts of both Argentina and Chile, with the Andes mountains separating the two countries. More research and photos produced images of snow, glaciers, lakes and wide-open spaces devoid of habitation, much of it semi-desert. Now that…!

At the time it looked too difficult, too daunting, especially on my own. Even getting there looked like a journey of problems: several flights to negotiate, accommodation to find, getting from place to place. Then recently, an email appeared in my Inbox from Collette, the American company I travelled with to the U.S. last year, advertising a single tour – *Patagonia: Edge of the World.*

Fortunately, I like flying because there were four flights between Perth and Buenos Aires, a total of 30-odd hours of travelling. I was met at Buenos Aires airport by Alex who, between chatting to me about his city and talking to someone on the 2-way radio, threw the odd comment and instruction to the driver. At the hotel, I met Enrique who would be our tour leader, and who immediately took charge of my check-in and took me to my room. Enrique looked a bit like a pirate captain's 2IC. Swarthy of complexion, he wore heavy black-rimmed glasses.

His shock of black curls, wild and free at that stage, was later contained in a bandana. He only lacked a cutlass strapped to his belt. But he was a great guide – always on hand to answer questions and smooth the way.

A day to myself to recover worked well, and I was ready the following day to start the adventure. Eight of us – seven Americans and me – were taken on a morning tour of very few of the numerous sights of Buenos Aires. On the journey from the airport, we'd driven along the "widest street in the world", Avenida 9 de Julio honours Argentina's Independence Day, 9th July 1816 – 140 metres wide, up to seven lanes in each direction, four traffic lights for pedestrians to cross.

Looking back, I remember Buenos Aires (no, time to see much) for its modernised European-style buildings as well as wall-against-wall apartment buildings, communication wires flowing down the outside, big open spaces and wide roads, trees (especially Morton Bay figs) and parks, and multiple dogs on leads. Oh, and statues – on corners, in parks and squares. People love their statues. Two things impressed me: the Recoleta cemetery which was crammed with huge mausoleums along sometimes very narrow passageways, some adorned with elaborate life-size religious statues. The tomb of Eva Peron (Evita) in contrast is a very large speckled black marble cube.

We were given 10 minutes to explore the biggest library I've ever seen. Housed in a former theatre, books occupy shelves all through the ground floor and two mezzanine balcony floors; also down an escalator to the floor below. Ten minutes was probably enough – the books were all in Spanish. Of course! Why would I expect otherwise?

During the afternoon, Enrique took four of us in search of a warm jacket for me. I'd failed to pick up mine when I left home. We walked … until he found what he called a flea market: a warehouse holding individual stalls selling mainly jackets, but also shirts and trousers. I knew what I wanted – a puffer jacket, with hood, fleece-lined, zip-up; preferably navy, not red or black. We marched from shop to shop with Enrique producing one jacket after another for my inspection until Jo pounced on one that ticked all the boxes. It had no labels and looked brand new, "Probably was," said Enrique. "Stolen!" And the cost of this treasure? AU$20.

My fellow-travellers were a delight. I couldn't have asked for a more likeable and agreeable group of people. They varied in age from early 40s to middle 60s, and after the first day we "clicked". Interested and enthusiastic about everything, if we were offered a chance to see or do something, they'd be in it, and they insisted I be in it too.

It was a 3-hour flight to El Calafate, gateway to Patagonia. Our hotel stood on a hill overlooking the town and the lake, to the snow-capped mountains in the distance. The houses scattered around the hotel were painted in bright colours. It was the same in Alaska and Greenland. Maybe so you can find your bright red house in the snow on a winter's night? Ask Mr Google. One explanation given for Greenland is that the colour of the house indicates the occupation of the resident: yellow for all medical occupations, green for tradespeople, and so on. There are other explanations.

Seventy-odd kilometres from the town, within the Los Glaciares National Park, the Perito Moreno glacier is one of the few in the world that is advancing. Five kilometres wide and rising 74 metres above the surface of Lake Argentino, this gigantic glacier sometimes blocks a narrow channel that flows into the lake, thereby raising the water level temporarily. We boarded a ferry-style boat and headed for the monumental face which seemed to grow larger as we drew closer. Not too close: it regularly and unpredictably calves off massive icebergs, causing great waves that could swamp our tiny (comparatively) vessel. The ferry moved at tortoise pace along the length of it, stopping occasionally to effect a 360° so that the mad photographers (all) had a chance to see and click.

On shore again, we drove to a high vantage point from where we could see the entire glacier, from its stunning façade, back between high peaks to the source in the distant mountains.

Onward from El Calafate, we all piled into our minibus and headed for Puerto Natales through a big, open, undulating country, sparsely vegetated with scrub. On the way, we called into a "gaucho estancia", literally a cowboy ranch. The farmer runs about 3,000 sheep on 58,000 acres, with the help of his "happy, loyal, hard-working farm hands" – 10 border collies. Responding to whistles and hand signals only, the dog with him shot off like demons from hell were after him, towards a clump of bushes some distance away. We heard scuffling and a few sharp barks, then seven frazzled-looking sheep emerged and were herded, in tight formation, to the farmer.

A demonstration of shearing was a first for my companions and when I asked a few questions, saying I was from Australia, he told us that the record was set by an Australian a few years ago – 17 seconds to remove the entire fleece in one piece.

We arrived at the border post between Argentina and Chile - a couple of buildings out in the sticks - where we had to unload ourselves and our luggage, go through Security, then climb aboard again (luggage and all), drive about 100 metres, and repeat the process on the Chilean side. After the trouble I'd had obtaining a Chilean visa, I was nervous of what might happen, and I think Enrique was too. He told us to stay in line and don't speak. But all was well. We met our Chilean guide (Sol) and driver (José), climbed aboard the Chilean minibus while the driver handled the luggage.

We checked in to our hotel, Remota Patagonia Lodge. Remote it was, some distance from the town of Puerto Natales which is the port for boats touring the Patagonian fjords. Living in Perth with only Rottnest and Garden Island off our coast, we can't imagine over 40,000 islands along the coast of Chilean Patagonia, and Puerto Natales lies within that archipelago. From our hotel, we had views across scrubland and water to the island on the other side and mountains beyond, snow-covered, of course. Puerto Natales is also the gateway to the Torres del Paine National Park.

Because of my own stubbornness, I nearly missed out seeing the very thing I went there to see. By this, Day 7 of my trip, most of it travelling, I was tired and decided to take a day off, stay in the hotel and rest. Thankfully my companions, including Enrique, thought otherwise and all but dragged me onto the bus.

The 80-kilometre road through Torres del Paine National Park was rough: corrugated and potholed. During the one-hour's drive, the sun shone, clouds descended almost to the road, it rained, it snowed, and the wind… always the wind.

Finally, there they were, the Torres del Paine or, in English, Towers of Blue: high jagged peaks, so big, so grand, viewed across a couple of lakes, blue and turquoise in colour. I could now die happy! There was more, but my head was so full of that awesome image that all else faded into insignificance.

Back at the hotel, I was glad I hadn't stayed behind. The first thing I saw on entering my room was two 2-gallon bottles of water, one marked Face and Hands, the other, Toilette. On the dressing table was a note saying "Sorry, the main water pipe to the hotel has broken, but we've supplied 2 large bottles of water for your use". The shower at the other end of the hotel was functional if we chose. I chose to have a "good wash" out of the bathroom basin. The toilet was another matter, and I think we were all happy to be leaving the next day.

More driving (did I mention Patagonia is big?) took us to Punta Arenas where we boarded our ship, the *Ventus Australis*, for a 4-night cruise around the islands and channels of Tierra del Fuego of which there were very many. I'm not a great drinker but that evening I tried a Calafate Sour – I wouldn't get one of those at home. Made with lemon juice, sugar, powdered Calafate berries and Pisco (fermented grape juice), it is peculiar to Patagonia where the Calafate shrubs grow. Served in a champagne glass, it was pink and tasted a bit like a sour Lemon, Lime and Bitters: refreshing and pleasant but perhaps an acquired taste. Any and all alcohol on board was included in the price.

Our ship was comparatively small, holding a maximum of 250 passengers, but there were only 80 on our cruise, which meant shorter waiting times to board the Zodiacs. At dinner, the Hotel Manager gave us a short talk and welcomed the guests by their nationality. We waited for her to mention Australia and when she didn't, my new friends, insisted on telling her, "You didn't mention the Australian in our group." Apparently the only one.

We were invited to visit the Bridge where I was interested to see a man sitting at the helm, never dropping his gaze from the water ahead. This was the pilot who steered the ship through sometimes quite narrow channels, mountains rising steeply on either side.

Nearly every day there were a couple of excursions ashore, accessed by Zodiac – it is too hazardous for ships to get close. One of the highlights was Pia Glacier which descends from the mountains in the Darwin Range into a secluded corner of the Chilean fjords. We were offloaded, ten at a time, to trek up the boulders alongside the glacier, to experience and enjoy a feeling almost of reverence for this mighty feature of nature.

We were supremely lucky with the weather. This part of the world is often cloaked in cloud, rain and fog, the reason it's not an advertised area to view the southern lights. The weather, generally, could hardly have been better – warm, most often sunny, only growing cool to cold as we travelled south where it sometimes snowed and, of course, the mountains were snow and ice-covered.

Our excursion onto Navarin Island revealed another surprise, for me anyway. The people native to that area are called Yahgans, sometimes spelt Yagans. I was struck by the name – was there a connection to the Western Australian aboriginal man, called Yagan? Later, I read that the British had put a bounty on these people, ordering that some of the heads be sent to England to prove they had indeed been killed – "a price on his head" enacted.

Yes, there are penguins on a couple of islands in Tierra del Fuego and some of the passengers elected to go and see them. We were told it might be a bit rough because the Zodiacs would be going out into the ocean. Not for me, thank you – my tummy doesn't like bouncy water, but for Jo, whose favourite animals are penguins, it was the high point of the tour, in spite of returning to the ship sopping wet, and freezing.

People were eagerly looking forward to going ashore at Cape Horn. We spent a morning sitting around in the 5th-floor lounge, life jackets at hand, waiting to be summoned to the Zodiacs, while the guides took several trips from ship to shore to check on conditions. Each time the report was that, owing to the high tide, with consequent rough seas, it was too dangerous for passengers and Zodiacs to land there.

Cape Horn was earning its reputation. Over 800 ships have sunk at this spot, and more than 10,000 people have lost their lives [figures taken from Britannica website]. I had no intention of going ashore anyway, wasn't keen on climbing 140+ steps to the first stage, continuing with more to the lighthouse…in freezing weather and gale-force winds.

I tried to go out on deck to take photos but soon realised that I would be blown over to Cape Horn, freezing to death before I got there.

Our last night in Patagonia was spent in Ushuaia, in a modern hotel overlooking that most southerly city in the world. Our ship had arrived the evening before but had to wait for a place to become available on the jetty.

Back in Buenos Aires, we were treated to dinner and a show featuring Tango (flamboyant, athletic, wild) and band, a female singer with a Very Loud voice, and an excellent 3-piece Peruvian band, pan pipes and all. Most of us ordered steak, Argentinian beef having a name for its excellence. Mine was so tough I couldn't get my knife through it, let alone my teeth.

And finally, four flights, five airports, 30-odd hours, 11 time zones, and it was all over. At home that night I slept for 14 hours.

Pat Fletcher

Time Travellers

People ask me what I want to be when I grow up. They get a big surprise when I tell them I want to be a time traveller. They probably think the son of a hot-shot lawyer should follow in his father's footsteps. My father Henry and I are on different levels of the totem pole. In fact, we're probably on different poles altogether. He's always finding fault with me. I guess that's because I'm not the clever son he always wanted.

He also disapproves of Gran even though she's his mother. Delusional, left of Centre, away with the birdies, are some of the nasty comments he makes about her. He refers to her as 'The Witch', but she must be a white one because I often hear her talking out loud to God.

I guess Gran's a tad weird, different to most people I know, but heaps more interesting, especially when it comes to travel. She's top of the wassa at geography, and studies her big atlas like some Christians study the bible. Foreign countries fascinate her. Gran's a mind traveller, and in her imagination, she visits all the countries in the world.

At some stage on her journeys, eastern ideas tipped over into her beliefs. She's a full bottle on astral travelling. "When you go to sleep, Boyo," she tells me, "that fine astral body of yours leaves your heavy body to go a-wandering here, there and everywhere." This info kinda freaks me out.

"That sounds great, Gran, but what if you can't get back into your body? That'd be a tad scary."

"Don't you be worrying about that, young man. Both bodies are joined by a strong silver cord which caters for the comings and goings of the astral body. As you're awakening, it tugs it back into the physical body quick smart. Most people don't remember their wanderings only in jumbled dreams."

Gran considers reincarnation and karma strong possibilities. "Otherwise,' she says, "how can you explain the unfairness of life? Here's me on my merry way to eighty and some wee mite has already passed on into the great beyond. And how is it that some poor folk, no matter how good they are or how hard they try, suffer terrible misfortune? Who knows, Billy, they may be paying for misdeeds in their past lives."

Time is another subject Gran knows heaps about. She tells me, "The flow of time isn't constant. Time can slow down, but like Superman, you must go super-fast for this to happen. The funny thing is the faster you go the slower time passes. If you get into a spaceship and fly fast enough you could swing back around toward the earth and watch yourself take off."

"Gee, Gran, I find that hard to get my head around."

"Think outside the box, laddy. Practise some of that lateral thinking the good lord's been good enough to grant you. Your mind, Billy, is trapped in linear time, time invented by man for convenience's sake. If time stands still, there is no yesterday, today or tomorrow; everything is happening now, right now."

Reality, as I know it, flies out the window as I battle to understand. "What's it all mean, Gran?"

'It means there is no time as we know it. Time isn't moving – it's us that's moving, Billy, through space, and we can alter time by changing the amount of space between objects or changing our rate of speed through space."

Gran reverts to reincarnation and carries her ideas a step further into the realms of the unbelievable. "Imagine, Billy, you have a life or maybe many, but you only live one at a time, but listen in. If time stands still, you could be living multiple lives all at once."

My mind boggles as I try to imagine other Billys in other places living different lives to mine. I shake my head, trying to make sense of it all.

Gran pats me on the shoulder. "Don't you be worrying your poor head about it all. Just get on living this life. With a father like our Henry, that's more than enough to contend with."

My father must have been eavesdropping because he suddenly appeared, interrupted our conversation, and ordered me inside. I hear his voice echo from the kitchen. "She's filling William's head with a whole heap of esoteric claptrap. Good God, as if his brain cells aren't deficient enough without filling him with all that nonsense."

"Like it or not, Henry," my mother replies, "those two are peas in a pod, made from the same clay, fashioned by the same sculptor, and there's nothing you can do about it."

I guess that's why Gran and I get along so famously. I'd much rather be like Gran than my father. Gran opens my mind to possibilities. She helps me question my ancestral beliefs. In that respect, she's taught me more than my teachers, or my brainy father ever could.

Good old Gran, when she leaves this world, I'm sure she'll be somewhere in the great beyond, learning, investigating, questioning, and still chatting with her God.

Robin Giraudo

The Determination to Ski

I was fortunate to win a trip to Vienna in February 2024. It was to attend the Zero Project Conference[1] at the United Nations. It's a global conference for people with disabilities to share ideas and innovative solutions to barriers. As a woman with a physical disability and a power wheelchair user, I won because of a video about my pointer stick that I use to help me do everyday tasks. The judges thought I was an innovator for inventing a simple solution which had a profound impact on my independence.

The conference organisers wanted me to fly in the day before, stay the four nights, and fly home the day after the conference.

"Do you know how far Austria is from Australia?" I asked. "They may sound similar, but the two countries are on opposite sides of the world from each other, plus there's a seven-hour time difference."

Fortunately, there was an Australian (who now lives in France) on this Zoom call, who agreed it wasn't fair to make me fly 17 hours each way for only four nights. They agreed I could stay longer, as long as I flew in and out of Vienna and paid for the extra nights myself.

So how many nights did I want to stay? I checked my annual leave balance at work and found out that I could go for three weeks.

My flights and accommodation were only confirmed four weeks before I left. So it didn't leave much time to plan my trip. One thing I really wanted to do was ski in the Austrian Alps. If I'm going to go in winter, I may as well go skiing.

Yes, people in wheelchairs can ski! I've skied twice before:

once in Japan and once at Mt Buller in Victoria. It is so much fun that I recommend it to everyone. Even though I hate the cold, it's worth it.

I made some inquiries before leaving, and booked a tentative date with a disabled ski school in Schladming, a town a three-hour drive away from Vienna.

When I arrived in Vienna, I asked the hotel staff to research some accessible transport options for me to get there. They came back to us a few days later: a taxi costing €930 (over $1,500)! Plus, if I was to stay overnight, I had to pay for the driver's accommodation, dinner and breakfast! I said no thanks.

My ski booking was moved to the Sunday after the Zero Project Conference, which gave us more time to plan. The first thing was transport. Amy, my support worker, didn't mind if she had to drive us there. But it meant going up the day before and returning the day after. It was too far for a day trip. If someone else had been driving, we could have done it in one very long day.

We made numerous phone calls and got lucky with Hertz in Vienna. They had one wheelchair-accessible vehicle for hire that was available for the weekend, would allow Amy to drive it (but needed to pay extra as she's under 25) and would cost about €250. A bargain compared to the taxi.

With transport sorted, we needed accommodation for two nights. We called the Schladming Tourist Centre and asked them to find something for us. After two days they hadn't found anything, and the weekend was fast approaching. We spent that morning on the phone, calling every place close to the ski school. On our fifth or sixth attempt, we got lucky: a wheelchair-access room with two separate beds, available for the two nights and not too far from the ski school. We couldn't believe we got transport and accommodation sorted at last.

But a few hours later, Hertz emailed me to say our hire car had technical problems and was off the road! And it wouldn't be fixed before we needed it. Yep. Just when we thought we could relax and look forward to the trip to the mountains.

So, it was back to square one. We called a lot of disability transport providers but none could help. In desperation, I tracked down the lady who booked my airport transfers. Her name was Eva and she was at the conference. Maybe she could help?

Unfortunately, we'd already tried the company she used and they weren't available. "But I might know someone who has a van," Eva said. We left it with her and asked everyone we met at the conference as well.

That night we emailed the hotel to say we had transport issues and couldn't confirm the booking just yet, but would be in touch soon. On the Friday, we still hadn't heard back from Eva, so we found her at the closing ceremony of the conference. She made a phone call while we waited in front of her.

Her friend of a friend had a wheelchair van we could borrow – for free! We couldn't believe our luck. The only catch was that we had to go to a country train station to pick it up, and have it back by 3 pm on Monday. Easy, or so we thought.

With transport sorted, we emailed the hotel straight away to confirm our booking. At 10 pm, and as we got into bed, I received a reply from the hotel. It read: "You no longer have a booking with us as you did not confirm in time."

Oh dear! (Not exactly what I said at the time but too explicit to write). It was as if the universe was against us going skiing. We tried calling the hotel, but there was no answer, so emailed them asking if they had another suitable room available. I was only going for two nights and wasn't taking my shower chair anyway. As long as the room was accessible and had two beds, I didn't really care what the bathroom was like. Not at this late stage when we were leaving the next morning!

We had an email from them in the morning with a choice of two rooms. I chose one, clicked on the link that said "Confirm" and a webpage opened that said "Thank you for confirming your booking". All sorted, I hoped.

We finished packing, pushed the hoist down to the station, found the train we needed and bought our tickets; only we missed our connecting train as it didn't have wheelchair access (plus we didn't know where we needed to go or where the lifts were). Some of these stations were huge with changing platforms so you have to check the display boards (like at the airport).

We found staff that could help us get on the next train, but we were late picking up the van by about an hour and a half, especially since we couldn't even find our way out of that station!

We met up with Mr Harrer, who didn't speak much English. Amy and I had started learning German on Duolingo only ten weeks prior, so we weren't very capable of communicating with him. But he'd brought a friend with him and she could be our interpreter.

After removing some of the back seats so I could fit, and folding up my hoist, Amy was handed the keys. Our dream of being in the mountains was about to come true.

It was Amy's first time driving on the wrong side of the road, in a left-hand-drive vehicle (we didn't tell Mr Harrer that). It was the little things, like having to use your right hand to change gears, and the indicator switch on the opposite side that confused her the most. I kept guiding her to stay within the lane and which lane to go in when turning. But two hours later we arrived at the hotel surrounded by snow. We had no idea that they'd had snow the night before – the first after about four weeks with none! It was amazing timing for us.

We entered the warm reception, and the lady asked, "Can I help you?"

I told her my name and she looked confused. "You didn't confirm your booking," she said.

I showed her the confirmation I got on the website on my phone. Turned out there was a glitch in her system and she didn't receive a notification.

"Well, do you still have a room available?" I asked.

"Yes," she replied, much to our relief.

She had housekeeping prepare our room while Amy got things out of the van. In my rush and desperation to book accommodation, I never asked about clearance under the bed for my hoist. I could see in the photos that one bed didn't, but the other was a sofa bed. *All sofa beds have clearance, right?* I'd thought. When we got up to the room and checked, I was wrong. Neither bed had space underneath for the hoist legs to go under. How would I get into bed and out again safely?

We decided to go down for dinner and leave that problem for later. But putting it off wasn't going to solve the problem. After dinner, Amy sat on both beds and decided she wanted the sofa bed as the other was too soft, even though the sofa bed was the easiest to get me onto with the hoist. The other bed was built into the wall, so it couldn't be moved or raised. I did consider sleeping in my wheelchair, but this was an expensive hotel so I wanted to sleep in their bed.

We moved some furniture around to make space, but still couldn't get close enough. One piece of furniture was a large wooden coffee table and it just happened to be the same height as the bed.

"What if we hoisted me onto the table, then slid me onto the bed?" I asked Amy. She sat on the table to make sure it was sturdy. *It might actually work*, we thought. We put the hoist side-on to the bed, I drove underneath and she hoisted me up. Then Amy moved my chair back and put the table underneath, and covered it with the duvet and my poncho which was slippery on the outside. She lowered me onto the table, disconnected me from the hoist, then ran around the other side of the bed and pulled me with the duvet. It worked! We were excited but exhausted, and to think we'd have to do it again for both mornings and nights. But we had a way which worked, and our reward was to ski the next day.

There was no way I was going to be late for my ski booking at 11 am, so we set the alarm early. We had no idea how much longer it would take to get me off the bed again. When Amy got up, she opened the blinds. The view took our breath away. It was 7 am, and the sun had just touched the top of the mountain range we could see, highlighting the snow. There was still snow on our balcony balustrade too. It was like waking up in a fairy tale book; we thought we were dreaming. It's the kind of scene you'd only see on a calendar or postcard. And here it was, right outside our hotel window, on a trip that almost didn't happen. It made us forget all about our problems and go out and enjoy the day. We had made it.

The view from our hotel window

Melanie in her sit-ski with her guide, Sevie

Melanie Hawkes

Love is in the Airport

Airports weren't romantic.

Dominic strode toward his departure gate. He flew frequently for work, every fortnight, in and then out again. It was known as *FIFO*. He knew the schedule and the boarding protocols; he could recognise the flight crew by now. He knew exactly how much time to allow, unlike the frenzied passengers rushing around him, spilling coffee and crumbs from their breakfasts.

A woman suddenly crossed in front of him and they collided. Hard. She would have fallen if he hadn't grabbed hold of her elbow.

"Are you okay?"

She looked up at him, eyes wide, stunned. He was struck by how charmingly beautiful she was with her hair piled on top of her head. His heart rolled over.

"I'm okay," she replied, blinking.

They didn't speak as they righted themselves. No apology, no accusation. They moved apart at the same time as if they were doing a kind of dance. Dominic hesitated but she was already turning away, the moment lost. He went to move towards his gate again, but then she glanced back at him. It was all he needed to take the risk.

"Can I get your number?"

"I don't usually … I mean, I guess so."

"Thanks," Dom said, as she typed her number into his phone. "What's your name?"

The blonde with the gorgeous blue eyes replied, "It's Elle."

And, that's how it started, just before they parted ways.

***

Elle checked the clock on her computer again. Only three minutes had passed, but it was getting closer to five o'clock.

Danica, who sat across from her, noticed Elle's uncharacteristic edginess. "Do you need to be somewhere?"

Danica was Elle's best friend at Sandpiper & Stone, the austere law firm where they both worked as research assistants to the lawyers. They had started on the same day about two years ago, which was enough for an instant bond, helped by the fact that they were the only two research assistants in the corporate team.

"I do, actually." Elle could not restrain the coyness in her voice. It was a novelty to finally have something to share, after months of unsuccessful dates and introductions.

"Ooooooooooh!" Danica's eyes widened. "Tell me everything! I need vicarious excitement!" Danica loved spin classes and champagne in equal measures but her social life was currently on hold. Her boyfriend, Josh, was training for the City-2-Surf half marathon. He was passionate about health and fitness. That meant no drinking, no takeaways and no late nights until the race was over.

Danica stood up from her open plan desk. She scooted over to Elle's spot on the other side of the partition for a closer discussion, which also effectively blocked Elle from escaping.

"Is it Airport Guy?"

Elle had let slip some weeks ago about her encounter with the good-looking stranger at the airport and how they ended up exchanging details.

"He has a name!"

"I think Airport Guy has a better ring to it!" Danica played with her ponytail of dead straight black hair.

Elle rolled her eyes with a smile.

"Is that why you're dressed like that today?" Danica perched herself on Elle's desk and swung a leg back and forth and she scanned Elle up and down.

"Yes."

Danica crossed her arms. "You look hot."

"Thanks," Elle exhaled. She hadn't been sure – the dress was outside her comfort zone of black pants and white t-shirt.

"Will you update me later?" Danica asked with a raised eyebrow.

Elle lowered her gaze, a blush flooding her cheeks. "I'm not sure." This thing with Dominic was too fledging – Elle wasn't sure it could withstand scrutiny this early.

Danica pursed her lips with a nod before returning to her desk.

***

As soon as the last search had been completed, and the results emailed to the awaiting solicitor, Elle left, not even finishing off her timesheet or waiting for Danica.

The elevator doors opened and there he was, standing in the foyer. He was wearing a button-up shirt; the sleeves rolled up to his elbows because of the weather. He would have had time to change before coming to meet her. He'd shaved, too; she could tell by the smoothness of his cheek. God, it was so special having him here after another two-week separation with nothing but texts and silly memes to sustain them.

"Hey," he said, with that crooked grin. He opened his arms and Elle let herself be swept up for a hug.

"It's good to see you," Elle said into his neck.

Dominic set her back. "Ready to go?"

"Yes, let me check on the Uber." Elle had ordered it before getting into the lift, so she opened up the app to check its location.

***

Looking at Elle as she frowned at her phone, her hair loose around her shoulders tonight, Dominic was glad that he seized that moment in the airport, despite his doubts that he could pursue a new relationship as a FIFO worker.

Elle looked up and broke his reverie. "What are you thinking about?" she asked.

"Just how we met," he admitted with a wink. There were certainly no real prospects on site. He worked at a location called Doolgunna, which was about a two-hour drive from the nearest town, Meekatharra. Meekatharra only had about five hundred residents, and the airport which flew the workers in and out each week for the various pastoral and mining projects in the Wheatbelt region. He had some good mates, and plenty to occupy himself, but it could still be lonely.

"I hardly ever fly," Elle remarked.

"Such a stroke of luck we crossed paths." He pressed a kiss to her forehead which earned him a smile. "You never told me where you were going – or arriving from? – that day?"

"No, I didn't." Elle tucked her hair behind her ear. "I was coming back from visiting my grandmother in Adelaide."

"Adelaide? I've never been there." Dominic had moved to Perth from Sydney because it was the best place for FIFO work.

"It's lovely. Like Perth, but with more beautiful buildings and wider streets. And churches of course!" Elle looked at her phone. "The Uber is about three minutes away."

Dominic put an arm around her shoulders. He wasn't going anywhere right now. "You can tell me more about Adelaide while we wait."

***

Elle beamed at Dominic across the table. He was back again, and she had snared a booking at a buzzing new restaurant called XO Fuse, an Asian/Australian offering in Northbridge, close to the CBD. A movie was tempting, but she was conscious to reinforce the vibrancy of the city to Dominic on their dates.

"What do you think?" Elle watched the waiters weaving through the crowded tables.

"It's noisy!"

Conversations around them were loud over the clattering of dishes from the kitchen, punctuated by a periodic burst of flames from a fry-pan. They ordered quickly and included some cold beers. The restaurant's air conditioning was struggling to overcome the humidity outside. The food arrived almost instantly. After a few minutes of silence, while devouring the dishes, Dom put down his chopsticks. He ran his hand through his hair to move his heavy fringe of brown waves off his temple. Elle loved it when he did that.

"I know what you're doing."

"What?" Elle took a sip of water.

"This." Dominic indicated the room. "You're choosing trendy places to remind me of what I am missing out on when I'm on site."

Elle squirmed. He was right, but she was also trying to give him reasons to stay in one place, to not leave. She wasn't arrogant enough to think that she could be enough.

"I just want it to be fun." Elle moved her hand to her beer bottle and ran her fingers up and down over the condensation.

"I appreciate it. There's only so much of an unlimited buffet a guy can take." He had told her during one of their phone calls about the extensive catering provided for every meal. No FIFO worker ever went hungry.

His gaze dropped to Elle's fingers. She drew her hand away and put it in her lap.

"Have you had enough?" he asked, motioning to her plate where she'd left a few pieces of chicken behind.

He could have been referring to more than just her meal. This on-or-off thing was exhausting. She had to consciously suppress the urge to blurt out to Dominic that she could never have enough of him, that she yearned for more time. A feeling she never imagined possible with anyone. Maybe it was her limited relationship experience. Maybe it was the fleeting and erratic nature of their encounters so far. But her world was shaken every time he returned, and then she was left behind and bereft when he flew out again.

Elle felt a tangible pull at her heart each time his plane took off. Her dad used to travel a lot when she was younger. He had been a sales rep for Ford which meant visiting car dealerships across the country. She'd never gotten used to his absences.

She didn't say any of that though. Instead, she waggled her eyebrows in a playful way. "I've had enough to eat, if that's what you mean, although I could find room for something sweet."

Her obsession for dessert had become a standing joke between them, after Elle had told him how much she adored Haigh's chocolates which came from Adelaide. A factory tour had been a highlight of her recent trip.

"In fact, I may even have a Haigh's chocolate frog at home still."

"Do you think I could take a bite?" Dominic's grin was teasing.

Elle blushed in response but pretended not to understand his meaning. "Sharing is caring, except when it comes to chocolate!"

Dominic chuckled. He dealt with the bill then held out his hand to her.

"Let's go," he said. "I'll take a chance you'll have something to satisfy me."

***

Another fortnight later, Elle messaged Dom. He should have landed by now. She checked the app for his flight status. Cancelled? That couldn't be right! Takeoff had been delayed, but Dom had messaged to say he was on board and would see her soon.

She had driven to the airport to pick him up. It would be so annoying if he wasn't here. She flicked her indicator to pull out of the pick-up zone, and her phone rang. She answered it via Bluetooth.

"Dom?"

"Hey, gorgeous."

"Where are you? Has your flight been cancelled?" She could hear a crackling on the line at Dom's end.

"Yeah, yeah, sorry," Dom said. "I tried to get a message to you but it didn't go through when we disembarked. We were all on board, ready to go, but the plane couldn't take off. There's a cyclone coming."

That would explain the noise. "Really? And you couldn't have tried to let me know before I drove all the way out here to pick you up?"

"The wifi has been dropping out, Elle. I had to get back to site as part of our crisis management protocols. I'm pissed off too."

"Are you taking a later flight?"

"Elle, I can't fly out tonight. There's no planes leaving Meekatharra. A cyclone is too dangerous. The airport is closed."

Elle blew out heavily. "So, you're going to miss the party?" Sandpiper & Stone was holding an end-of-financial-year event, and employees were allowed to invite a plus one. Elle had been looking forward to introducing Dom to her bosses and hanging out with Danica and Josh.

"Well, yeah, I can't magic myself there."

This was so frustrating! "The whole point of me coming to the airport to get you was so we could get to the party on time, together. Now I'm going to be late, and alone, again."

"I'm sorry, Elle; it's not my fault."

"Couldn't you have checked the weather? Maybe asked for an earlier shift or to finish up so you could try and beat the cyclone?"

"Elle."

She was being irrational, but this had tipped her over for some reason after months of being able to cope with the uncertainty, the absences, and the distance. "It's fine, I get it. It's not your fault. Don't worry. I'm sure there will be someone for me to talk to at the party." She wouldn't flirt with another man, but she wanted Dom to think that she might.

"I'll get a flight out tomorrow morning, I'm sure of it."

Dom's calm voice didn't help with Elle's frustration. "I'll wait to hear from you," she said tightly, trying not to let this escalate into a full-blown fight. She pressed the red button on her steering wheel to end the call.

The romance was definitely "off" for now.

Elle joined the line of cars heading towards the city. She felt like a total cow for not asking if he was safe.

***

Dominic used to love fly-in-fly-out work and the extra money. He had applied for it when he was single and had no reason to be in one place all the time. He enjoyed the break from his flatmates, and the rigours of the city every two weeks to go off to somewhere remote and less overwhelming. Doolgunna was definitely remote. It was dry, dusty and flat. Nothing could be seen on the horizon, just the red earth meeting the sky.

Then he met Elle. Now FIFO sucked. They could not find a rhythm to their relationship, turning it on when he flew in, turning it off when he flew out. He was glad they had managed to find a way with technology to stay connected during the two weeks he was away. But there was no substitute for physical connection.

This was the first time his flight had been cancelled and they'd lost a day of valuable time together. Air travel was always unpredictable, but it was hard to accept delays when every second counted.

Dominic bent to look outside of the plane's window as he stood in the aisle and waited to disembark. He was back again. As he stepped off the flight, he tried not to break into an undignified run towards the exit.

***

Dom loved his job as a project manager and flying to the site regularly. Elle knew that. He loved getting out of his company's office in West Perth from time to time. He did interesting work, the latest being renewable energy and the dismantling of a solar farm that had reached end-of-life. But it meant that they really had to plan their periods of time together and savour it. And she had to endure a long period of waiting in between.

The separations and reunions were initially thrilling. However, the exhilarating aspects of their fly-in, fly-out relationship were getting stale. It was emotionally draining to be so happy to see Dom again, to orchestrate an artificially perfect fortnight together, and then to suppress the feelings of abandonment as they had to say goodbye again.

"Is he here this weekend, or not?" Danica asked after Elle had returned from lunch. "It was such a shame he missed that work party! It was wild."

Elle hadn't enjoyed it as much as Danica. She had still been simmering over the cancelled flight at the time. "He's coming back tonight," Elle said. No inclement weather. Everything looked to be on time.

"Hey, you haven't asked me about what I have on tonight, you know!" Danicia flung her ponytail over her shoulder in mock offence.

Elle smacked her forehead with her fingers. "Of course! The race is over! Josh must be emerging from his self-imposed hibernation I assume?"

Danica gave a little wriggle. "Yes, especially because he was stoked he ran a good time. We're starting at The Royal straight after work with some of his mates – you know you're more than welcome – then we are heading off for more drinks later at one of those new bars on James Street. And he's promised me we can grab some Thai along the way! I can't wait!"

"I'm so happy for you, Dee," Elle responded. Her friend had been a supportive girlfriend the past few months and deserved to celebrate. Elle slumped heavily back into her seat. The thought of an airport pickup was more of a chore than a delight. She'd rather grab a sparkling wine with friends than battle traffic alone.

***

"Thanks for picking me up," Dom said. He could charge a taxi back to his company account but Elle always offered and they greedily grabbed the extra time it gave them together.

Elle barely glanced over at him. "No problem." She shifted in her seat. Her dress pulled tightly across her thighs and she regretted wearing it. She should have just worn leggings.

Dom looked across at her. "Is everything okay?"

Elle inclined her head slightly. "Of course, just a long week."

Dominic touched her shoulder. "It was pretty shit that the wifi was so poor on site this week. I missed our usual Zoom time together."

"Same," Elle responded. She craned her neck ostensibly, not to see how many cars were in front of them but because it gave her an excuse to avoid eye contact. She stopped herself from saying that even with good wifi, sometimes a remote connection was just that – remote.

"You didn't have to come out here on a Friday night, you know, Elle."

"I know," Elle said. She abruptly indicated to turn onto the Reid Highway in the hope it would be quicker. "Danica was going out to drinks after work and invited me but I said I had to pick you up."

"Oh."

The silence sat between them as they stared straight ahead. Could that flicker of resentment be quashed, or would it simply grow uncontrollably, getting bigger every time Dom flew out and left Elle alone?

***

Another two weeks and she was at the airport again. Dom said she should wait for him at her apartment. Elle insisted she come – she didn't want her previous churlishness to take their routine off course.

Elle's heart skipped a beat at the sight of his handsome face coming out of the terminal, his hair flopping over his forehead as usual, his bag swung over his broad shoulders. She had missed him! A huge smile broke across her face.

Dominic opened the door and slid inside. "Hi, gorgeous!" He leaned across for a deep kiss.

"Welcome back."

***

Dominic watched Elle put the car into drive, glad that her mood was lighter than last time. He suspected that she was also making an effort to gloss over the fact that this arrangement – even with a reliable wifi connection and flight schedules – was wearing thin.

"Can you turn left here?" Dominic motioned with his hand as they approached the intersection.

Elle swivelled her head to look straight at him. "Why? Wouldn't that take us back to the airport?"

"Yes, but we'd actually be going around the back of it."

"Oh, Dom." Elle bit her lip. "That would be a major waste of time. It's quicker if we take Great Eastern Highway."

"I know." Dom reached out to squeeze her hand. "Just let me show you something first. You didn't have anything booked for us tonight, did you?"

With a sigh, Elle turned left, and the road became empty and darker almost immediately as they left the other vehicles and travellers behind.

Dom pointed forward. "Follow this road for about a kilometre."

Elle indulged his request. They drove past the terminals and hangars and the freight areas. After business hours, there was not a lot of action. Soon they came upon barriers and temporary fences indicating a construction zone.

***

"Is this safe?" Elle asked nervously. She'd never come this way before. She peered through the windshield and wondered if high beam was advisable. She could see a crane and a bulldozer in the distance.

"Absolutely," Dominic said. "You can pull over here if you like."

Elle checked her rearview mirror. She pulled over and put the car into Park. "What are we doing here?"

"A proposed development."

Elle's brow furrowed as she thought about recent news articles she had read. "You mean the new runway construction?"

"Yes, it was planned for 2026 but the government has decided to bring it forward to 2025."

"Next year?" Elle asked.

Dominic nodded.

"Okay," Elle said slowly. She didn't exactly follow his meaning. She waited with raised eyebrows. "And? So what?"

Dominic laughed. "I know I'm being a bit obscure but I'm just so excited!" He unbuckled his seatbelt and turned to face Elle. "They are starting to resource the team for the first phase of construction. I saw the advertisement online and made some enquiries."

Elle's heart started to pick up pace.

"I applied for one of the project manager roles," Dominic continued, "and I got it! I got the job!"

"What does that mean?" Elle pressed her lips together.

"Basically, it means no more FIFO, Elle!" Dom put his hands on her shoulders. "Elle, I'll be here now, every day, every week. No more flying."

"Oh my gosh, that's the best news, ever, truly, Dom." Elle gave a messy laugh of relief and joy and leaned in for a hug. "I can't believe it! Really?"

"Yep," Dom confirmed. "And it's for more money because of the accelerated timeframe. I start in six weeks, so I will finish up my current job in the next month, have a short break, and then get into this project straight away."

"Oh my gosh, should we take a holiday together, go somewhere? We could fly to Adelaide and indulge in Haigh's and big Barossa reds?"

Dom shook his head. "No way. No more planes. Not for a while."

"Fair enough! A staycation!" Elle put her hand to Dom's cheek. "Dom, I can't believe you did that, I know you loved being on site."

"Elle, I did, but I love being with you more." Dominic put a finger to her lips. "Please, don't deny it. It was hard on you. I saw it. I felt it."

"I missed you so much, but I thought we were coping with the Zoom calls?"

Dom almost growled in response. "I can't look at a laptop the same way again. I'd rather be in person with you, with my hands all over your body, caressing every single damn inch of you."

Elle laughed. "I prefer the real thing too."

Dom started to nuzzle her neck. "Not here!" Elle stopped him. "This is your future workplace!"

"You're no fun," he said jokingly as he sat back up.

"Can I take us home now?" Elle turned the ignition.

"Absolutely," Dom's mouth raised at one corner in a devilish grin. "Let's get started."

Elle sat there with her hands on the steering wheel.

"Elle?" Dom nudged.

Elle took a second before responding. "I need to tell you something."

"Okay." A hint of worry crept into his tone.

"I think I love you," Elle said.

Dom breathed out. He took a strand of Elle's hair and tucked it behind her ear. "That's good to hear. I wish I could say the same thing."

Elle froze. Had she gotten this horribly wrong?

"I don't think I love you. I do love you. So much."

Elle squeezed his hand then turned the wheel. Their journey together was taking off in a new direction. On the ground. Elle made a face at the air control tower as they drove past. She was glad they wouldn't be back here any time soon.

Airports weren't romantic.

Caroline Hayward

Cruising with a Wheelchair

"Why don't you take a cruise?" suggested friends.

"But we're not the cruise type," I protested. "We don't do bingo and karaoke."

"Well, get a cabin with a balcony then you can read a good book in splendid isolation. At least you can push the wheelchair around, you won't have to shop, cook, and clean, you can wear a pretty frock or two and you'll have people helping you."

It made sense, so we started to plan. Swayed by his tastes in musicals, my husband chose to cruise in the South Pacific. There was a logic to this that quelled my antipathy to cruising because the best way to visit islands is by sea.

After five years of pushing a wheelchair, I now know what to look out for: "No, we can't take that ship," I told our travel agent. "Look! It has a box-like swimming pool with metal ladders. He'll not be able to get in."

I booked when I thought we'd covered all bases. I emailed the cruise company twice before departure to ensure special assistance with embarkation. "Noted," came the reply. "Just ask when you get to the departure lounge."

So, already frazzled by coping with a Sydney taxi driver who wanted to rip-off the wheelchair-bound by charging three times the normal price, and already exhausted pushing a husband weighed down by our hand luggage, I requested help as soon as we entered the departure lounge.

"Just go to the lady at the desk and she'll help."

This proved to be normal check-in, but so far so good. I requested help again.

"Just take this and go through immigration," she said. After my next request, I was instructed to "Just go through security." Getting through security was a nightmare … the hand luggage, the wheelchair, his walking stick … "Laptops in or out of bags?"

Suddenly I was at the bottom of the ramp. I stonewalled: "I can't push this weight uphill and I requested assistance, which hasn't been forthcoming."

A passing employee pushed the wheelchair to the top of the ramp and dumped us.

"What do we do now?" I asked of anyone wearing a uniform.

"Well, you can't get into your cabin until 2pm and it's now 11am."

"So that's what I can't do. Now, please tell me what I can do."

"Well, a buffet brunch is being served on Deck 8."

"Which deck are we on now?"

"Two."

"So, how do I get from Deck 2 to Deck 8 with a wheelchair?"

"Take the elevator."

"Where are the elevators?"

Once settled into the Deck 8 buffet, I went to see what help might be available for finding my way to the cabin: None. Have you ever tried pushing a wheelchair along a narrow corridor lined with suitcases? Still, it was good practice because, thereafter, I'd be pushing the wheelchair almost the full length of the ship to reach the lifts whilst negotiating the cleaning carts that lined the route. I needed sonar to navigate the narrow gap. The cheerful cabin attendants squeezed against the wall as I staggered past. No help was offered. To be fair, though, they did all seem keen for me to "Have a nice day". Oh yes, and there was that nice officer who watched me struggle through the large, heavy door to the pool deck.

"You should go through backwards," he advised. "Do the same when you drag the wheelchair over that metal rim on the floor." Nice of him, wasn't it? At least somebody on board cared! That was the first and last time I wore a pretty frock, because I ripped it on the brake handle of the wheelchair.

When we arrived in the cabin, we were quickly into the practice run for emergency evacuation of the ship. The instructions were clear: Go to Deck 6 and do NOT use the elevators. So, I rang Guest Services.

"How do I get from my cabin to Deck 6 with a wheelchair without using the lift?"

"Just use the elevator, Ma'am. It's just a practice"

"But what if it were real? What would I do then?"

When we got to our emergency assembly point, we were lined-up in rows of six as we arrived. By chance, we were at the back. No particular problem in that except that it was impossible for my wheelchair-bound husband to see over the heads of the five people in front to see how to put on his lifejacket. Still, it was just a practice.

Our cabin was located at the stern, hence the lengthy corridor walks. It was an inappropriate booking, but we were not to know that at the time. Any cruise ship organisation with half an eye to the needs of those pushing wheelchairs might have provided better advice. A briefing about getting around the ship with a wheelchair would also have been welcomed. On our first evening aboard I did what I knew to date. I used the lifts to the Deck 8 buffet, which meant circumnavigating the swimming pool. By now it was dark, the swimming pool was overflowing onto the deck, and the wind was rising. At this point, I discovered that my husband and his wheelchair serve as a kite when the breeze picks up. He took off with me in tow, skidding through the water. Good job I can water ski.

Even though it's on the flat, it's heavy work pushing a wheelchair on carpet, and it's surprisingly skiddy. My husband started to ride shotgun, one hand out, ready to protect himself as the wheelchair careered into walls. But it was only six trips a day, to and from breakfast, lunch, and dinner – a novel version of Meals on Wheels. There was no other reason to emerge from the cabin. We don't gamble, so no need to go to the casino. Ballroom dancing and the men's bellyflop competition were clearly out for us, and we had already vetoed bingo and karaoke. With one exception in nine days, the films in the theatre were all of the action movies that didn't interest us. There was disabled access to the main pool, but this was packed with hordes of kids. The adults-only pool was not accessible.

The best of a South Pacific cruise is the snorkelling and swimming, so maybe we'd chosen unwisely, but I had asked about tours at the time of booking. Yes, these were available, and most buses were accessible. Great, I booked two tours. Only after our first scheduled stop did I realise that my husband wouldn't actually be able to get to the buses because the ship anchored offshore and he couldn't get in and out of the tender boats that ferried passengers to the jetties. So back to Plan B: relax with a book, but as our balcony faced outwards from the stern of the ship, it was never in shade. So, cabin-bound, we flicked through the channels on the TV. Apart from BBC World and CNN, there were some American programs dubbed into foreign languages and a few channels showing ship-board events. At least I found-out what a belly-flop competition is – and the surprising number of people who are interested to watch it. Well, what about a cuppa? No: There are no tea or coffee facilities in cabins (nor even potable water) and passengers are discouraged from walking around the ship with hot beverages.

"Well, I'm not pushing you back along the corridor just for a cuppa."

"Try room service," suggested our cabin attendant. Good idea! Maybe this is the solution to pushing the wheelchair several kilometres a day. Not really, the menu is limited and unchanging, presumably to discourage overuse. When I did ring for a cup of tea, I was told there would be a forty-minute wait. Not much spontaneity in that, is there?

"I think we'd be better having a holiday at home," I grumbled to my husband. "At least you'd have your newspaper and a choice of TV channels and cooking and cleaning would be easier than wheelchair marathons."

"Look on the bright side," he said, eyeing the load of laundry I'd just hand-washed in the bathroom sink (no launderette on board). "At least the balcony is so hot that'll all dry pretty quickly."

Lynne Hunt

Piddling on Cultural Boundaries

On a recent trip to Crete, I was the only Australian among a group of British travellers – most from the south-east of England. I didn't think much about it because I'm British by origin. I thought I knew the ground rules. However, I soon discovered that I was something of an oddity in their eyes.

"Do you always wear black?" a sister traveller asked, referring to my traveller's uniform of black T-shirt and jeans.

I thought this a bit rude and judgemental, so I turned the tables and asked if she always wore coloured clothes. I aimed to be sarcastic, but she thought I was engaging in deep and meaningful conversation. "Well, I do wear coloured clothes. However, at home in England, I wear a lot of navy blue. I even buy a special laundry detergent for washing navy blue clothes." We were in a lift. There was no escape.

The Crete tour was busy. After visiting a few archaeological sites each day, there was little time to spruce up for dinner, but, on the last night, I had time to slip on a pretty frock. Then it happened again! A woman I didn't know leant across the table at dinner to observe, "Oh, I see you do wear something other than black!"

How did this get to be her business? This group of English travellers had a clear understanding of who's in or out of their culture and they felt entitled to judge the out-group.

"They're not quite PLU, are they?" a fellow traveller asked me as he looked askance at the hordes of British tourists disembarking from the cruise ships anchored in the bay of Santorini. "**P**eople **L**ike **U**s," he explained when he saw the blank look on my face. I was floored by this comment. I can't stop talking about it. I can't imagine hearing any Australian talking about 'PLU' – ever.

Lest I alienate UK family and friends, I should note that I ran the 'She's dressed in black' and 'PLU' stories past a few of them. They were equally gobsmacked at the rudeness of such superior comments. They, like me, had British mothers who taught them not to pass comment about other people's appearance unless it's favourable. So, I'm not suggesting that these conversations were characteristic of British culture, but my fellow travellers did appear to be beating the boundaries of their in-group and marking their southern English cultural territory by piddling on the borders of their dress codes. I began to feel very Australian even though similar snobbishness exists in the Antipodes. I discovered this when I admired the blouse of a woman who saw herself as part of the Queensland elite. "It's Versace," she replied, "You wouldn't be able to afford it."

I once read a book called 'Watching the English.' It purported to study English culture. It was actually a collection of amusing anecdotes which showed how the English drew cultural boundaries, particularly those pertaining to social class. Does one say 'sofa' or 'settee'. Is it 'napkin' or 'serviette'? Do you go to the 'loo', 'toilet', 'lavatory', or 'bathroom'?

I still remember the TV comedy sketch in which tall John Cleese represented the British upper classes. Ronnie Barker, of average height, signified the middle classes, and shorter Ronnie Corbett was the working-class man. Standing in height order, John Cleese announced, "I have lunch in the executive dining room." Ronnie Barker had lunch in the staff cafeteria, and Ronnie Corbett said, "I don't have lunch. I have me dinner."

Take care when travelling in England because your use of language will indicate the extent to which you are 'in' or 'out', as Greek PhD student, Nikos, found when he arrived in Liverpool (UK) in the mid-1960s. His research was about ecumenism, so he was introduced to the hierarchies of the different faith groups in Liverpool. Soon after his arrival, he was invited to Sunday lunch with the Bishop of Liverpool.

"Would you like to go upstairs before lunch?" the bishop's wife asked.

"No, here will be fine," Nikos replied, looking around the dining room. Now that really would have been piddling on cultural boundaries, but how was he supposed to know that going upstairs meant going to the 'loo', 'toilet', bathroom', or 'lavatory'?

My travelling, working and family lives have been one long negotiation of the boundaries between cultures.

"Oh, Gawd!" I exclaimed as I tried to find my way into a new university job in Queensland in 2006.

"Don't say that here!" a new colleague cautioned. She explained that the campus is located in a region with strong Lutheran and evangelical traditions. I shouldn't blaspheme. My cultural boundary lines were being redrawn. It had been the same thirty years before when I first started working in Australia. I needed housemates to share the rent and mentioned in a staff room announcement that male or female applicants would be fine by me. I'd been in share houses with male and female co-renters in Liverpool (UK) and thought nothing of it. I was taken to one side and informed that I'd ruffled a few West Australian feathers. Co-ed house shares were not the done thing in Perth in the early 1970s. It was the start of learning my new cultural identity in Australia.

Culture cossets. After travelling, most people are happy to return home where they know the rules of engagement and where they speak like those around them. In fact, my Australian husband actually asked me to change aspects of my language and British pronunciation because he was keen for his children (my step-kids) to speak with Australian idiomatic expression. (Lollies in Australia is sweets in the UK is candy in America). My father-in-law, Jack, was a walking dictionary of 'Strine' – Australian English. When the Macquarie Australian Dictionary was first published in the 1980s, we sat down with Jack and let him yarn-on, checking his use of language against the new publication. In one evening, we found a number of Strine expressions that hadn't been included. We sent them off to the dictionary which subsequently appointed us 'Friends of the Macquarie Dictionary.' I was starting to feel quite PLU in Australia.

Since then, Australian culture and language has changed. Perth friend Vince, now in his nineties, recalls a move in the 1950s to introduce Southern British Approved English (SBAE) to make Australian use of language more formal. Fortunately, it didn't get off the ground, but I'm sure my fellow travellers in Crete would have nodded in approval if it had. They were very SBAE themselves. The reality is that, in Britain and Australia in the 1950s, most radio and TV announcers did speak SBAE. I'm always interested in stories about the well-known Australian humanitarian lawyer, Geoffrey Robertson. Apparently, he didn't speak until he was five years old, but he'd spent a lot of time listening to radio announcers who spoke SBAE. So, when this little Australian boy spoke for the first time, he sounded as English as he still does. The British magazine, Private Eye, described him as an Australian who'd had a vowel transplant.

Things have changed and regional accents now abound in the media. Australian culture and language have changed as well. Equal opportunity legislation now inhibits the use of some idiomatic expressions because they are derogatory, racist, or sexist. Culture has become more inclusive of diversity to the point where individuals can now forge their own cultural and personal identity and self-identify at will. As a 'portly' elderly woman recently declared, "I have an announcement to make. From now on, I want to identify as twenty-five and slim." And I want to identify with the Beatles song: 'She's dressed in black'.

Lynne Hunt

Travel when you can

In memory of Ruth Hunt (1982-2020)
and her dad, Lyall Hunt, (1933-2018)

In 2003, my husband, Lyall, and I purchased round-the-world airline tickets that resulted in us spending many a boring hour in South American airports waiting for eternally delayed planes. To pass the time, we started to make lists and tables of the countries we'd visited in our lifetimes. Our two kids each had their own columns in the tables because they were already well-travelled, having accompanied us on two previous round-the-world adventures before they were fifteen. We had rules of inclusion for the lists of countries. For example, just passing through a country didn't qualify as a visit. At that stage, I'd been through Switzerland about eight times by train, but I'd never stayed. So, Switzerland was off the list. When we arrived home in Perth, I threw the list into a catch-all basket in my study and forgot about it. Two years later, I rediscovered it, decided it was interesting, and typed it up to share with my family.

My daughter, Ruth, always a bit of a bush lawyer, like her dad, was prepared to argue the toss about anything. Incensed, she hurtled into the room accusing her father of triple-dipping. "You can't claim the Soviet Union, Uzbekistan, and Kazakhstan as three countries. They were all in the Soviet Union. That's one country!"

My friends were impressed when I told them the story. "Wish my kids understood world politics like that," they exclaimed.

Ruth was so busy shirt-fronting her dad that she failed to spot the loopholes in *my* list. I had (and still do have) East Germany and Germany as two countries because when I went to East Germany in 1973 it was a separate country. In contrast, in the last few decades, I've been to Czechoslovakia, the Czech Republic and Czechia three times and, each time, it had a different name. I haven't claimed three countries. I'm not sure what to do about protectorates like New Caledonia or Easter Island. Are they countries? I went through passport control, so that's good enough for me. They're on the list.

I've listed England, Scotland, and Wales as three separate countries rather than the singular 'Britain'. Each country now has its own parliament, so I think they're legitimate claims and, when I go to Northern Ireland later this year, I'll reach my eighty-ninth country. Even so, I was raised in Britain, so it does seem a bit weird. When I left in 1973 the ethnic identities in Britain hadn't crystalised into nationhood as such. Now, when I return and watch the news on BBC, the announcers throw to the 'news around the nations,' when they wrap-up the national component of the day's events. It takes me by surprise. Which nations? I always have to work out what they mean. Counting countries is a shape-shifting exercise.

So, what began as an idle pastime in South American airports became a lengthy discussion in my family about countries and borders. When we started this discussion, I didn't realise that league tables associated with travel are a 'thing'. There's even a One Hundred Club for those who've travelled to one hundred or more countries. I've even met a member of the club. He went to San Marino to celebrate his fortieth birthday just so that he could hit the ton. He was one of the tour leaders on my Arctic voyage and he'd previously been an adventure tour leader in Africa – a useful continent for clocking-up countries.

Friends engaged with my list of countries. Peter, in Germany, encouraged me to go to the former Yugoslavia because I could visit six countries in one hit. I've already visited Croatia and Bosnia Herzegovina, but travel isn't really a quantitative thing for me. Adding Montenegro or Serbia would just mean more churches and cobblestone streets, and there's only so many of those that a girl needs to see in her lifetime. Even so, I find a sense of completeness in round numbers, so I took my wheelchair-bound husband on a South Pacific cruise hoping that he could reach fifty countries. Unfortunately, a cyclone hit Vanuatu. We couldn't land and Lyall died at an unsatisfactory forty-nine countries. I'm currently at eighty-eight countries with Northern Ireland yet to come, so I'm tempted to visit Lichtenstein next year so that I can reach ninety countries before my travel legs wear out.

Beating the boundaries is a traditional ceremony in England, which involves walking the geographic boundaries of a parish to maintain the memory of where the borders lie. It's a way of saying "This is us."

In my travels around the world, I've found that ethnic identity can hold more sway than nationality. These ethnic boundaries are beaten through shared language, literature, art, and music regardless of countries separated by passport control. My point of view was reinforced when I saw 'The Slav Epic' which comprises twenty huge canvases painted by Mucha. He wanted to strengthen a sense of Slavic (not necessarily Czechian) identity. Mucha shaped Slavic identity by painting themes such as education; religion; historical events; 'The magic of the word'; and geography – the original homeland of the Slavs, which doesn't accord with the country I listed called Czechia.

In contrast, my guide in Dresden spoke of the importance of culture in defining countries. He told tales of the 'Baedeker Bombings' – WWII attacks by the Luftwaffe against historic towns and cities in Britain. Their objective was demoralisation through the destruction of cultural heritage. The targets were informed by the German Baedeker travel guides which pointed the way to buildings of British cultural significance. The subsequent bombings of German heritage towns, like Dresden, were seen as Allied reprisal for the Baedeker Bombings. Either way, the intent was to smash countries at their cultural core. Who would have thought that travel guides would become instruments of mass destruction?

Churchill kept the Dresden bombings a closely guarded secret because the British aristocracy would have opposed the plan. They were fond of the city which they included in their grand tours of Europe. In fact, it was the city in which many finished their education. Strange to think that in those days English ladies and gentlemen could roam freely across Europe. They carried papers, I know, but strict country borders and passport controls were less evident. Fortunately, the development of the European Community saw a return to such freedoms in a united Europe, but I still count each country separately in our lists of the countries we travelled to when we could.

Lynne Hunt

Always for the Moment

So here I was, standing in the cattle yards in the bowels of LA International Airport, herded along by stern-looking security guards and hoping they would come my way and unclip and re-clip the drafting lane and redirect the flow, thus shortening the queue. With planes arriving every five minutes, passengers from numerous flights had all jammed into the lanes, each as eager to get clear of Customs and continue on their way; there seemed to be a thousand of us all with the same hope.

The backpack, in the last hour, had mysteriously doubled its weight, as had the camera bag, which was now chockers with junk food from the plane – you can indeed only eat so much on a fifteen-hour flight through the night, and much of that eaten out of boredom and discomfort from sitting so long unmoving. Sleep had come in dribs and drabs only to wake in even more discomfort for doing so. But that part of the journey was thankfully over and I was on my feet and moving again – albeit in a shuffling motion that would eventually see me and my passport scrutinised by an even sterner security guard.

I breathed a sigh. The drafting gate had been redirected: I would soon reach the desk, suffer the scrutiny then sidle forward to the carousel to retrieve my small trolley bag (small because I had vowed to travel light) then I'd launch myself out into the unbelievable world beyond that was Los Angeles.

Here I was living only for the moment and each new moment thereafter for the next three weeks.

Security check complete, I bustled my backpack and long camera bag through the metal barriers, found the appropriate carousel, one of twenty or so, and searched through the crowd for a glimpse of purple and yellow geometric patterns. Ahh! it was there, jiggering along the conveyor saying 'Grab me, Mummy, grab me!' And that I did, feeling closer to debarking into brilliant LA sunshine.

It's amazing you know just how heavy light can be; even more amazing just how much computer equipment you can cram into one small trolley bag – of course safely wedged amongst socks, undies and a pair of summer pyjamas. But being the computer addict I am I had to have it all – the weighty inverter for computer use and recharging in the vehicle while driving; the spare camera, the dash cam, a whole sward of flash drives, mini SD cards and collapsible keyboards, and of course my American mobile phone. So gathered and hauled, I approached the Customs security, and shuffled forward to be asked, "Do you have any food, drugs or contraband in your luggage?"

"Yes," I answer proudly.

The burly Latino looks up from my declaration form and raises an eyebrow.

"I have vegemite and a jar of Nescafe coffee ... in case I can't buy it here."

He smiled – you know, that smile that says 'you Crazy Australians.'

He thumbed towards the brightness beyond the glass doors. I was free to go. I had made it. I had fulfilled a lifetime dream to travel to America. Until now I never thought it would happen – it was always just a dream. Even catching the plane from Perth to Melbourne to make the Los Angeles connection couldn't convince me that it was actually happening. Something would surely go wrong. Until I stepped on American soil, I was waiting for a spanner, always expecting the worst would happen, but now I was here, it didn't matter what went wrong – I would deal with it because I was here.

As I stood in line to exchange Aussie dollars for US notes, my thoughts drifted back to the two years of planning, the scraping and saving to stow away enough cash to pull this off, the constant battle with Lindsay over doing this trip alone, the late nights trawling the internet, planning the route and stopover points. I wished Dianne was here. When I had first announced to the group I was going, Di had said, laughing, "I'm coming with you."

"Too right!" I'd said. This had, after all, been our dream all these years, our dream as far back as I could remember, in primary school, through high school. I guess we grew up sometime during the next three decades and lost the dream. Lindsay's sudden announcement that he had a dream to go to NASCAR and up and did it just like that, alone, without any thought of finances, was enough to rekindle mine. I rekindled it big time. It became a raging urge that kept fuelling the fire during all those months of planning.

So here I was, without Di. Her husband's milestone birthday would fall in her absence and she felt committed to be with him on his 70th. I would do this for us both, having added her points of interest into our travel plans before she had cancelled out, to ensure we both experienced what we wanted to on the trip. I remember her face in the crowd at Perth airport – we had all gone for a Bon Voyage meal, kicked on at the Airport till my midnight flight boarded. I kissed Lindsay goodbye, but it was Di who got the last wave – this should have been us – us who had never given up on our childhood dreams, just lost them for a while.

I exchanged colourful Aussie dollars for grey bills and stepped out into the LA air, headed for the taxi stand, thinking: "This is for us, Di. Three weeks across America."

I slid onto the back seat of a yellow cab, the door held open by a crowd marshal who now had no crowd – the massive crush inside the terminal seeming to have vaporised while I'd stood gathering play dough. The morning was warm and bright and I realised time was running backward. I had flown out of Perth at five minutes past midnight on the 1st of May – the three-hour flight from Perth to Melbourne landed at 6.00 am on the 1st of May – I flew out for Los Angeles at 09.30 am and fifteen hours later I was here in Los Angeles catching a taxi at 7.00 am on the 1st of May. If this kept happening, I could be young again. And at 58, nearly 59, years old, I was indeed feeling young again. I felt like a backpacking teenager doing what I never had the chance to do when I was young. And I daresay I would make all the mistakes I might have made back then – only now I hoped I had more common sense and would deal with it wisely.

The taxi pulled out. First stop, to research the location in one of my novels. I said to the driver, "Rodeo Drive please." Mentally, I said as I sat staring out the window, wishing I was standing up through the sunroof, fists punching the breeze: "Yooohooooo! We're on our way, Di. We're on our way."

WALKING THE WALK

With my trip planned down the last second, I was glad to be sitting in the taxi heading away from the airport. At eight in the morning, the peak hour traffic on the freeway was hectic, a kaleidoscopic crush of metal all vying for a space in a lane that was going a multitude of somewheres. I gazed out the window, tried to be comfortable with being on the wrong side of the road – hell, everyone was on the wrong side of the road. I shuddered that in several hours that would be me behind the wheel, sitting on the wrong side of the car, driving on the wrong side of the road. I had indeed pictured this for the past two years during the planning stage, every day on Australian roads brainwashing myself till it became automatic to 'just keep your window arm closest to the white line, regardless which way you turn'. That was going to be the whole crux of driving for the next few weeks. This amount of traffic, however, was bringing up a whole heap of doubts that I could do without. Six lanes of traffic, high speeds and cars pouring into the lanes from all directions to congest and contest space even further. How would I know which lane, which off ramp to take, where the hell I was going?

I shelved those thoughts for the moment as Los Angeles slowly unfolded on either side of the road. I started to wonder what the fascination was with LA. It looked like Perth, a sprawling metropolis of low-slung houses, three to four-storeyed apartment buildings, green suburbs and people walking dogs. So, if I stayed off the freeways, I should be fine. For now, though, the focus was on researching my novel - *Mel Bailey's Men* – set in Los Angeles and the rich and famous set – so first stop was Rodeo Drive. The taxi cost $60, plus of course the tip. Tipping was something else I would have to get used to.

Rodeo Drive was green and clean. With palm trees. Palm trees down both sides of the road. Palm trees down the wide centre island, garnished by hedgerows of prolific white roses. Note: cross only at the lights.

The driver set me down around the corner on a side street: Brighton Street. This was fine as I now had time to rearrange my luggage, get the laptop out of my backpack to lighten the load on my back and into my trusty trolley bag. The long camera case alternated between slung over my shoulder and secured between the handles of the trolley bag. Regardless of its mode of travel, it was cumbersome, and I regretted bringing it, but it had been Mum's (silently, she too was with me on this trip as she used to like to travel but never made it overseas), and therefore, I wouldn't shed it.

So, the aim was to get the feel of the setting – stroll along the boulevard, (window) shop like the rich and famous, pop into Gucci, and Prada, look interested in something chic in Bulgari – dressed like a tourist? ... yeah right! This tourist first needed a cup of coffee after leaving the herding yards at LAX.

Tossing up between the excitement of walking the pavement where film stars and millionaires had walked before me and the need for strong stimulants, the stimulants won out. I went in search of a coffee shop ... found none. I did however find the flat fronted facades of Prada, Gucci, Bulgari, the ornate and slender structure of Stefano Ricci on the way to Wilshire Boulevard; I watched store windows being decorated with exquisite clothes, toyed with the idea of buying something decadent – a 'must do' a every location so I wouldn't forget a single minute of this unbelievable episode of my life.

The importance of research pressed

home as I tried to walk in the footprints of my high-flying characters – but none of the stores were open, and it was nine o'clock already. A passer-by advised stores don't open till ten. This was going to seriously cut into my time and I had planned everything down to the second. It also meant my story would be more credible knowing the rich and famous don't bother surfacing till somewhere closer to noon. Which is why they also didn't bother with coffee shops. And so, with trolley bag following like a tired toddler, I headed south. Next stop, downtown LA to walk the Walk of Fame.

It was while walking that I realised a couple of absent items on my inventory – one, I didn't have a map, nor a blind clue of where I was going; secondly I didn't have a phone (well, I had an American phone but no service yet); and my GPS was in the very bottom of the trolley bag which seemed to be getting heavier and floppier for no good reason. I realised almost immediately I should have brought a more solid carry-all with bigger wheels and these tiny plastic rollers objected to pavement cracks and any sudden movement in direction. I decided to walk only until I found a taxi stand or a pay phone where I could ring a taxi – only I didn't have any American coins, nor did I have the phone number of a taxi company. These little tricky bits of annoyance were enough to jar my thoughts and make me wonder if the queasiness growing in my stomach was nerves at being in a strange country all alone with no one to call on if things got out of hand, or if the airline food or the lack of a decent breakfast was having an adverse effect on my body. Nevertheless, I kept walking.

Next bit of vital research information: America, it seems, doesn't have taxi stands. And pay phones are almost non-existent. I walked the ornate narrow pavement passed Stefano's, passed The Wilshire-on-Wilshire-Boulevard, headed down Wilshire Boulevard, and just kept walking. I hoped it would bring me closer to my next destination, the Hollywood Walk of Fame. The distance, however, did little to bolster my growing apprehensions – I had no idea where I was heading, only hope, and I began feeling more ill with the distance. To make matters worse, my trusty trolley bag decided to do a quick waltz every time I crossed a road or negotiated a curb, and there were many of those, so I had to resort to dropping the handle and carrying the load by hand across roadways, which became taxing. I walked for about two hours, mentally absorbing the sights and sounds, willing a taxi stand to appear out of nowhere. After five miles, I gave up hoping and turned back. Hailing a taxi on this high-speed six-lane roadway was an impossibility – there was simply nowhere to pull up.

About two miles back towards my starting point, while crossing North Crescent Drive, I spotted a taxi heading down the hill towards me. I tried to hurry, but with a backpack hunching me over, the camera bag bashing against my hip so I had to carry it by the handle, and the trolley bag almost in carry mode, it was difficult to cross the road and flag it down. I was in the middle of the road when it passed me, dashing my hopes, but it stopped just before the intersection. I hurried to the driver, jostling my load. It must have been a sorry sight for, even though he had passengers in the back seat, he popped the boot, climbed out and dropped my bags in the back. I climbed into the front seat beside him, a rarity in America, for passengers never ride in the front. Expressing my thanks to the two Japanese businessmen for allowing me to encroach on their ride, I remained silent until we arrived at their destination.

The driver then gave me his full attention – where did I want to go? How long had I been in LA? What did I want to see in LA? Verizone was the best company for Internet access and AT&T for the phone. Lots of phone shops in the area I was going. He pointed some out as we passed. Suddenly, the six lane roadways became narrower and leafy, bordered by high fences and stately homes. We were in Beverley Hills, just cruising up and down streets. My driver pointed out homes of the rich and famous, or homes they had once lived in before selling out to high-priced lawyers and bankers and moving into the hills. Had it not been for this wonderful man I would never have experienced Beverley Hills, which also featured in *Mel Bailey's Men.* Relinquishing his role of impromptu tour guide, at half noon he pulled up outside the Capitol Record building on Vine Street.

"There's the start of the Walk of Fame," he said, and wished me a great experience on my drive across the country. He charged me $10 even though we had been driving around for over half an hour sightseeing. 'Courtesy of the previous passengers,' he added.

The time driving had given my arms a rest from my luggage, but it was now time to start walking again, slowly and reflectively, as I located stars of my childhood – William Boyd (Hopalong Cassidy), hoot of Hoot, Roy Rogers, James Arness. I found Mario Lanza; Marlon Brando (for Merrill), Bobby Darin (for Dianne) – a photo taken for each one I knew or had a soft spot for. It was a slow, slow walk down Vine, till it ran out of stars, then back up the hill towards Hollywood Boulevard, my stomach churning more and more by the minute. I guessed I was still hankering for that cup of coffee.

Soon enough I reached the corner of Hollywood and Vine – another milestone of my tour – and there was a Starbucks. I had promised Di we'd have a coffee at Starbucks, so in I went, shuffling my luggage ahead of me. Keeping an eye on my stuff, I ordered a Frappe – it was hot outside – but no, they can't change a hundred-dollar bill. What is wrong with these people!! It's only a hundred dollars! And my purse was full of them. So I shuffled my bags back out the door and headed to the bank down the street, then shuffled back to pay for my order. *Note: break all the hundred-dollar bills down if you want to buy anything.*

Sitting sipping down this $5.00 icy, thick, sickly sweet caramel milkshake, I had time to study the map I'd bought from a tour company on the way to the bank; it gave me a chance to gain my bearings, plan my route, for my next stop was the Mann Chinese Theatre on Hollywood Boulevard. It was now 1.00 pm and I would soon have to catch that elusive taxi out to Carson to pick up the 27-foot RV, but the Mann Theatre had been a top favourite on my list of Must Do's, and I was *this* close.

Ignoring the rumbling in my stomach, and noting the decrepit state of my floppy bag and its wonky wheels, I started the long trudge east. Every second store offered Tours of the Stars, a two-hour bus run around Hollywood and Beverley Hills.

I politely said: "Sorry, I don't have two hours to spare." I did, however, buy a stack of I LUV LA t-shirts in a souvenir shop – three for $10.00. I passed Hard Rock Cafe, saw the Hollywood sign on a distance hill between buildings, gave way to Darth Vader and Captain America crossing a crosswalk – *could only happen in LA*. Twenty minutes later I glanced back. I'd just passed a taxi stand, with two taxis parked up. And in the distance on the other side of the road was the Mann Theatre – I could just see the ornamental facade. Taxi? Mann Theatre? Taxi? Mann Theatre?

Mann Theatre won out and I kept walking, one of the wheels of the trolley bag now buckled and refusing to turn. Every step became a decision opportunity – go on and cross something off my list, or abort and rush back to the taxi stand before they leave. The Chinese-style facade loomed larger. And larger. And then there I was, feeling a whole lot worse for wear for the walk on a queasy stomach topped off by a sloshy Frappe, right out front, albeit on the other side of the street, but I was here. Only four lines of traffic to cross over, but the taxis were drawing me, and my stomach was warning me not to push it any further. A big moving van was parked out front of the Theatre – I took the photo anyway, truck and all, then turned on my heel and hurried the hundred metres back. Thankfully, the taxis were still there and I grabbed the first one, just as the wheel fell off my trolley. I know how the bag felt. All I wanted now was my RV and a bed. I had made it to the ending side of my second 1st of May. I would see more of LA tomorrow.

Helen Iles

From my travel diaries, Road Trips – USA or Bust – *to be released in 2025*

Das Kimberley

Western Australia has a land area of approximately two and a half million square kilometres and is the second-largest country subdivision in the world, surpassed only by Russia's Sakha Republic. Ninety-four per cent of its entire population of two and a half million cling like limpets to the southwest corner of the state. I am one of those limpets. One wet July day, whilst drinking a cheering ale at The Brass Monkey in Northbridge, my husband and I got chatting to a young German couple. They had travelled all the way down from Darwin, traversing the entire length of Western Australia on a motorbike. They talked rapturously about 'Das Kimberley', a region which we knew only for its mining and cattle stations, a place we considered as being just 'up north'. We felt ashamed that we had never given a second thought to visiting this place which excited our German visitors so much, a place which was on our very doorstep, a place that offered months of warmth and endless sunshine at a time when Perth was cold, wet and gloomy. We determined then and there to toss comfort aside and go visit this wonderful 'Das Kimberley'.

Preparation is the key to a successful and safe camping holiday, so we researched distances, roads, caravan and camping sites, towns and, of course, the climate, making long lists of absolute essential items, not-so-essential items, and luxury items. The most important decision to make, though, was when to go and that depended very much on the weather. The Kimberley is located north of the Tropic of Capricorn and boasts a tropical monsoon climate. It has only two seasons – the wet and the dry.

The dry season runs from May to October with clear blue skies, easterly winds and balmy days averaging 29°C. It does not rain! However, the wet season, as the name suggests, is an entirely different story. The north of W.A. is affected by big low-pressure systems bringing intense heat and violently unpredictable weather. Thunderstorms can dump incredible amounts of rain on unsuspecting travellers whilst lighting up the sky in spectacular shows of raw electric power. Flooding is common and dry river beds can fill and overflow in a matter of hours, even roads and the main highway can get cut off for days at a time.

We decided to go in June. Everything we read assured us that all roads would be open, the countryside still lush and green from monsoonal rains, the temperatures pleasantly bearable, water levels in rivers and creek crossings would have dropped but cascading waterfalls would still be a spectacular feature; most importantly, there would be no rain! However, tourists would be on the move as grey nomads took to the road to escape winter in the South West. Our destination was the Gibb River Road, one of the two major roads that dissect the Kimberley region.

The Gibb River Road was named after the geologist and explorer Andrew Gibb Maitland, an Englishman, who, at the tender age of twenty-four, was assigned Assistant Geologist to the Geological Survey of Queensland in 1888. He went on to become the Government Geologist in Western Australia and in 1901 joined Drake-Brockman's expedition to the Kimberley. The Road stretches 660 kilometres through vast untouched wilderness, traversing magnificent deep gorges and majestic mountains, rainforests and thermal springs, mud and salt flats. It was constructed in the 1960s to transport cattle to Wyndham from the outlying cattle stations of Home Valley, Drysdale River, Argyle Downs, Ivanhoe, Mount Barnett, Ellenbrae, Glenroy and El Questro. From Wyndham it leads down to the port of Derby, linking Kununurra to both these towns. The road is mostly unsealed, but well graded, giving travellers easier access to some of Australia's most stunning country and scenery. Even so, it would be a very brave, or very foolish person who would travel in anything other than a four-wheel drive as road conditions are at the mercy of the weather and water crossings can quickly become treacherous.

We spent two weeks packing and prepping, working our way through numerous lists of water, food, medical supplies, clothing, bedding, and absolutely essential equipment to repair punctures or radiator leaks. The Cruiser had been serviced and four new tyres installed. We left Perth at 6 a.m. on June 5th in our Toyota Land Cruiser, heading for the Great Northern Highway and Meekatharra; there was to be no going back for anything. This first part of the journey was a walk in the park: travelling along a sealed road, scenery ranging from tall stately River Gums and red earth to scrubby bush and red earth. There were a few slight showers but nothing that would excite the farmers to expressions of joy.

We were only a couple of hours into our journey when my heart sank. I had left a crucial item behind – my CD collection! My husband, on the other hand, had brought numerous Country and Western CDs and I was being regaled by the likes of Jim Reeves, Slim Dusty and Charlie Pride, hour after hour after hour. I cracked.

"Bob," I complained, "if I hear one more song about a lonesome, broken-hearted cowboy and his faithful, four-legged critter, I'll slit my throat."

Short of handing me a knife, Bob took the lofty view that *This is my car and I'll play what I want.* We compromised. He'd play only one CD a day and I'd refrain from singing along in my 'worse than a cane-toad with laryngitis' voice. Travelling is also about compromise.

We were pleasantly surprised with Meekatharra, the largest town in the Murchison region. This one-time gold rush town was well kept with wide roads and colourful gardens, the caravan park was clean and tidy and even boasted a camp kitchen. We left early the next morning for Marble Bar and, after checking road signs, we turned onto an unsealed but graded road and were on our way. This proved to be a long, uneventful drive through interesting but unspectacular scenery and in 8 hours only one other vehicle passed us, going in the opposite direction. We could almost have been the last survivors of the human race.

As the sun began to set, we pulled off into the bush and set up camp. We were on the edge of the Great Sandy Desert just a few kilometres north of Jigalong Aboriginal Community reserve. The sky spread above us like a huge dot painting of a million glowing stars, the air was so still you could feel it pressing on your skin. I tiptoed around, praying we were not trespassing on an Aboriginal sacred site haunted by malevolent spirits.

Marble Bar is Australia's hottest town. In 1923 it had 160 consecutive days of 100 °F temperatures. Our first port of call when we arrived – dusty, hot and thirsty – was the heritage-listed Iron Clad Pub, where an Irish colleen, working her way around Australia, served up two icy cold beers. Although Marble Bar's gold rush days are well over, it boasts some magnificent government office buildings made from local Jasper which, in 1895, was mistaken for marble, hence the name.

We pressed on along more dirt roads, passing through amazingly beautiful countryside where water abounded. The creeks and rivers were full and the Fortescue a running torrent. We stopped at a billabong for lunch but, alas, nary a Waltzing Matilda to be seen. Just outside Port Hedland we rejoined the Great Northern and made for Indee Station where we had booked two nights' accommodation. The entrance to the station is through a metal gate followed by a five-kilometre bumpy drive.

I was the designated gate opener-and-closer and was kept busy hopping in and out of the car as we made our way through the station. At the homestead we were greeted by an English backpacker who gave us a whirlwind tour of the facilities, explaining that the owner had gone to town and left him in charge. The 400,000-acre cattle station, he told us, had an air crash memorial, a walking trail along the river and a huge red granite outcrop with a series of fresh water pools and ancient Aboriginal rock art. We enjoyed two relaxing days exploring the station and dodging cattle, then headed off for 80 Mile Beach Marine Park and Pardoo Station.

Located in the Pilbara Region 160 kilometres east of Port Hedland, Pardoo is a mecca for anglers, birdwatchers and anyone just wanting to chill. After locating our designated camping site, Bob grabbed his fishing rod, I grabbed the bottle of wine and glasses and we made our way to the beach to watch the sunset and maybe catch a Barramundi or three. We were not alone. There were grey nomads everywhere, ambling along, glasses in hand or sitting in the sandhills, glasses in hand, quaffing their Chateaux Cardboard as if there was no tomorrow. The sunset was spectacular.

Our destination the next day was Broome, the gateway to the Kimberley. Catastrophe struck as we drove along the Great Northern. Bob detected oil leaking from the rear hub, a potentially serious problem if you are in the middle of nowhere, as we expected to be in a day's time. We turned back to Port Hedland and the nearest garage, only to learn that their mechanics were booked out till August. However, they kindly organised a mechanic in Broome for us, so once more we were on our way.

The mechanic in Broome had bad news for us. After a quick examination of the problem, he told us there was a three-day wait before it could be fixed. We headed for the free camping area at Willie Creek opposite Kailis's pearl farm where, surprisingly, we were the only campers there. It was a welcomed, restful three days. We lazed on the sandy beach and waded through freezing cold water in the mangroves, catching fish and crabs. We could hear the voices of the pearling boat operator floating across the inlet, boats going up and down the ramp, and helicopters chugging in and out. The world passed us by as we waited but I was not idle. I ventured into some serious camp cooking, taking advantage of the unlimited supply of driftwood to stoke up the fire. Utilising the camp oven, I made cakes, pizzas, even a roast lamb dinner: food had never tasted better.

At last, the car was ready and we began the 220 kilometres drive to Derby. Located on the edge of King Sound, Derby is famous for having one of the highest tides in the world – 11 metres rushing in and out every six hours. I was surprised at just how spread out the town was. We did a quick drive along the coastal road, inspected the jetty and a straggle of shops, called in at the Tourist Information Bureau for maps and a permit to go on Aboriginal land, stocked up on water and supplies and headed for the Gibb River Road. After seven days travelling to get here, I was feeling quite excited at the prospect of tackling this famous road.

Apart from dodging cows, who stared indignantly at us for having the temerity to drive on their property, the Gibb River was a bit of a letdown. For a start, the scenery was flat and empty apart from the aforementioned cows, but the road itself was sealed, which made it no different from the highway. The roads to Meekatharra and Marble Bar had been more challenging, a fact I pointed out to Bob. I should have remembered the old adage "Be careful of what you wish for". After an hour's travelling, the sealed bit ended abruptly, and the dirt road began, the dips and corrugations so bad I was bumped up and down till my teeth were rattling in my head. However, we still managed to average 90ks an hour which was good going.

Darkness comes suddenly in the outback so we began looking for a suitable camping place while it was still light. We spotted a narrow track leading off the road and followed it to a clearing which was ideal. We soon had all our camping gear out of the car and dinner on the go. The sunset that followed was unbelievably beautiful: thousands of fiery red cirrus clouds flew across a pink and purple sky. Lost in admiration at the wonders of nature we did not realise that this was an omen of 'things to come'.

Things came at 5 in the morning when we were rudely awakened by the staccato hammering of rain on the roof of the Cruiser. We got soaked dragging everything back in and waited, shivering, for the rain to ease. A couple of hours later, we were back on the road driving through the magnificent King Leopold Range under the stern gaze of Queen Victoria's rock.

There are many gorges in the Kimberley but the most famous ones are: Lennard River, Bell, Adcock, Manning, Barnett River, Windjana, and Geikie. We didn't have time to do them all of course, but we were determined to see as many as we could. The first we came to was the Lennard River Gorge and, according to our map, not to be missed. We drove along the track as far as we could then walked the remaining 3ks to one of the most dramatic gorges in the Kimberley. Here, the Lennard River plunges over 300 metres from four cascading waterfalls into a narrow chasm, forming a huge pool. As the rain had eased off, we clambered down and spent a couple of hours walking through the gorge. Clambering back up the cliff, the rain started to pelt down again and by the time we reached the car we were soaked. The track was now deep red mud, very bumpy, slippery and treacherous.

It pelted down all day. Our plan to visit more gorges was put on hold as all access tracks were closed. We pushed on through extremely bad conditions, fishtailing from one side of the Gibb River Road to the other, visibility practically zero as the sea of red mud we were slithering through washed over the roof and windscreen of the car.

"Good job we're the only car on the road," I remarked.

No sooner said than through the rain and mud, a caravan loomed up straight in front of us. It had broken down and was stuck in the middle of the road. To brake in these perilous conditions would have been disastrous. Bob, with no hope of stopping, managed to scrape past it on a prayer and an inch to spare.

As the light rapidly faded, it was imperative that we found somewhere to camp. We drove down a side track and parked on a high bank next to a pond and prepared to see the rain out. It rained all night and all the next day.

"If this is the dry season, I'd hate to be here in the wet," Bob grumbled as we debated whether to stay in our bush sanctuary or risk the road. I looked nervously at the pond, which by now had doubled in size, and wondered how many crocodiles also found it a sanctuary. By midday, cold, wet, and miserable, we decided to chance the road. At least we could put the heater on.

Five long, weary hours later we pulled in at Drysdale River Station behind a small bus and three other mud-splattered vehicles. Station Manager Pat informed us that the Gibb River Road and Kalumbaru Roads were closed until further notice from the Shire of Wyndham. We were marooned, along with about thirty other travellers, on this one-million-acre working cattle station which boasted excellent facilities for campers but, more importantly, a licensed restaurant – all supplies, including fuel, are trucked in via the Gibb River Road, but they have an airstrip and the mail plane flies in twice a week, weather permitting. We soon found the most popular place on the station – the huge campfire in the beer garden where a hardy group sat underneath market umbrellas, sheltering from the rain and swapping stories. Most of them were anxious to leave because of various commitments: one couple was booked on a cruise out of Darwin in three days' time; four Aboriginal men were on their way to Kununurra for medical treatment; a young couple were heading for a wedding in El Questro where the girl was to be bridesmaid; six Americans were travelling around Australia in a small Cessna and were booked into the Kimberley Wilderness Camp. They were stuck at Drysdale River because the pilot's license didn't allow him to fly in cloudy conditions. Bob and I felt ourselves fortunate that we had no pressing commitments.

The rain poured down for five solid days and Bossy Boots Pat refused to let anyone leave the station until the Shire opened the roads. The penalties for being caught on a closed road are steep: a $1000 fine per wheel, and, should you be unfortunate enough to have an accident, you are not covered by insurance. Meanwhile, things were getting tight – the bar ran out of red wine but there was still some beer and one or two bottles of white; the camp shop was down to seven loaves of bread and a few cartons of long-life milk. Everyone was running low on food. I did a stock-take: I had enough rice to feed China, five tins of tomatoes and two tins of lentils. In breaks between heavy showers, Bob went fishing with his new friend Paul and came back with black brim for tea. I found a packet of sultanas and flour and made a boiled fruit cake in the camp oven. After seven days, a few people who were in dire straits were faxed permission to leave the station by the Shire of Wyndham. Paul had run out of heart tablets and was allowed to leave. We waited. The rain had stopped, and the clouds disappeared, but the roads were still impassable. We waited. The Americans took off in their Cessna and the roads remained closed.

Rumours flew around the campsite: the road to Kununurra would be open at 8 a.m. the next day but closed at the Derby end, and the Kalumbaru and Mitchell Plateau Roads would remain closed. Crisis time. Bob was all for leaving and heading towards Kununurra, calling in at El Questro. I wanted to stick to our original plan to visit the Mitchell Falls, we might never have the chance to do this again. We waited.

The next day, it was smiles all round as Pat announced the Shire had opened all roads. We filled the tank with our ration of fifty litres of diesel, waved farewell to Pat and the other station hands, and headed north on the Gibb River Road. A couple of hours later, we waved goodbye to 'Das Kimberley' as we turned onto the Kalumburu Road, our destination The Mitchell Plateau.

Jacqueline Kelly

A Second Chance in Edinburgh

Emily is in Edinburgh for her sister Abigail's destination wedding. The very last person she wanted to see was her ex-boyfriend, Cal. Now that he was suddenly a part of the bridal party, Emily had no choice but to let the past lie. Can Emily spend multiple days in Scotland avoiding him? Will he be too preoccupied with his date to even notice her, or will she be forced to confront him (without creating a scene, of course) and handle the past?

Of all the places for Emily Hawkins to run into Cal Reid, her least favourite ex-boyfriend, it had to be there – at her sister's wedding rehearsal. On the other side of the world in Edinburgh, Scotland, no less. Emily and Cal had a complicated relationship. That is to say, Emily hated Cal, and she was certain the feeling was mutual.

The bottom of Emily's dress fluttered in the cold night breeze while she stood outside of the pub, Maggie Dicksons, in Edinburgh. She pulled her jacket closer to her chest. Her family and friends were having a drink, and she had stepped outside for a bit of quiet. At that moment, she didn't care that her lilac dress was clashing with her tan jacket – it was cold.

'Are you excited, Em?' Abigail, Emily's sister, came to stand beside her.

Emily nodded and lifted her shoulders to keep her neck warm. 'So excited!'

Abigail raised her brows as she observed her sister. 'It's not that cold, Em.'

'It's easy for you to say! You've lived here for two years. I'm from Sydney, remember?'

Abigail laughed, and they fell into a comfortable silence. Emily turned to examine her sister. They never did look alike. Unlike Emily's long brown, wavy hair, Abigail always wore her hair in a blonde bob. Emily had curves, whereas Abigail was slender and did yoga twice a week. Emily would only accidentally ingest vegetables.

Emily couldn't believe that Abi would be a bride soon. It was crazy to Emily, who felt like they were playing in the backyard with the sprinkler only a few years ago. She smiled. She was over the moon for Abigail and her soon-to-be husband, Mark. They were an adorable pair, and they restored Emily's faith in the potential of a happily ever after.

'I need to make a confession.'

Emily scowled. 'Why, what happened?'

'It's not so much as what has happened as 'what is about' to happen.'

'Meaning…?'

'Cal is coming to the wedding.'

It took a few minutes for Emily to process the news. Cal Reid was not someone she wanted to see. Ever. They had a bitter breakup less than five months ago, and if Emily was honest with herself, she was still coming to terms with it. Emily and Cal had only been together for six months, but it was quite possibly the best six months of her life. She was certain she loved him and had even talked herself into thinking they might end up married with the white picket fence. Apparently, the feeling was not mutual.

'Why?' Emily could barely form the word.

'He's standing in for one of Mark's groomsmen who can't make it.'

Emily hated the look on Abigail's face. It was pity. Her sister pitied her.

'It's fine, Abi. I'll just ignore him or be cordial if I have to. Don't worry about me.' Emily wanted her sister to have the best wedding imaginable, and Emily and Cal's disastrous relationship wasn't going to be the thing that ruined it.

'He's bringing a date. Don't freak out.' Abigail rushed out. She put her hand on Emily's arm and gently rubbed her bicep. As if Emily needed comforting.

Cal's bringing a date. Emily wanted to roll her eyes. Of course, he was. Of course the man would have a date ready to up and fly to Edinburgh with him with little to no warning. He was insufferable, and his date was likely to be just as bad.

'It's fine!' Emily reiterated, trying to calm her sister's nerves. 'It is totally fine.' At this point, she was mostly trying to convince herself.

'I'm sure you'll barely see them.'

Abigail was lying through her teeth. The next few days were going to be like a festival of love, requiring the bridal party to spend many, many hours together. So the likelihood of not seeing Cal was almost zero. Emily could forgive Abigail's lie. After all, it was Abi's wedding, and she was only trying to keep things civil. It's not like Emily was going to cause a scene when she saw him – she wasn't dramatic like that. No, Emily would be more likely to get so angry that she cried and tried to run away instead of actually confronting someone.

'Hi, Abigail. Hi, Em.' A deep, smoky voice permeated the night and broke Emily out of her daydream.

She heard him before she saw him. His voice still did things to her. Damn him. She turned to face Abigail, and there he was. All six feet of him, dressed in a grey suit that fitted him like it was moulded specifically to his gorgeous frame. His dark hair was longer now, and it curled around the collar of his white shirt in a way that made Emily want to run her fingers through it. So much for barely seeing him. Emily wished she could vanish into thin air. She actually focused her energy in an attempt to physically vanish. When she didn't, she knew she had to respond.

'Hi, Cal. You well?'

Abigail looked between the two of them nervously.

Cal lifted one corner of his lips in a grin. 'I am, thank you. You look well.' He stared at her intensely, from her face to her toes, and back up again.

Emily had to refrain from shivering under his scrutiny. 'I *am* well.' She responded almost defiantly. 'I am very well.'

A woman with shoulder-length brown hair appeared at his side. 'Hi, I'm Casey!' She beamed.

This must be 'the date'. She wanted to throw up. Casey was stunning, and Emily had to stop herself from groaning loudly over the fact.

'Hey, Casey, nice to meet you!' Abigail said warmly. They exchanged smiles until Emily mumbled a hello.

Cal's eyes never left Emily, and she felt like she was under a microscope. What did he want? How dare he look at her like that now when he had made it clear she wasn't enough for him before. Their relationship had been great until Emily saw him on a date with another woman. He had texted her to say he was working late and was going to miss her promotion dinner, but it was too late. She had already seen him having drinks at a bar with *her*. Emily could still remember the moment vividly. He sat with his back to the doorway while his date laughed and put her hand on his leg. She never confronted him about it; she never dared. She was too hurt, too upset, and too devastated to hear him lie and deny it. She just wanted to be done with him and move on. He called a few dozen times and texted over the next week, but must have eventually gotten the message when she changed her number. He turned up at her apartment twice, but she pretended she wasn't home. He sent flowers, apologising for missing her promotion dinner. But she couldn't forget what she had seen. She just cried herself to sleep and continued to ignore him.

'Well, I better go, early morning tomorrow and all.' Emily turned to Abigail and hugged her. 'Goodbye, Cal. Casey.'

She turned and left, bracing her shoulders to stand up straight instead of huddling into a ball and crying, which was what she wanted to do.

The next morning, Emily awoke in her hotel room, got ready for her day of tourist activities with the bridal party, and then examined herself in the mirror. She didn't want to, but she couldn't help but wonder if she looked cute. You know, just in case she ran into Cal (she was definitely going to see Cal). She wore a pink, blue, and yellow pinstriped shirt dress and a denim jacket. She had pulled her hair back into a high ponytail and put on a touch of makeup. While the sun was out, it was still brisk, so she packed a scarf into her handbag and left her room to meet the others in the foyer.

She saw Abigail immediately, and her eyes lit up. Her sister always managed to look cute and chic, from the ski fields to the beach. If she wasn't her sister, Emily was sure she would hate her. She walked over and put her arm around Abigail's waist, kissing her on the cheek.

'Good morning!' Abigail's smile took over her face. 'Are you ready for the yacht?'

The sound of the lift door opening caught Emily's attention, and she turned to see Cal and Casey walk out. Seeing him took the air out of her lungs and left her feeling like she had been punched in the stomach. Why did he have to be so charismatic? She brought her attention back to Abigail before Cal could notice her.

'I'm very excited, but are we going with 'the yacht'? I feel like Her Majesty would prefer it be addressed by its full title.'

'Oh, very well then,' Abigail continued in her best English accent, 'Her Majesty's Royal Yacht, Britannia.'

'Very good.'

They all left the foyer to see a white coach at the entrance to the hotel. They boarded, and a short time later they were at the tourist centre for the Britannia. They collected their audio guides and made their way onto the yacht.

Abigail hung back to walk with Mark, so Emily went ahead, keen to explore. She was on the top deck, examining the view and memorabilia when a shadow cast over her. She noticed someone had come to stand beside her.

'Isn't it beautiful?' Cal stood close to her – too close. He stared into her eyes while his eyes dropped to her lips. She licked them, feeling the weight of his attention. She gathered herself to reply.

'You're interfering with my audio guide. I don't want to miss anything.'

'You can replay it, Em.' He finally looked away from her and out into the basin.

'But then I'll hear the same thing twice or maybe miss something.'

'Is it really that important?'

'Queen Elizabeth loved this boat, Cal. She loved it, and I'm going to show it respect.'

He scoffed. 'You're just being difficult.'

'And you're just upset because your date is more interested in the Corgi toys like a five-year-old than she is in talking to you,' she countered, thinking of when she'd seen Casey gleefully pointing out the various toys throughout the exhibits.

Cal turned back to face her. 'Can you at least set aside five minutes of your time at the castle?'

She had to wonder why he was so keen to speak to her after all this time when he clearly had other women to be preoccupied with.

She stuck her chin in the air. 'Maybe. But I think they have an audio guide too.'

Cal chuckled. 'Screw the audio guides, Em.'

'Well, that's just rude. Now I've lost the number.'

Cal leant forward, holding his face precariously close to hers, to look down at the screen. 'It's three.' He spoke softly, almost into her ear. 'See you soon, sweetheart.'

She managed to avoid Cal for the rest of the tour. It was more skill than luck. She deliberately gave him a ten-minute head start on the guide and then took as long as she could at each exhibit. The last thing she wanted to do was give him time to talk to her. He could talk to his date, as far as she was concerned.

She had less luck avoiding him at Windsor Castle. It was just after lunch, and the sun had decided to hide behind clouds for the afternoon. Emily thanked herself for bringing the scarf and quickly wrapped it around her neck. The tour guide welcomed them to the castle and informed them all about the reason the entry was designed on a slope (as a battle tactic to make it harder to invade the castle).

A hand grabbed her elbow and pulled her to the back of the group. Instinctively, she knew it was him. He was holding her firmly but without force.

'You promised me time at the castle,' he said softly into the shell of her ear.

She recoiled, pulling away from him. 'Why are you talking to me?'

'I think the more important question is, why are you still *not* talking to me?'

'Why am I not talking to you? Are you kidding me? Why would I want to talk to you? You're an asshole.' She had lost her patience. He had plenty of people to speak to; he didn't need to talk to her. They hadn't been together for a while now; he needed to move on. Her chest constricted at the thought of him with someone else.

'I'm the asshole? I didn't just ghost someone after dating for six months, sweetheart, that was you.'

'I did not *just ghost you* for no reason.'

'Hmm, let me think. Yes, yes, you did.'

'I didn't, and you're annoying me. Please go away.'

'No, I'm not going to *go away*. What are you, twelve years old?' He laughed dryly while she tried to cover her reaction to that laugh. Why could he always get a rise out of her like that?

'It's my sister's wedding and I promised I wouldn't make a scene, but you're really pushing me.'

He pulled her to a stop and maneuvered her so she faced him. 'Then let's get out of here. Let me buy you a drink. Make a scene somewhere else. Just talk to me.'

They were dangerously close.

'You have a date you should be having drinks with.' Emily tried to push down the hurt that arose when she thought of him having drinks with another woman.

'I don't want to talk to her. I want to talk to you.'

'Does she know that?'

He released her arm. Emily was certain she saw a flicker of hurt flash across his face.

'This isn't over.' He took a step away from her.

'Yes, it is!' she called out to his back as he walked away.

Thankfully, the rest of the tour was uneventful. She caught herself momentarily – just momentarily – wishing she would run into him again. Any excuse, really, to be as close to him as she was outside. So she could feel his breath on her face again, and that would be enough for her to want to slam her lips against his to see if the spark was still there. She just knew it would be, but being in denial was easier than dealing with the heartbreak.

The rain pounded against the windows of her hotel room that evening as she dressed to go to a local cultural show. The show was thankfully indoors and was a highlight of Edinburgh, according to various tourism websites. The cast sang; they did a Highland dance, and guests were served traditional haggis.

Emily applied pink lipstick and a bronze blush to her cheeks, then surveyed herself in the mirror. She wasn't as pretty as Abigail or Casey, but she thought she looked good. Maybe she could pass as cute, even. Emily picked up her phone to check the time and was horrified to learn she was late and had missed the bus. She needed to hustle if she was going to make it to the show on time.

She grabbed her bag and hotel key, quickly shutting the door behind her. She called the lift and waited impatiently. The lift doors opened, and there he stood.

'Running late too, sweetheart?'

She rolled her eyes.

'For the sole purpose of getting there on time, we can share a taxi, but let's keep the chit-chat to a minimum, please.' She was in no mood for him tonight. She was pedantic, and the thought that she was late was mortifying enough.

'Yes, ma'am.' He saluted.

Luckily, there was a taxi waiting outside the hotel, and they jumped in. Emily was only exposed to the wind and rain for seconds, but already her hair was a mess. She tried to brush it with her fingers, but the wind had done too much damage. She left it alone with a huff.

The taxi was going to be a fifteen-minute ride into the city to the venue. She had no intention of talking to Cal. He sat beside her, looking as good as ever; completely unphased by the rain.

The taxi suddenly stalled, jerking them forward. Cal put his arm out to stop her from coming too far forward, and her chest was pressed against the back of his arm. She was too touched by his gesture to say anything. He was trying to protect her. *It could have been reflex, something he would do for anyone,* she chastised herself.

The taxi slowly came to a stop in the middle of the street.

'Sorry, wee problem…' The taxi driver continued to speak, but Emily didn't understand a word of it. His accent was too thick, and the rain was too loud against the windows. She turned to Cal and shrugged.

'We've broken down, sweetheart. There's a pub right there. We can wait while he calls for another cab to come to get us.' Cal opened the door and the rain rushed in.

Without hesitating, Emily pushed open her door and followed him.

They walked into the crowded pub, soaking wet and shivering. The fire was blazing near the bar, and Cal motioned for Emily to sit down at the counter nearest to the fire so she could warm up.

'So, I'm finally getting that drink.' Cal took a seat next to her.

'I guess you found your silver lining. Where's mine?'

Cal sighed and shook his head, his desperation becoming apparent. 'Please talk to me, Em. I can't keep this up. I can't do … this whole thing where you hate me and I have no idea why.'

Emily was taken aback. Did he really have no idea? She was equal parts angry and confused. She guessed this conversation had been put off long enough. 'I thought we were good,' she admitted. 'I thought we were happy. And I saw you. At Preston's Bar. With her. She was all over you, and you were all over her. You told me you had to work. You lied to me.'

His brow furrowed. 'What are you talking about?'

'The night of my promotion dinner that you missed because you had to work. I saw you.'

His face was drawn as he processed what she was telling him. Emily noticed the line between his eyebrows that she wanted to smooth over with her finger. She caught herself before she did it. *He's a cheater*, she admonished herself.

Recognition flickered across his face. 'Emily, no.'

She shook her head. She didn't want apologies and excuses. 'Don't. We don't have to do this. I didn't want to hear it then, and I don't want to hear it now.' She reached into her bag to grab her phone – anything to distract herself.

'Emily, *please* listen.' He reached down and pulled her hand out of her bag. He held it in his as he stared into her face, his eyes dark and serious. 'Please don't do this. It was my boss, Lauren. Nothing happened. A group of us went for drinks after work, and she hit on me. I said no, Em. I told her I loved my girlfriend. Nothing happened.'

'I saw her.'

'You saw her hitting on me. Did you stay and watch what happened, Em? Did you see me turn her away? No. Because I did. I wouldn't cheat, not on anyone, especially not on you. Ever. I promise, sweetheart.' He pulled her hand closer to him. 'Trust me.' He turned her hand over and kissed her palm. '*Nothing* happened.'

Emily's chest constricted. Before that night, he had never given her any reason to believe he was 'that guy'. Looking into his eyes now, all she saw was sincerity and desperation. She believed him. 'I don't know what to say.'

'It's okay.' A faint smile slowly crept across his face.

'Wait. You're here with me, and you have a date?'

'She's my friend.'

'Really?'

'Yes!'

'Does she know that?'

'She definitely knows that. She's not interested in me at all.'

'Have you seen yourself in the mirror?'

Cal laughed. 'She's more attracted to you than me.'

'What?'

'She's a lesbian, Em.'

'Oh.'

'Yeah.'

'So…she's not really your date?'

'She heard I was coming and wanted to tag along. I didn't see any harm in it. But if I'd known she was going to make you jealous, I would have paraded her in front of you sooner.'

'I am *not* jealous.'

'Oh yeah, jealous.'

Emily reluctantly smiled. 'I am not. You wish.'

They fell into a comfortable silence.

'You loved me?' Emily couldn't help but ask.

'Entirely. Obsessively.' He squeezed her hand.

'I thought it was just me.'

He reached forward and placed his free hand against her cheek. They stared at each other for a moment before he leant forward and placed a delicate, soft kiss against her cheek. She turned into his palm, feeling safe and comforted, like they had never been apart.

The barman knocked on the counter and said, 'Your taxi's here.'

They broke apart awkwardly and headed towards the door. They didn't speak on the way to the show. Too much had happened, too much had been said, and they both needed to come to terms with it.

The wedding was beautiful. Her father delivered a heartwarming speech, and the best man managed to keep his speech bride-friendly. The only missing piece was Cal. She hadn't been able to speak to him at all that day. She had barely seen him apart from the ceremony. After the cake-cutting, she was officially free. Her bridesmaid's duties were done.

'Can I have this dance?' Cal stood in front of her, handsome as all get out in his suit.

'You may.'

He took her hand and led her onto the dance floor. Within seconds, they embraced, with her hands on his shoulders and his around her waist. It felt right.

He nuzzled into the curve of her neck, and her breathing stopped. 'Can I have this dance and all the dances, forever?'

She laughed nervously, feeling his breath on her neck. 'What are you saying?'

'I don't want us to be apart anymore. It's still there. Tell me you can feel it too.'

She took a deep breath and nodded. 'I do.'

A wide smile lit up his face. 'Have dinner with me?'

'We're already having dinner.' She raised her brow.

'Move in with me. Marry me. Have a drink with me. Any of them, just be mine.'

Emily laughed. While she wanted to immediately jump at his proposal, the reasonable part of her brain jumped in. 'Let's start with dinner and see how we go.'

Emily and Cal eventually became engaged on their first anniversary, when they were holidaying in Scotland. Edinburgh wasn't traditionally known as the city of love, but after her time there, Emily knew that she would always look back and remember how much love was not only celebrated but also rediscovered.

Marina Kelly

Aftermath

The soft young voices drifted through the damaged cathedral, perfectly unaware of the terrible past. They were children living in the aftermath of a war-torn country, too young to appreciate the world outside of their everyday existence.

A little girl squirmed on the stage, pulling at her skirt, uncomfortable and shy. Her attention wandered. She was out of tune with the others in the small concert group. I judged their ages at around five or six years, though one child stood taller than her classmates. Her long black hair and quiet manner indicated she was older. A sweet little girl wearing glasses held her hands together tightly, eyes downcast, I imagined she was waiting for instructions, their brilliant yellow and black uniforms a stark contrast to the devastation just outside the church walls.

There was a break in the recital. I smiled at two young girls jostling each other. They looked bored. A teacher stood nearby, watching her charges. They had been waiting more than an hour for the visitors.

My attention was drawn to a small piano near the rear, barely visible from our seats. The music was light and refreshing, and then the children continued their performance. They sang in their native Croatian, strange to the audience of holidaying Aussies but nevertheless charming. The teacher had a pleasant voice, leading a mixture of tuneless youngsters.

No one cared. We all clapped as the concert concluded.

The teacher stepped forward and introduced the mayor, a portly older man with a heavy beard. The serious intensity of his manner and dark piercing eyes grabbed my attention. He spoke broken English. Turning to the teacher for assistance, she smiled and nodded.

Through his interpreter, he spoke about the war, drawing attention to a display of photographs showing the terrible destruction of the cathedral and buildings throughout the city. The city was slowly being restored, in the aftermath of the bombings.

It was 2011 and we were in Vukovar, Croatia, a charming Balkan town sitting comfortably alongside the peaceful Danube River, its small population still recovering from the traumas of war.

The mayor spoke with shifting emotions, stopping briefly to wipe his eyes. He drew a handkerchief from his pocket, took a deep breath and continued. Through the interpreter, we heard about the devastation wrought on Vukovar in 1991, when the city was totally destroyed by the Serbs during the Croatian War of Independence.

We were told that Serbian gunners lobbed more than a million shells into Vukovar during the war, destroying 15,000 homes and causing around $2.5 billion in damage.

A sigh of disbelief was heard among the visitors when the mayor said more than 3000 people were killed and another 20,000 were subjected to ethnic cleansing. Those who could, fled to other parts of Europe. Families were now returning to their homeland to resume their lives, but there was a great deal of damage to repair and little money. Of the 44,000 people in the city before the war, less than 23,000 now remained.

To support what turned out to be an appeal to the visitors for help, the mayor screened a disturbing video taken during the atrocities. The full extent of the death and destruction flashed across the portable screen. We squirmed in our plastic seats.

Bombs fell, people screamed, and buildings collapsed. It was difficult to understand why the mayor showed us these disturbing images. We were tourists, and few in the group were wealthy. No one was likely to return. His reasoning lost our compassion.

The mayor's words droned on. My mind wandered. I was deeply disturbed. We had been so looking forward to this destination. There was a destination briefing as our boat moved quietly up the Danube. The cruise director spoke briefly about the conflict – but nothing prepared us for Vukovar.

Our boat docked on a cool Balkan afternoon, showing brief glimpses of an approaching summer. There was little sign from the dock of the devastation we would confront on a walking tour from the dock to the church. The boat was late, and a children's choir had been patiently waiting for us.

We were met by a young Croatian man in a colourful national costume. He was quite striking, in a long red coat with white ruffled shirt. Speaking with a controlled passion about his beloved town, he lifted his arm, revealing white frilled cuffs escaping elbow-length red sleeves. The coat flared from the waist, stopped at his knees above gold pantaloons, and white stockings. His shoes caught my eye, most unusual for a man, red pumps, with a small heel, cut high on the instep with a small ruffle. A wide-brimmed silk hat, topped with white ostrich feathers, completed his costume. Very medieval, very welcoming.

I watched with interest when he spoke emotionally about the history of Vukovar, briefly touching on the war. Our guide held our attention explaining the devastation and terror his family endured. He revealed that he and his brother, ignoring their parents' warning to remain indoors until they departed, crept closer to the action raging around their city. Hiding near the soldiers, they leapt in fear when a bomb landed a short distance away. They ran in terror towards the river. Those in our group held their breath when he said they swam to safety and hid among the trees on the far side of the Danube River. Their parents, packed and ready to flee the danger, missed the boys and mounted a frantic search. He smiled when he told us his parents were so happy to find their two sons in their hiding place, the boys escaped a beating. He and his family fled to Germany and only recently returned. He funded his university studies with work as a tour guide.

We were Australians living in a safe country, and fully aware of the devastation this war created. It was big news in Australia, a country with a high number of Yugoslavian immigrants. But no one understood the politics of such a conflict.

On our way to Vukovar, our cruise up the Danube took us to Belgrade, the capital of Serbia. It is one of the oldest cities in Europe, and our hearts were touched to observe the aftermath of the war. As in Vukovar, new buildings stood alongside bombed-out structures. There appeared, at that time no plan to demolish the ruins.

The mayor completed his presentation, and through his interpreter invited the visitors to view the restoration work inside the cathedral. The church was nearly restored, however, high gothic arches with new white paint, partially covered the side chapel, exposing the remains of the war. The roof, destroyed during the bombing, was now repaired. Fortunately, the church walls survived the bombings. A terrible sight.

Our guide thanked the mayor, gathered his group, and led us on a tour of the city. It was a terrible sight. The extent of the destruction opened before us, not far from the cathedral. It was strange to walk down the empty streets. Shops were shut. No cars or people were about. It was a Sunday, though, and no doubt people remained in their homes. Our group moved quietly, some of us emotionally affected by the devastation. Buildings destroyed by bombs nudged newly constructed homes and shops. I imagined the authorities were slow to demolish the ruins, a stark reminder of that terrible time.

The overall damage was horrific. In the twenty years since the war, little appeared to have changed. We walked past beautiful European buildings with familiar red gable roofs, still partly destroyed and barely visible screened behind metres of crudely erected fencing. Shabby structures briefly held together by hand-made bricks left an indelible reminder of the ravages of war.

It was not hard to see that this was the first European city completely destroyed since WWII.

As we walked, our young guide spoke with emotion about the healing and attempts to put the past behind them as people returned. However, it was very evident that forgiveness was still a long way off as these people struggled to rebuild their lives. In the aftermath of such a pyrrhic victory that inflicted such a devastating toll, nothing made sense.

Our guide said Vukovar was now a symbol of peace. Its people showed great courage during a terrible conflict. As a result, it now held a high place in the creation of an independent Republic of Croatia.

His words brought a smile to our faces and a reminder that young people would establish their future alongside the persistence and bravery of those whose lives were destroyed by the terrible conflict.

We returned to the ship in a deeply subdued mood, but the visit to Vukovar set us thinking. We found a renewed respect for human suffering.

That evening over dinner, our companions agreed the visit instilled a new understanding of a complicated period in history. And, of course, history has shown us, nothing ever changes.

Dale Kerford

Stranger in a Strange Land: Concrete Beds

Scene 1: Cubicle Camping

A khaki plastic travel cape kept the rain off the fire and pushed the smoke into our damp, dirty faces. The spirit from the flames was more important than its ability to heat us, or the water for the dehydrated food we carried. Once the blaze in the concrete barbeque had been coaxed into life, some of the group searched for more wood in the rain-sodden Serpentine National Park. The others checked the toilet block for shelter and if we could refill our canteens. We'd reached the pick-up point at around midnight. Unfortunately, we weren't being picked up until 8.00 am. After hiking about 140 kilometres on part of the Bibbulmun Track, from Kalamunda to near the Serpentine Falls, we were knackered.

In 1980, a small group of 14-17-year-old Venturer Scouts had hiked on the one-year-old track named after the Bibbulmun people. We brought food, water, and dry socks. No camping equipment. We travelled light. Regaling each other with tales of drop-bears and hang-spiders, we walked along pea-gravel tracks lined with varieties of Eucalyptus (Gum) trees. Many were Jarrah trees which can grow to 50 metres high. In the daylight, wildflowers pushed through soft grasses and prickly native vines. The flora faded to grey at night, and we heard the fauna's thump, squeak, and rustle. Headlight eyes stared into our torch beams. The maps and compasses ensured we ended up at our endpoint landmark. A brick toilet block. Our thoughts were, *shall we sleep in the Ladies or the Gents?* My head faced the urinal, my feet – clad in dry socks – pointed at the cubicles, I slumbered on the concrete until dawn, using my backpack as a pillow.

Scene 2: Bad Shandau

We forgot to get a Czechoslovakian visa to cross from Berlin to Vienna so we were escorted onto the Bad Shandau train station platform at about midnight. It is a spa town. In German, Bad means "bath." After getting kicked off the train, "Bad" just meant bad. Bad choices, bad days, and bad luck because we'll be sleeping on a concrete railway platform. It was like time had frozen in 1950.

The station was closed, and all the staff were tucked into their beds hours ago. The few items under a glass counter – single packets of chewing gum, razors, and matches – would not be out of place in a museum. I peeked out the front doors, and there was more moonlight on the roads and houses than streetlights. The tramp, who had also been kicked off the train, buttoned up his khaki greatcoat, re-arranged his frying pan and kettle, and tucked his arm under his head to continue sleeping.

Beate spoke German, so she understood the two old drunk guys chatting about leaving the pub to travel to the end of the line and then return to Berlin. We consulted the Lonely Planet and settled on going back to Berlin and then to Munich for Frühlingsfest (Springfest). Our *kleine bier festival. Prost.* Using our packs as pillows, we dozed on the concrete and waited for the next train back to Berlin. I never went to Vienna.

Scene 3: Roma Ostello

After avoiding the thieving children, we lugged our backpacks onto the Roma train station platform. A bottle of aqua in hand, we caught a bus to the youth hostel. The ride went past monuments that made Australia's colonial buildings look minutes old. Our accommodation was in the YHA Ostello di Roma. A five-star ostello della gioventù (youth hostel) sounded like a dream after some of the dives we'd stayed in while on our European odyssey. There was a small bar – the benefits of a five star venue. Due birra (two beers), we could only afford one each while in Rome. Saluti, we said. Beate's accent was better than mine because she had studied Italian when we were in high school. The restaurant served meals with meat, pasta, and vegetables, a change from our poor backpacker choices to date. Unlike the cheaper hostels where we previously stayed, we didn't have to cook, clean, or share a communal kitchen. This converted ex-Olympic village of the 1960s was feeling luxurious. They boasted of sleeping up to 334 people in dorms. However, I think that's how old the beds and mattresses were. Or that many people had slept on my mattress. We soon understood why others had pulled the mattress onto the concrete floor. It was more comfortable. The bedding looked suspect, so I used my unique hostel bedding (an all-in-one sheet and pillowcase). At least it was a barrier between me and any bed bugs. Now, at the end of our Eurpoean Oddysey, I put away the Lonely Planet and pulled out the map of our next destination, Bali. Snug in my sleep-sheet, I dozed off as others scratched their night away.

Kathleen Knight

When Your Goal is Gaol

I want to go to gaol. I want to see how the original prisons of Fremantle, Western Australia (WA), have been absorbed into the metropolis and what vestiges of them are still recognisable. This is easy to achieve because the developers of the City of Fremantle incorporated the original structures as they created the city. Up until 1991, if you committed a crime, you could have been tried, convicted, and incarcerated all within a fifteen-minute walk of the Fremantle Town Hall.

It is a lovely stroll to visit all the sites, and you can have a coffee or lunch in a heritage building along the way. If you have more time, you can catch the number 532 bus service (which runs in both directions every 15 minutes). It is convenient as a self-guided hop-on, hop-off tour. All the locations are within easy walking distance of the bus route. The Swan River Colony was founded on 2nd May 1829 by Captain C.H. Fremantle, and the City of Fremantle was named after him. The first mention of this new venture is a paragraph in the 10th April 1829 newspaper, the Colonial Times. The report that "Captain Dance is appointed to command the Sulphur bomb" (a type of sailing vessel) with a shipload of craft persons is optimistic. Then, during the same year, over 600 Europeans arrived. However, the land was already occupied by the area's original inhabitants – the Whadjuk people – who call the area Walyalup. Nowadays, both names are used to acknowledge the history of all the people who have lived in the area. Unfortunately, the clash of cultures often led to conflict and death. And, when you have unruly people, of course, you need a gaol. You've got to love colonial thinking.

The Marquis of Angelsea (1829-1830):

A Profitable Wreck

The first prison was the shipwrecked hull of the Marquis of Angelsea (as documented by the WA Shipwrecks Museum). It is also quoted as "Anglesea" in other records. Angel. Angle. It seems such a minor difference until you search for it in various documents. Interestingly, the newspapers of the time called it the Marquis of Anglesea. Is this another way that something old has been absorbed and changed by the new? Or is it how spelling varies when you have a 19th-century education and can't check information on the internet?

When I was first trying to locate information on the ship, I came across "The 'Dancing Marquess' of Anglesey". He was the 5th Marquess and a dandy of his time who loved a tiara and a fancy-dress party. The ship was named after his predecessor, Henry Paget, the 1st Marquess of Anglesey. It was launched in 1815 (when Paget received his title). The vessel was stranded on 4th September 1829 while transporting people and goods on its first voyage to Fremantle. A storm caused the ship to drag its three anchors, becoming beached. Fortunately, there was no loss of life, and they had unloaded most of the cargo. George Leak purchased the stranded hull and made a profit by leasing it back to the government as a ready-made structure. One wonders if he understood the irony. It was (among other uses) the Governor's residence, the Post Office, and where they would lock up the refractory (stubborn or unmanageable) servants. How out of control were they when there was nowhere to run except into the wilderness to starve? Was it the demon drink that made them rebellious and prevented their masters from receiving their perceived due deference and service? Try taking me to the early colony as a servant without choices, and I, too, may have become a refractory individual.

Later, the Marquis of Angelsea housed up to twenty-seven prisoners as a gaol. It is thought that the hulk finished its journey at Point Anglesea (which is probably true because it appears the area was named after the shipwreck), which is now incorporated into the reclaimed area of the Fishing Boat Harbour. The closest you can get is to walk or sunbathe on Bathers' Beach. The little strip of sand faces west and gives an uninterrupted view of Rottnest Island and beautiful sunsets. The Fremantle Doctor – the afternoon sea breeze – is pleasant. There are plenty of fish and chip establishments or gelato to the south where you can watch people, boats, and seagulls. Nothing of the ship remains. After more storm damage, perhaps people dismantled it? It was probably absorbed and repurposed by the residents. It may still be a part of the buildings in the area. After all, back then, you couldn't knock back a good piece of seasoned timber close to the coast. The only real presence of the ship is when it is mentioned in the database of the WA Shipwrecks Museum. They had never heard of the first gaol in Fremantle, and I had to find the information on the internet. Perhaps, this is because the museum has a more significant focus on earlier shipwrecks where adventurers found historical treasures. It is always easier to interest the public in items they can see or touch.

The WA Shipwrecks Museum is well worth a visit (entry is free). The Blue Cat bus will let you off in front of the building. There is a magnificent line of glossy black ships' anchors in the courtyard. A limestone façade takes you back in time, and there is a part of Joan Campbell's '1833 Shoreline' artwork of bright blue sea creatures.

The entry part of the complex is through the Commissariat (an army store to provide provisions), which was constructed in 1852. It was among the first places built by convicts who had started arriving in 1850 to answer the colony's need for manual labour. In 1878 it was converted into a Customs House and Bonded Warehouse. They must keep those goods safe and ensure all the taxes are collected. Designed by James Manning, it is now part of the Western Australian Maritime Museum. There is an extensive collection of shipwreck artefacts, personal paraphernalia, and the Batavia Gallery housing the 1629 wrecked remains of the VOC ship Batavia in a temperature-controlled environment. In the Gallery, there are an elevated viewing deck, a skeleton of one of the murdered crew members from the ship, and a reconstructed portico façade (archway) recovered from the ocean floor. As you traverse the museum's rooms, don't forget to look beyond the information boards, display cabinets, and modern amenities. The original limestone walls, brick arches, and roof beams have been sympathetically left exposed alongside the electric lighting, fire extinguisher, and emergency exit signs. The building has been absorbed but not obliterated.

The Fremantle Round House (1830-1850):

A Monument to the Pernicious Pioneer Prisoners

There may be no trace of the first gaol in Fremantle, but you can't miss the first permanent public building of the colony on its limestone cliff. At the end of High Street, the Round House (a 12-sided structure with eight cells and a freshwater well in the middle) demands your attention. Stripped of any external penal trappings, it now glows in its beribboned glory of signalling flags like a miniature Sacre Coeur. Its original purpose has been absorbed, but the outstanding architecture, designed by Henry Willey Reveley – and built in about six months – has kept it in plain view. It is the buffer between the city and the Arthur Head Reserve. The Whalers' Tunnel that was constructed underneath in 1837 takes you through to Bathers' Beach. The strip of white sand allows views of Rottnest Island on most days and uninterrupted views across the Indian Ocean towards Africa. Nothing but salt water for days. The ocean trapped the early settlers on one side, and unsurvivable (by their standards) bush hemmed them in on the other sides. Indeed, that would have been a deterrent for me, so they would not have needed a prison. The dedication to preservation in the precinct means there are many heritage buildings nearby, such as the four Pilot's Cottages, the District Gunner's Quarters, and the Kerosene Store. It isn't one of those villages where you pay at the gate to enter for a trip back in time. There isn't a shop with costumes so you can take an old-timey photo. Instead, it is a step over an invisible boundary into the past.

The violent actions in this area are spelt out on plaques and guided tours. It is a very sanitised way to absorb that John Gavin, a 15-year-old charged with murder in 1844, was publicly hanged and buried on the site. It is documented that he killed his indentured master's son, but there are contemporary doubts that he committed the deed. He has the (doubtful) privilege of being the first and only European settler to be executed at the Round House. Gavin's execution would have been used as an example to the populace. A shame that it didn't work. There have been 154 people hanged (the method of execution in WA) primarily for murder. The last person was in 1964, and the death penalty was abolished in 1984. There's also a total of 442 people who have been sentenced to death, but they were not hanged. Again, most of the crimes were murder.

After Fremantle Prison was built to house the felons, the Round House had several roles. It was the police lock-up, living quarters for a chief constable (his wife and ten children), and a tourist attraction. A tradition was started in 1900 of dropping the time ball and shooting the cannon at 1 pm to give an exact daily time to mariners and residents. It's fantastic to think that the view has hardly changed since the first settlers arrived. Apart from the solar panel on the pole, the flotilla of boats, and the cars in the carpark, it's hardly changed. Welcome back to the present.

The Fremantle Prison (1850-1991):

Where Your Ensuite Is a Bucket

Edmund Henderson of the Royal Engineers designed the Fremantle Prison. Built between 1852 and 1859, it dominated the landscape. Today, you can drive past the back of the site on Hampton Road. You may not even realise the significance of the expanse of the high limestone wall. It could be the enclosure surrounding an exclusive suburb. That close to Fremantle, the real estate would be worth a fortune. The razor wire deterrent is mainly gone. The guard towers look like an architect's interpretation that didn't quite work. A brown tourist sign indicates to drive between the towering stone wall of the prison and the grey concrete multi-storey car park of the Fremantle Hospital campus. You'll come out changed from either place. The prison parking lot is an excellent contrast to the magnificent main entrance facing west. You could be approaching a castle, although there's no royal welcome or expectation of luxury.

In the past, some of the crimes and sentences of convicts transported to WA were highway robbery (life), throwing a cap at an officer (14 years), and stealing turnips (7 years). They were probably shocked when they arrived and saw the landscape where they had to live and work. At least, in the beginning, before the cells were built, they had the opportunity to grow and steal a turnip. The guards controlled their every movement, function, or action. That is the exact opposite of the guest's experience in the areas turned into the Fremantle Prison YHA. After the daily regimen, the prisoners had tea and were locked up from 4.15 pm until the following day at 7.00 am. There were no toilets in the cells. They used a slop bucket (quaintly called a "shit bucket" by the prisoners in the documentary that plays in Gallery). It needed emptying in the Toilet Bucket Drainage facility in the Exercise Yard during the 7.00 am to 8.00 am ablutions time. The backpackers who choose to sleep in a cell may not have an ensuite, but they can leave the room to use the toilets. A bucket is not part of the kit when you pick up the room key. Speaking of what you get on arrival at Fremantle Prison, all prisoners were issued with the basics (soap, dental hygiene products, and one pack of coffee). There was one, and I repeat, one pair of underwear. You can only hope that they were swapped out for a clean pair every day.

It was lights out at 11.15 pm for the inmates. When you are confined to your cell and have seven hours to kill until the building is dark, it's good to have a hobby. The inmates' well-executed pieces of art on exhibition in the Prison Gallery demonstrate their artistic abilities, award-winning talent, and ability to generate income for the individual artist prisoners' fund. The West Workshops were transformed, but there are still traces of their previous use when you look upwards. The rafters and ceiling have a thick new coat of paint, there is studio lighting and air conditioning. The bars on the window could be protecting the collection of exhibits, but we know they were there to keep the prisoners inside.

During the 139 years as a working prison, the range of "inmates included imperial convicts, colonial prisoners, enemy aliens, prisoners of war, and maximum-security detainees." The Aboriginal Heritage Management Plan for Fremantle Prison addresses the disproportionate number of Aboriginal people who have been through the Fremantle Prison system, have died in custody, or were displaced from the area. The *Wirrin Yira Koorl (Up Spirits Go)* Plan is named after a smoking ceremony on the site that invited spirits to leave if they wished to.

Fremantle Prison moved its last inmate to Casuarina Prison on 31st October 1991. It's only thirty years since prisoners did a daily slop bucket run. While the Fremantle Prison may have merged into the city's landscape, it still has a six-hectare footprint. Nowadays, you can pay for a guided tour of the cells, the tunnels, or experience the creepiness of the gaol at night. Admission to the Gatehouse and Entry Complex is free and a fantastic place to visit by themselves. Within the area are the Visitor Centre and Gift Shop (previously the Contact Visits Area), the Prison Gallery (previously the West Workshops), and the Café (previously the armoury). There are displays of memorabilia and archaeological finds; you can have a coffee and cake at the No Escape Café, or go next door to purchase books and knickknacks at the Gift Shop. The raw grittiness of this place of imprisonment has been covered by tourist and safety items. The bars of the gift shop doors display convict and uniformed prison guard soft toys, a beige telephone hangs on the wall next to the fire extinguisher, and the emergency evacuation procedures are between the exposed plastic conduits for the lights.

All these sites are heritage listed (as they well deserve to be for their historical and architectural value). The Fremantle Prison is also on the UNESCO World Heritage list. The city may not have started as a penal colony but they sure have a good collection of prisons. At least they have been absorbed into the municipal precinct. So, if you decide you want to go to gaol, you have a short amount of time, and a dislike of being locked up for years, then I suggest coming to Fremantle.

Kathleen Knight

Two Arabian Nights

Having bid farewell to Paris's romantic charm, Tom and Donna embarked on a thrillingly contrasting adventure in Abu Dhabi. This new destination, where they were to spend a few days with friends, offered a stark contrast to the allure of their previous stop, piquing their curiosity and sense of adventure.

Arriving at Abu Dhabi's Zayed International Airport, they were immediately enveloped in the city's grandeur. The airport, emblematic of Abu Dhabi's luxury, was just the beginning. They exited the terminal into extreme heat, a vivid departure from the crisp Parisian air they had left behind.

Any initial discomfort soon dissipated as friends warmly greeted them and ushered them into a sleek, sporty Porsche. Tom sat next to Nenad, while Donna and Patricia squeezed into the back seat.

"Wow, mate. I've always wanted to know what it feels like to be driven in a Porsche, it feels great, just as I've always imagined," Tom said as he adjusted his seat.

"That's how I felt when I brought it; luxury cars are cheaper here than in Australia. However, while you're here, I've arranged for my driver, Sutir, to use the BMW limousine, which is more comfortable." Nenad reassured Donna that she wouldn't be squashed in the back seat.

Tom and Nenad were colleagues at Rio Tinto in Western Australia. However, when Nenad completed his doctorate in electronics, he got a job at the Barakah Nuclear Energy Plant. The offer was too lucrative to refuse, so they moved to Abu Dhabi.

Driving through the city, Tom and Donna were impressed by Abu Dhabi's ultra-modern skyline, a visual feast with the city's Muslim heritage, where magnificent mosques sat on the town's periphery. Tom was in awe of Abu Dhabi's modern architectural wonders, a stark contrast to its past as a modest island with a scattering of simple palm frond huts along the coast. The discovery of freshwater pearls and oil catapulted the UAE into becoming one of the wealthiest small nations in the Middle East.

Half an hour later, they arrived at their friend's apartment.

"What a stunning penthouse!" Donna exclaimed, her eyes wide with awe as she took in the unique pieces of furniture finished in high-gloss lacquer, and the walls covered in gently textured silk. It boasted five bedrooms and three bathrooms, epitomising modern opulence with interiors graced by a contemporary take on Arabesque designs. The living area had a modern design with silver lights that hung over an elegant marble dining table, complemented by light lavender velvet chairs.

The expansive floor-to-ceiling windows and the views were just as enchanting from the outside. The seamless blend of the interior with the exterior offered a connection to the world beyond, from the unspoiled beaches to the enchanting skyline punctuated by whimsical skyscrapers.

This lavish setting left Tom and Donna in awe, and they were eager to explore more of Abu Dhabi's luxurious offerings.

Nenad popped the cork of a Dom Pérignon Champagne bottle while Patricia brought chilled crystal champagne glasses and some appetisers, prepared earlier by their housekeeper.

After a resounding reunion toast, they relaxed in white leather armchairs and slowly drifted into small talk. Donna wanted to know how Nenad and Patricia had settled in a new world so different from Perth.

"During the summer months, the heat becomes oppressive in Abu Dhabi. Despite all the luxuries, I miss the most refreshing afternoon breeze of the *Fremantle Doctor*. I still have fond memories of delightful times lingering at Cicerello's on the Fremantle boardwalk; the evenings there were so pleasant for sitting outside, unlike here, where the heat remains dry and stagnant even at night," Patricia said with obvious nostalgia in her voice.

"What do you do while Nenad is at work?" Donna asked.

"When home, I do very little. In Abu Dhabi culture, housemaids are part of life, not paid much, but we tip them well. This is an Arabian fantasyland; it's a pure Hollywood lifestyle." Patricia smiled.

"Nothing is wrong with that!" Donna interjected, smiling widely.

"But when I get bored, I go to air-conditioned shopping malls to wander around and buy the latest fashion designs." Patricia rose and spun around, displaying her new Christian Dior dress and Gucci handbag.

Nenad shifted slightly in his seat, saying that he thought his wife spent too much on designer clothes.

Patricia's body tensed. "What else would we spend our money on? Come on, stop wasting time. Let's go and do some shopping and sightseeing," Patricia said with urgency.

"That sounds great. We have only two days, but that will be enough to shop until you drop. How convenient that we are in Abu Dhabi this year to buy something special. This year, the Gold Plate award theme is Arabian Nights. We need to buy something special for that gala night at the Hyatt Perth."

Ready to shop and go sightseeing, they walked straight from the lift to the car park, where Sutir, the limousine driver, was waiting. The first item on the agenda was shopping to escape the heat. Abu Dhabi featured over 200 stores, a food court, and a cinema. The biggest shopping centre complex connected to the Beach Rotana Hotel, providing the convenience of a direct entry from the hotel, so there was no need to step out into the heat. Guests at the Rotana Resort had a selection of restaurants offering a range of dining experiences without braving the outdoor temperatures.

After exhausting shopping, the friends settled down at the Rotana Resort air-conditioned rooftop bar. There, they relaxed and savoured some well-deserved refreshments.

"So, Donna, what do you make of all this shopping razzmatazz?" Patricia asked.

"Exhausting. As of today, shop-till-you-drop has taken on a new meaning for me. It's never like that at home. I couldn't even imagine it to be so luxurious." To toast this success, they lifted their glasses.

In the late afternoon, the friends arrived at the designated spot where their limousine chauffeur was waiting. With the car boot full of shopping bags, it was time to do some sightseeing. The amiable Indian driver, Sutir, spoke fluent English and possessed an extensive knowledge of Abu Dhabi. He informed his travel companions that Abu Dhabi was comprised of over 200 islands featuring a variety of landscapes, from coastal islands with famous attractions and beaches, to expansive desert views. It served as a centre for many attractions and cultural landmarks.

Sutir then drove them to see the magnificent masterpiece *The Sheikh Zayed Grand Mosque* on an island.

'It is the largest mosque in the country and serves as the principal place of worship for daily prayers in Islam. The Sheikh Zayed Grand Mosque is a monumental architectural masterpiece, blending diverse Islamic architectural styles. It features 82 domes, over 1,000 ornamental columns carved from white and semi-precious stones, and floral designs crafted from mother of pearl,' Sutir said.

The chandeliers, plated in 24-carat gold, resembled the date palm tree indigenous to Abu Dhabi. It also housed the world's largest hand-knotted carpet, positioning it among its grandest mosques and a magnificent embodiment of exquisite beauty.

Sutir saved the best for last with the Emirates Palace, a more grand and expansive structure than Buckingham Palace. Nestled in the heart of the UAE's capital, the Emirates Palace featured a pristine 1.3-kilometre private beach, exquisitely landscaped pools, a private marina overlooking a natural bay, a sumptuous spa with unique offerings like a 24-carat gold facade, and some of the world's most prestigious restaurants. Open for public visits, guests could take a guided tour of the palace's most private quarters while enjoying a luxurious coffee experience. The Emirates Palace was a testament to Arabian hospitality, with most of its rooms lavishly decorated in gold and marble.

Tom and Nenad had a fantastic journey that ended at Burj Mohammed Bin Rashid, a magnificent 92-story residential building surrounded by two luxurious shopping centres. They took a break at a cafe with a stunning view of Abu Dhabi while Patricia and Donna explored high-end fashion outlets with price tags exceeding the value of Donna's car. They also visited shops that sold traditional handicrafts, henna, spices, jewellery, Arabic fragrances, and local attire. Donna bought some handcrafted jewellery displaying Arabian motifs and a few perfumes with the scent of Arabian nights.

Returning to the penthouse, it was time to unload the shopping bags. Following a rejuvenating shower, they indulged in ready-made meals and a selection of wines. Tom and Donna marvelled at the grand sunset beyond the skyscrapers. The sunlight bounced off the windows, cascading from one structure to another. As the final beams of light disappeared behind the horizon, the sky erupted into a breathtaking display of orange, pink, and purple hues.

"You must be exhausted," Nenad said. "It's best that you get a good night's sleep because tomorrow, we will do some serious partying."

***

The following day, the friends got all dressed up to party all night long. Donna insisted Tom wear his new tuxedo, and she wore her new red dress and red stiletto shoes – all dressed to impress. Nenad promised them a gala night, and they were all excited and ready for a fun time ahead.

The chauffeured limousine arrived on time, driving them to a magnificent seven-star hotel. Nestled beside a wall adorned with genuine gold leaves arranged in intricate Arabian motifs, they indulged in seafood and drinks, taking in the surroundings with appreciative eyes.

The first stop was a Russian-themed restaurant on the top floor, radiating with the ambience of live entertainment. After scouting for the prime location, Nenad secured a table near many charming Russian ladies who were engaged in animated conversations and sipping vodka. Nearby, three burly men resembling bouncers sat still, their brooding expressions etched onto stern faces, primarily concentrating on the beverages before them.

The atmosphere was lively, with girls dressed in traditional Russian costumes performing to pulsating music.

With a cheeky smirk on his face, Tom couldn't help commenting. "They are probably the working girls with plenty of wealthy Arabs to choose from."

Nenad smirked, saying. "Abu Dhabi is a cosmopolitan city; it caters to all nationalities. Alcohol is not forbidden, but it is expensive."

Nenad ordered a platter of authentic Arabian seafood with special spices and herbs. Tom reciprocated with French champagne. Music played, pulsating tunes as a part of a live performance by girls dressed in traditional Russian costumes.

After the show, Nenad made a suggestion.

"After we're done here, let's go to the rooftop. It's something you have to see for yourself, and the night is just beginning. Are you ready for more thrills?" he inquired.

"We're here to play, so let's have fun." Tom smiled.

Tom took Donna's hand and walked her ceremoniously behind Nenad and Patricia to the elevator. As they stepped onto the open-air rooftop to cope with dry heat and enjoy cool, exotic cocktails, the colourful buildings lit up the sky; the light reflected the beach below.

Donna exclaimed, "Wow, what a stunning view of the city skyline!"

Nenad secured a table with clear views near the dance floor. The venue bustled with guests lounging on vibrant ottomans under remarkable tents, enjoying hookahs, large water pipes with flavoured substances. The atmosphere was fragrant with an enticing blend of herbs, aphrodisiacs, and essential oils emanating from incense smouldering in towering torches.

The warm, gentle, and balmy breeze seductively caressed Tom and Donna's flushed faces. Sipping on Champagne and indulging in seafood dishes, authentic Arabian musical instruments tempted them to yield to the alluring oriental delights around them. Both Tom and Donna felt transported into the Aladdin cave, their spirits lifting as if flying above the clouds on the magical carpet.

Tom was his old self again. With a rising sense of potency and euphoria, he whispered to Donna as they waltzed around the dance floor, "Don't you feel sexy on this erotic Arabian night?"

Donna pinched his arm. "Sure, I always do when you are next to me, my feisty Arabian prince."

"Hey, you two lovebirds, let's get further up to get the best spot. The fireworks are about to start." Nenad waved his hand with an amused look.

Startled, Tom and Donna drew apart and giggled as if sharing a secret. Their friends joined them and they watched the fireworks together with sudden interest. Everyone turned and looked at the marvellous display of vibrant colours exploding in the dark.

Donna looked at Tom and placed her hand on his. It stirred Donna's memories and she turned to Nenad and Patricia.

"Do you remember when we watched fireworks together from your apartment? It had a lovely view of Langley Park and the Swan River."

"Oh yeah, those times were something special. We miss Perth," Nenad said.

They settled back at their table just as a sudden gust of sea breeze threatened to extinguish the flame of the frangipani-scented candle in the centre. Although the candle flickered back to life, its glow was not as bright as before.

Tom and Donna enjoyed their evening in that beautiful location, feeling the warm and gentle breeze against their flushed faces.

"I must say, this is something extraordinary. I've never seen such unrestrained indulgence anywhere we've travelled before; I can't believe that we are in a Muslim country," Tom said.

"Yeah, mate; here in Abu Dhabi, nightlife goes on 24/7. The city never sleeps. Let's go … I booked my driver to pick us up after midnight."

***

In the morning, they all rose listless and lethargic, the exuberant feelings from the previous days seeming somewhat lost. However, after a few cups of strong coffee, some vigour returned to their lazy limbs. Tom shaved and took a shower and checked that his travel documents were all in his inside jacket pocket. Donna fussed with the presents in the new suitcase, not entirely happy with how she'd packed them earlier, excited that in a few hours, they would fly back to Perth.

After refreshing orange juice and strong coffee, the friends sat around the table chatting about the good old days.

"What happened to that apartment?" Tom asked.

"It's rented to a Rio-Tinto executive, and we'll never sell it because Perth will always be in our home. We sure had some good times in Perth, especially in Fremantle when we met with our friends at the Sail and Anchor. I fondly remember those days and evenings," Nenad said.

Patricia looked up. "We would sit there on the balcony and have a meal, drink cocktails, and have fun."

For a second or two, Tom seemed deep in thought. Then he livened up. "Have you come any closer to deciding about retiring and coming back to Perth?" Tom inquired, his interest rekindling.

Nenad rose from his seat and lifted his hand, seeking everyone's attention. To Patricia, he became animated. "In a few years' time … but I will probably have to work longer because Patricia keeps buying all these designer clothes that will send us broke," he laughed.

Patricia smirked back at him and made a sarcastic remark. "What about your Porsche convertible? We only managed to open the roof once because the heat was unbearable. Most of the time, we use the limousine as it's more comfortable."

Right on time, as planned, Sutir drove Donna and Tom to the Abu Dhabi Airport to catch their flights back to Perth. Once they passed the security and passport check, while seated comfortably early anticipating a boarding call, Donna squeezed Tom's hand and said, "Oh, Tom, I must say that I feel sorry for Patricia."

"What on earth for? She has everything money can buy," he responded, puzzled.

"Patricia is trapped in the world of wealth and opulence, like a bird within a gilded cage. I wouldn't exchange my humble Perth lifestyle for all the riches Abu Dhabi could provide."

"Well, dear, some people believe that money can buy happiness, convinced that the grass is always greener on the other side …"

"While in Abu Dhabi, I have only seen many concrete buildings, with hardly any grass in sight," Donna exclaimed, happy to go home and water her beautiful green garden.

Nada Lubay

Yucatan Adventure

It's four in the morning. I'm lining up among a small group of passengers summonsed to check in in-person for international connections. The majority of travellers, wearing hi-vis, are dropping their bags, already checked in for their regular commute to places never heard of unless you work there, holes in the ground where the riches are dug out of the Western Australian soil, fuelling the economy of the state and the nation. The Qantas lounge looks like the mining companies have outsourced the breakfast canteen to the airline. I feel inappropriately attired amongst the blue and yellow uniforms; an outsider in a club I don't belong to.

Our anticipation of a pre-flight drink is unfulfilled. The bar does not open until midday; why would it? The customers are almost all on their way to work; they won't be drinking. By noon, perhaps more mainstream passengers will inhabit the lounge, like us, on the way to far-flung holiday destinations, able to enjoy the first of many alcoholic beverages to be consumed in the coming weeks. I make do with a toasted sandwich and orange juice.

The boarding call for our flight suggests that it will leave on time, but we sit stationary for half an hour before the aircraft crawls, at walking speed, to the runway and sits once more, waiting for something unannounced. Finally, it rises into the air, heading east, away from the Indian Ocean, the blue strip that I can see receding behind us as we head up and over the tree-encrusted scarp and across flat, already dry Wheatbelt dotted with farm dams. Scars now pock the landscape – salt lakes resulting from over-clearing. Then everything disappears under a blanket of fluffy clouds, and it's time to explore the entertainment system until the billows evaporate, revealing rivers, roads, and dams.

The clouds have returned, thicker now, a soft, white doona beneath us until suddenly disappearing again over patchwork farmland as we head across the country towards the Pacific. Clearing again, a scattering of houses appears from amongst wooded country and grassland; the grass green here, instead of brown. Now more densely settled suburbs: Western Sydney presumably. Industrial units among winding streets of housing estates. A river heads towards the harbour. Bridges cross an estuary. Not *that* bridge. Beaches of yellow sand fringe the deep blue ocean. A peninsular, wilderness, cliffs in places. Then the conurbation of Australia's largest city. We fly across the iconic harbour; long sandy beaches and mangrove forests. Dappled water of blue and green. Paragliders in flight as we land.

After a few hours' respite in Sydney, we are queuing for the fifteen-hour long haul. It is slightly delayed, and we grow anxious; we know that we have a tight transfer in Dallas. We had been assured when checking in at Perth Airport that we must collect our bags on arrival there, an additional thing we need to fit into our schedule. The pilot assures us that we will pick up time in flight, and we do land on time – just.

The US immigration system, however, determines to foil our plans. Thousands of people line up chaotically to reach the screening counters. We are next in our line to be processed when the officer in the booth, to which our line is assigned, decides to take the guy ahead of us away for questioning and doesn't return.

"Wait, he will come back," we are told.

He doesn't. Eventually, we move to another line and wait to come to the front again. It takes all of a minute to clear us, we are transferring to another country but we've lost precious time and our flight is gone.

No more flights to Cancun tonight; we will have to stay overnight in Dallas and fly tomorrow. We ask if American Airlines, Qantas' partner airline for this leg of the journey, will cover our costs. We are told to direct our enquiry to Qantas as we booked through them. We phone Qantas, they tell us to talk to American Airlines!

"They told us to talk to you! And we lost more time because the Qantas staff in Perth incorrectly informed us to collect our bags in Dallas." I tell them. I am told I can fill in an online claim form, but they doubt it will be covered; our flight had not been delayed.

I call our travel insurance company. No, that doesn't cover it either, I am told. We have lost one of our three very expensive nights in an all-inclusive resort in Cancun, planned to facilitate recovery after the anticipated twenty-seven hours of travelling. We phone ahead, but of course, it is too late to cancel. We book an extra night to cover the one lost, meaning we also have to cancel a night in our next destination, and book a night in the Dallas Airport Hotel. Meanwhile our luggage is quarantined somewhere in the airport. Thank goodness for the spare undies and toothbrushes packed in our handbags. Frustrated, stressed and miserable, we go in search of food. We are in America where even airports boast decent restaurants. We find one and drown our sorrows.

Arriving at last at our beautiful resort, we are disappointed by a lack of empathy on our arrival. Our room won't be ready until 2:00 pm and we're advised to go and have lunch! While we had phoned ahead to explain why we would not be arriving until the morning, we had been designated a "No Show". We are unable to fathom how our room could not be ready when we should have checked in the previous night. It is fine to go and have a beautiful lunch in a very nice restaurant but I am still wearing the same clothes I've had on for the last two days. I just want to have a shower and get changed!

Despite this, we enjoy our three days in the luxurious resort; all-inclusive cocktails, delicious meals and quality entertainment. The weather is cool and overcast, at times delivering torrential rain. The sea is choppy. We spend little time in the lovely pools or the water of the gulf fringing the resort. At the end of our stay, I am ready to start exploring the *real* Mexico.

A private transfer takes us to our next stop, Playa Del Carmen, the starting point for our tour of the Yucatan Peninsula. Checking in to our colourful little hotel, we immediately meet one of our fellow travellers. Alex is a similar age to my daughter Freya, and the three of us quickly become friends as we head off in search of the beach.

Playa Del Carmen is touristy with all the usual American brand stores, the ubiquitous souvenir shops and market stalls. The beach nearest our hotel is lined with bars and marred by rocky reef and rough waves, but we manage a paddle before heading back for our 6 pm meeting with the rest of our group: fourteen travellers from all over the world and our wonderful tour guide, Roger.

Yes, his name, despite being Mexican, is indeed Roger. He speaks excellent English, is invariably helpful and highly knowledgeable. We are reminded that flushing toilet paper down the loo in Mexico is a recipe for a blocked toilet and that toilet paper belongs in the bin; Mexico, like many other countries, does not have an integrated sewerage system. It also does not have potable water from the tap. Fortunately, bottled water is easily available and reasonably priced, purchasing it, just a daily ritual.

On our way to the restaurant for dinner, we walk through the Plaza des Armas, the main square in all Spanish colonised cities, delightfully decorated for Christmas; a fantasy of lights and a tree. While enjoying delicious Mexican food, Freya and I come to know our new companions, sharing countries of origin and hopes for our common journey.

The next day we are travelling to the island of Holbox (pronounced Holbosh) with high expectations. Over the continual thrum of the engines, I hear the chatter of my fellow passengers but whether they are speaking English or Spanish, I am unable to decipher.

The smell of diesel pervades the cabin, where we sit on red vinyl-covered benches staring through the extensive windows, offering tourists a perfect view. Our luggage shares a room with plastic-wrapped turkeys, ready for Christmas dinners. I am glad that the journey only takes thirty minutes, for there is no cool room here for this precious cargo.

The sea is perpetually murky green, but today, it is flat, chopped only by tiny waves. On our left, the dense foliage typical of this coast reaches its tentacles into the sea. We have arrived, the ferry edging itself into its berth.

Holbox will forever be imprinted in my memory. To call it unique is an understatement. The flooded streets are traversed only by vehicles that defy description, half tractor, half quad bike, their huge wheels plough through the muddy sludge that passes for roads. The footpaths, for want of a better name, are raised a little from the level of the potholed roads traversed by our taxi, which wallows, hippo-like, towards our hotel. Later, we will walk these paths, where they exist, sometimes holding onto a fence post as we step onto a rock and round a corner to find a dryish place to cross the street en route to our destination, a small bar or restaurant. As in the rest of this amazing country, art is everywhere; murals on buildings, in restaurants, the sound shell, any surface is a canvas, enlivening the town with colour, augmented by brightly coloured flowering plants. Animals and scenes from history and past or present cultures abound. We try not to trip over street dogs as we walk. It is true that they do have homes and are never aggressive.

Our hotel epitomises its tropical location; the reception sits under a veranda, its construction enhanced by wooden poles and palm thatch. Comfortable outdoor furnishings adorn the reception area and upper balconies; it is everything it should be on a tropical island.

Walking along a sandy beach adorned with palm thatched umbrellas, deck chairs and cabanas, small bars offer cocktails. Further along, I see a plethora of brightly coloured para gliders gracing the sky. The wind whips at the palm trees. A small, thatched hut is covered in paintings of the wildlife to be observed in the reserve. Fishing boats and tourist vessels lie along the sand, and a colourful HOLBOX sign invites visitors to insert themselves where the L belongs for photographs. A net suggests beach volleyball but no one is playing today. We head back into town for a drink before dinner with our companions.

We eat outdoors in a courtyard restaurant. I order chicken burritos with mole, a savoury chocolate sauce. I do my best with the enormous serving and curious taste.

Next morning, we breakfast at a restaurant; the interior is furnished like a nineteen seventies living room. I recognise its contents from my adolescence; it makes me feel nostalgic and old – my life experience verges on history for the young.

A motorboat takes us to a small island, a reserve for birds where the sand is soft and the water warm. The sulphurous, muddy aroma of mangroves drifts in the air. In places, the sand sucks at our feet. We walk in shallow water; it feels like walking on a foam mattress; it becomes more efficient to swim.

A solo flamingo stands on a distant sandbar. I stretch my camera's telescopic lens to the max to take my shots. It is breeding season; I hope that he won't be alone for long.

On the other hand, there is no shortage of pelicans! Several species it appears, none of them white and black with pink bills like our Australian Pelicans. Most are brown but some have yellow or white heads; others are pure white with long yellow beaks. Confused, I seek advice from Google: The Brown Pelican does indeed come in several subspecies and changes its head plumage in the breeding season. The white pelicans are American White Pelicans. Well, that clears that up!

Then there are the ubiquitous double-crested cormorants, quite happy to share the trees with the diverse pelicans, snow-white crested egrets, and frigate birds, not quite ready to fill their red balloon pouches for breeding. And of course, there are gulls, pretty ones with white faces and dark eye makeup. I snapped one that turns photogenically to look at the camera while floating on the sparkling sea.

That evening, I dine on garlic fish at Viva Zapata. When on an island why not eat sea food? It is delicious and the restaurant as colourful as usual, with a full-scale statue of Zapata, seated on a bench near the entry.

Sadly, the next morning, we head back to the mainland, but excitement is high as we drive towards another much-anticipated highlight: Chichen Itza.

We walk down a jungle pathway lined with stalls loaded with tourist souvenirs but we do not waste time stopping to look. A magnificently preserved Mayan temple complex awaits at the end of the avenue. Intricate carvings of gods, warriors and eagles adorn its surfaces, their meaning lost in time. Statues of snakeheads and jaguars guard the sacred space. Fearsome skulls carved in stonework for perpetuity. Stone stairs lead to ritual platforms. A doorway, now closed to visitors, leads into the main temple. What lies inside is left only to the imagination.

Another building houses a court for a ball game. A stone ring attached high on the wall is where the players must aim the ball through a surprisingly small hole. The ball could not be thrown, rather it was hit by a bat or parts of the players' bodies. It seems an impossible task. Some say that the captain of the winning team will be sacrificed to the gods; an honour, apparently. Others believe that this sacrifice is to be made by the captain of the losing team; either way, it seems a dangerous game to play.

At the other end of the site lies the Temple of a Thousand Columns. A statue of a reclining man sits atop it, surrounded by intricately carved stone columns, which may once have supported a roof. In front of and to the side of the temple, stand many hundred more columns, their purpose now unclear. Perhaps they too were once covered?

Roger recognises my in-depth interest in culture and leads us aside to show us a traditional Mayan House. It is constructed of mud daubed over wooden poles with a palm thatch roof. The door, made of sticks woven together with rope, lies open but there are no windows. It is a simple oval-shaped building; the mud on the inside has been whitewashed, and the floor is compacted earth. Some simple wooden stools and rocks are all that remain by way of furnishings. I have noticed similar buildings as we passed by small, rural villages on our way here. They appear still in use.

We travel on to Izamal, a town with buildings painted uniformly yellow in celebration of a past papal visit. We visit a restaurant for a lesson in making tamales. Fortunately, the green dough has already been prepared for us. This is notoriously difficult to work with, Roger informs us. It is brought to the table already rolled into rounds on the banana leaves that will be our job to fold, once we have added the filling. We place our chicken and vegetables on the dough and fold it up, tying the parcel together with strips of banana leaf. Now they are ready for steaming.

While we wait for the tamales to cook, our host takes us on a walking tour of his pretty town. Horse-drawn carriages decorated with flowers offer rides to tourists. We find the ruins of an ancient pyramid, the reason for the town's original existence; a centre of religious pilgrimage. Some of us climb the ruins. I only climb as far as the first terrace; the rocks are large, crumbling and uneven. I am not sure-footed and don't want to mar the rest of the trip with a broken ankle. Still, the height provides a view over the town's houses.

We return to the restaurant via the main square, decorated as usual for Christmas. There is a difference here though; flowers have been planted to depict Christmas themes. We pass the cathedral and brightly lit shops. We enjoy our tamales before driving on to our beautiful hotel for the night, painted in the same yellow and surrounded by pretty gardens and a swimming pool. The reception area boasts paintings of Izamal and, of course, Christmas decorations.

Next morning, we are on the move again. Today we will swim in cenotes, underground caves in the limestone rock filled with water, unique to the Yucatan. Once changed into our bathers, we are provided with compulsory life jackets. We may choose to cycle to the cenotes or travel on a dray pulled along tracks by a horse. Option two, of course! Where else am I ever going to have that experience?

Our first cenote is completely covered, lit only by electric lights and entered by way of a wooden staircase. Tree roots reach down through the cave to the water. Despite the weather being cool, the clear water is a surprisingly comfortable temperature, perhaps kept constant by the rock covering. After an enjoyable swim, we move on to our second cenote, this one reached through a tunnel into the cave which is partly open to the sky and we enjoy the antics of Mexican vultures in a tree overhead. The remaining roof sports stalactites which reach down into the water, a magical place to swim.

Our third cenote is really a gorge in the rock, covered by lush green vegetation. We swim through the gorge to a wider pool before moving on to our fourth and final location, just opened today after refurbishment of the wooden staircase and platforms from which one may jump into the water if desired.

Returning on our horse-drawn train, we change before entering the restaurant for another delicious Mexican lunch: lime soup and empanadas.

Another long drive sees us arrive at Merrida in the late afternoon. We take a walk with our guide to orient us to the city, enjoying a fruit sorbet along the way. I choose a flavour called mamey. Orange in colour, it tastes nothing like oranges. It has a slightly tangy taste, sweet and creamy, perhaps a little like sweet potato. It is quite unique and takes a little time to acquire. *Perhaps I should have chosen the coconut.*

The next day we have free time in Merrida. Freya and I decide to share an Uber with a couple of our companions to see the Museum of Mayan Culture. It appears that the Spanish were not quite as successful at exterminating the indigenous cultures of Mexico as I had previously believed. Roger has informed us that the Mayan language is alive and well in the Yucatan Peninsula and is now being taught in schools. Where language survives, so does culture and it becomes clear that many traditional beliefs have been integrated into the Catholicism imposed by the

Spanish, with saints taking the place of gods for the newly introduced items that accompanied colonisation. The extensive museum includes items from the Stone Age or Archaic period (8000–2000 BC) along with beautiful pottery, stone carvings, ceramic figurines, statues, jewellery and other artworks from pre-classical (1000BC- 250AD), classical (250AD-950AD) and post-classical (950AD-1539AD) periods of Mayan civilisation. Items from the Chichen Itza site, including one of the rings for the ball game and other archaeological artifacts abound, along with displays of traditional burial practices.

After spending several hours in the extensive museum, we walk back to town along an avenue lined with beautiful buildings belonging to the French period of occupation. Sadly, many of these are in a dilapidated state. Ideally, they could be renovated to house embassies, exclusive restaurants, or maybe even apartments. We stop for another sorbet along our route. This time, I choose the coconut flavour. It's delicious.

This evening Freya and I choose to eat at *Museo Gastronomica*, a lovely restaurant set in a Spanish colonial building. The food is delicious but, as usual, we find we have ordered too much. Mexican serving sizes are often very large! After dinner we catch the end of a traditional Thursday night serenade in the park opposite our hotel. The audience joins in with the obviously well-known songs played by the band, providing a joyous atmosphere.

The final day of our Yucatan tour brings us to Tulum where we explore more Mayan ruins set on a coastal cliff top with a view of a sparkling azure sea. Iguanas make their homes among the ancient gods adorning crumbling temples.

Having settled into our pretty hotel, we decide to go in search of a particular ice cream parlour recommended by a friend. A walk into the town gives us a glimpse of the tourist mecca that is Tulum. By the time we return, it is time for the farewell dinner.

Held in a restaurant close to the hotel, it is mediocre and very expensive, unlike the food that we experience elsewhere on our journey throughout Mexico. We learn that Tulum, in general, is very over-priced and we are glad not to be staying longer. It is however, sad to be saying farewell to all of our companions and to Roger, whose company certainly made this part of our trip all the more memorable.

Amanda Perlinski

The Wonder of it All

Look up at night and imagine
floating away into galaxies. Our insignificance
emphasised with vast numbers of stars
as we pass by their shimmer and shine.
To finally enter a void of deep deep
space, all the while feeling a radiance

Yet today our sun's rays' radiance
and power, push winter's imagination
to the limits of recall, cold and chill so deep
that we might curl inside with insignificance.
We worry about this season's shine
Seeking answers above in skies or stars

For legends past arranged the stars
in patterns, figures, of coloured radiance.
At night, around fires did theatre and drama shine,
making sense of this world to imagine
and buffer an awe of human insignificance
To a more comfortable place, stories for culture sown deep

Then travel and wayfinding across oceans deep.
Travellers looked to measure and judge by stars
often uncertain in destination, insignificant
compared with hopes for wealth and riches radiant.
To escape hardness? Driven to imagine
something better for their children, a new shine?

Artistic creations inspired shapes with diamonds' shine,
jewellery keepsakes given from emotions deep.
Metals and gems taken and wrought to imagine
tranquillity, immensity from heavenly stars.
A mortal effort mismatched to energy radiance
highlighting our puny human insignificance

Bearing children, generations not insignificant
Each human contributes a speck, a shine
Aggregating knowing, wisdom and radiance
Though short millennia, our impact is deep
Viewed from the heavens a vantage of stars
Interpreting our home and stretching to imagine

So my child, of insignificance may your sleep be deep,
your time to shine soon to be reflected from the stars,
for human care and radiance can nourish, as you travel, imagine.

Tammie Reid

Chasing A Mirage

Mandy Jones aims a final kick of frustration at her car's rear flat tyre and sets off. The desert sun is scorching, desiccating and unrelenting, the road ahead, long and straight. A heat haze shimmers in the middle distance, giving the illusion of cool relief.

shimmering heat haze
oasis in the desert
false promise beckons

She knows its madness, but the car's interior resembles an oven. If she stays, even with all four doors open, no breeze means no relief and the added hazard of flattening her already dodgy car battery.

It's a risk she decides is worth taking. This morning, she left Coral Bay with no water, no hat, not even sunscreen to protect her face and arms. Her chances of survival now are equally slim whether she stays or leaves, and moving feels better than doing nothing.

An hour later, Mandy questions her sanity as she stands in the middle of the road where it forks. The diverging tracks appear identical in size and shape; twin heat hazes shimmer with equal intensity in the middle distance. She tries to recall the map that blew into the desert with the only gust of wind on this airless morning when she opened the passenger's side door.

The trip started so simply: a shortcut saving nearly a hundred kilometres. He never warned her the tracks on his hand-drawn map are all rough gravel. Nor does he know she is on her way. She's decided to surprise him, but she hasn't counted on city-soft tyres succumbing to the sharp, flinty gravel road. Or more tracks than he's drawn on his mud map, she thinks, standing under the baking sun, trying to decide which one to follow. At least she's had the sense to drape her jacket over her head for protection when she left the car.

plan for reunion
travel to experience
hearts reunited

dreaming of a shared future
in an outback oasis

A distant dust cloud rises skyward, catching her attention. Probably no more than a willi-willi crossing the road, but it's better than nothing. She takes the left-hand track and begins trudging again. Walking seems harder now, demanding more effort. Has she made the wrong decision after all? For perhaps the first time, she glances back at her car. It's out of sight, as if it never existed. She keeps walking.

Mandy has lost track of time when she stops again. Her feet barely move forward now, instead shuffling, raising dust with each dragging step. Slowly she becomes aware of something pressing into her back, threatening to send her pitching onto her nose. Irritably she turns to confront her attacker.

Her coat flies off her head.

At first, she stands uncomprehending. Dust swirls into her eyes and she blinks, trying to clear them. What has changed? When did those dark purple clouds creep up behind her? Now they fill half the sky. The wind gusts more strongly and pebbles scurry down the road. Remembering her coat, she turns again, in time to see it at least a hundred metres away and the wind lifting a sleeve to send it tumbling further. She is too exhausted to run after it, although she tries.

Mandy smells the rain before she hears it drumming up the road behind her, like an army on the march. She stops and turns again. The rain arrives and she lifts her face, fat drops manna on her parched tongue. She drinks their moisture as her clothes and body become drenched, but she didn't care. She will survive.

Lightning flashes and thunder explodes overhead. She jumps and claps her hands over her ears. The rain drums harder, competing with the thunder for dominance.

When it eases, she notices a steady light shining down the wet road and turns, not sure whether it's real or her imagination. A four-wheel drive pulls up beside her, the driver's window lowers about halfway, and a deep voice invites her to get in.

Mandy places her hand on the door to reassure herself it's not a hallucination. Then she scurries around the vehicle for the passenger's door and warm shelter inside.

"I'm Dan," the driver introduces himself as he drives on, leaning forward and squinting through the rain-lashed windscreen.

Apart from a quick stop for Mandy to retrieve her muddy coat, he continues slowly, lightning flashes punctuating the mid-afternoon, which is now as dark as midnight. Eventually, he pulls up outside a station homestead.

Mandy's heart dances at the sight of the man who emerges to meet them. She is about to leap from the vehicle and throw herself into his arms when he turns and calls to someone. Her hand freezes on the door handle as she watches a woman appear and the man place a protective arm around her.

were sultry whispers
in overheated moments
empty promises?

Dan climbs from the four-wheel drive first. He introduces Mandy to the couple, who will become her host and hostess until the weather clears and the district's many tracks and gravel roads become passable again.

Two days pass before Dan drives Mandy back to her car. He inflates the spare tyre, changes it for the flat one, and leads her to another highway via a different shortcut.

Once more, Mandy confronts a road stretching to the flat horizon. This time, no mirages distort the landscape. She is on bitumen again, following the narrow ribbon of tar south to the city, returning to civilisation and safety.

Shirley Rowland

Landfalls in Paradise

Kev, my husband, woke me at dawn for our first sight of land in eight days. The cruise ship *Astor* had been steaming west-southwest since leaving Acapulco in Mexico. Two days earlier we'd crossed the equator to re-enter the southern hemisphere and were now in the same half of the globe as our destination: Perth, Western Australia.

I kept glancing through our cabin porthole as I dressed and prepared to join the queues at the breakfast buffet. Later, I watched through an air-conditioned lounge window as the island grew closer and larger. Our vessel steamed into a deep inlet on the high, jungle-clad island of Nuku Hiva, and dropped anchor about a kilometre from the town at the top of the bay.

Nuku Hiva was in the Marquesas Islands, the westernmost of four island groups comprising French Polynesia. It was not an island the casual traveller visited as a destination. Instead, it was their first or final port, before or after traversing one of the emptiest stretches of the Pacific Ocean.

Kev and I queued again, to board one of the lifeboats the ship used to ferry passengers to and from the shore. Twenty minutes later, I stepped unsteadily from the lifeboat, rocking in a disconcerting half-metre swell, onto an unyielding concrete step leading up onto a wharf.

The act of walking on land was stranger than I expected. I found myself walking with my feet apart to overcome the sensation of being about to overbalance. Now I understood why sailors, accustomed to lurching surfaces underfoot, walked bow-legged!

My other surprise was the humidity. We were still in the tropics, so I should have anticipated it, but the combination of air conditioning and being on the ocean nullified its effects aboard the ship.

Kev and I walked across the foreshore park's neatly mown grass, laughing at each other's attempts to find our 'land legs'. In a quiet moment, I marvelled how this was yet another place I'd never expected to find myself in, despite my teenage goal of one day travelling around the world.

I'd read about Nuku Hiva in cruising yachting magazines. Recently I dug out my treasured hard-cover book, '*Landfalls of Paradise*' and wasted half a day re-reading about the exotic, remote, romantic islands scattered across the Pacific Ocean.

Two yachting friends, with their partners, had landed here on their way across the Pacific Ocean, heading west from the Caribbean to different home ports in Australia.

Years earlier, Kev and I had talked about sailing the world in our own boat. At the time, we'd owned a yacht capable of completing the trip, but *Alesig* was a heavy steel vessel designed by an engineer, not a sailor. After noticing the windless days around the equator, I was relieved we had not, in the end, attempted it on our own. A cruise ship took the hard slog of victualling (replenishing water, food and fuel supplies), and navigation out of our hands, leaving us with no responsibilities apart from amusing ourselves or joining in the onboard activities designed to beat boredom.

The town's small shopping centre was our first destination. When tourists arrive in another country, their first mission is obtaining local currency for spending, and we were no different. I withdrew local Francs from a French bank's ATM using my Australian bank's debit card. It was a quick and simple transaction.

From there, we wandered through the supermarket and chemist to see what they sold and then continued our walk around the bay. It was perhaps a kilometre to the end of the foreshore street. Clouds began forming over the mountain peaks behind the bay and, by late morning, provided cooling shade from the hot sun. We heard later that the passengers on a bus tour to an inland waterfall and lookout had been disappointed – they'd seen nothing but fog!

By the time we returned to the town's commercial centre, my legs and feet were aching despite my daily shipboard walks to maintain fitness. Fellow passengers hailed us from a bar, and we joined them for a non-shipboard lunch and imported beers.

Later, as we waited on the wharf for a lifeboat to ferry us back to the ship, Kev and I ate ice cream. Our first cruising yacht had had no freezer and we'd developed a ritual of eating ice creams in each port of call. While we ate, we critiqued the yachts in the bay. When one raised its sails and departed, I watched enviously – with other life choices, it could have been us deciding where to sail to next!

That evening the *Astor* raised anchor and continued steaming westwards. Two days later, we entered a modern port on the legendary island of Tahiti. Captain Cook would not have recognised the bay he sailed into in 1769 to observe the 'Transit of Venus', before sailing across the Pacific to discover New Zealand and the east coast of Australia. While we waited for the ship to berth, Kev and I entertained each other, mispronouncing Papeete.

I'm a keener swimmer than Kev, so I had booked a snorkelling excursion without him. Mid-morning I joined a dozen other passengers from *Astor* aboard a nearby powerboat. Our first stop was off the end of the island's runway, where two small boats and a plane lay submerged in shallow water. I was enchanted by the clown fish and clams amongst the coral on the limestone reef, and amongst the last snorkellers out of the water. The boat then took us outside the fringing reef to view freshwater up-welling. Perhaps I'm too accustomed to swimming over coral reefs from my own vessel, but the trip seemed to me more roaring at high speed to distant spots than swimming in the clear, warm water.

The islands of Tahiti and Mo'orea were less than twenty kilometres apart and visible across the sea. The *Astor* left Papeete wharf a little before 5 am and anchored before breakfast at Mo'orea, two and a half hours later.

Both islands were part of the Society Islands group, along with Bora Bora, arguably the most beautiful island in the world although Mo'orea also claimed that title.

We had booked a scenic tour of this island. After a half-hour delay for a 'no-show', we left in a convoy of small buses for a lookout halfway up the slopes of the volcanic mountain dominating the island's skyline.

The view over the peninsula separating two bays was a photographer's dream. Every vista was postcard picture perfect. Behind us, the towering, jagged-rimmed volcano was screened by huge vine-wreathed trees sweeping uphill. Low shrubs at the jungle's edge displayed vibrant blooms, and frangipani flowers perfumed the air. I tried and failed to squeeze all that beauty into a few photos, in the age of cameras with film.

Unlike Tahiti, much of which was inaccessible over land, Mo'orea had a road completely encircling it. This road boasted the title, 'Number One Highway'; as underwhelming of its state as the scenery was overwhelming. 'Rutted track' would be more appropriate, but it did allow us to travel around the entire island by road. By the time we returned to the resort that had been the starting point for our tour, we were suffering beauty overload. Oh, for something ugly to dilute the cloying sweetness of perfection!

But we had one more chore before returning to the ship for lunch. In Papeete, we discovered that obtaining the local currency was a breeze, but converting it back to Australian dollars was impossible! Our only option was to spend our remaining Francs on T-shirts and more ice cream. Paradise had a downside.

On Day 36 of our 54-day cruise from London, we were at sea once more, steaming towards Australia and home. Behind us, paradise waited to enchant other visitors.

Shirley Rowland

Why Travel?

I have a friend who hates travelling. He hates everything about it, packing, leaving the house, the airport process, flying – you name it, he hates it! He has a belief that there is nowhere in the world that he could go that he couldn't see better on TV. The ultimate armchair traveller. But is he right?

I may not be the best person to answer that question, because I love travelling: the researching, getting the passport, booking the accommodation, watching people at the airport, and not to forget, seeing new places. For me, it's all very exciting! But that's not the best thing about travelling.

It's the unexpected things, the things you can't plan. A chat with a local on a train, missing your bus stop because you couldn't get down the steps of the double-decker bus in time, these are the things that you remember, and you can't experience those things watching TV.

I took a trip with my son and his family to London and Paris this year. There were seven of us travelling, two nannas, two parents and three children. My eldest grandson is seven, my granddaughter had her fifth birthday while we were away, and my youngest grandson was eight months. You can imagine my trepidation, but I've already confessed that I love to travel, so not surprisingly I jumped at the chance.

Now, I could tell you all the places that we went to and the things we saw, but as my friend would say, you could see it better on TV. So instead, I'm going to tell you some of the things that happened and how we felt.

The luggage! With seven people you can imagine, and everyone overpacked. We were carrying, dragging, pulling, and rolling cases and bags for hundreds of metres. We searched for and crammed into elevators and hurriedly lifted all the luggage onto trains before the doors shut. Anxiously, we checked that everyone had made it on. Stressful at times, but satisfying too. We were in a foreign city on the other side of the world, taking public transport like the locals and getting where we needed to go. Of course, it was all thanks to my daughter-in-law who had pre-ordered oyster cards for us all and had worked out which trains to catch. It was no easy feat, but so much fun!

It's the wonder of travel that I love too. The thrill of being somewhere that you've seen in a movie or seeing something that just amazes you. The architecture, the history, the splendour. It's the way it makes you feel. It's the squirrels in Hyde Park, the statue of Paddington Bear at Paddington Station, taking a photo with your family at Buckingham Palace.

More than all that, it's the funny stories along the way, the private jokes that only the people that were there will know. Like can a Nanna be trusted to take a photo? Probably not, fingers over lenses and close-ups of gates rather than the whole building, yes, we weren't to be trusted!

Travelling with children can be tricky but can be lovely too. You get to see the world through their eyes and even feel like a child again. Does the Easter Bunny go to London? Of course he does! The carousel near the London Eye is twice as fast as the one at Elizabeth Quay and goes for much longer. You have to hold on extra tight. But do the horses jump off the carousel and ride off like in 'Mary Poppins'? Of course not, but I remember the look on my granddaughter's face when I suggested that they might. Priceless!

My eldest grandson spent his spare time writing about what we had done each day. He wrote pages and pages and was always asking how to spell certain words. I loved reading what he had written; he was very dedicated – unlike his grandmother, who did not write a word!

My favourite part of the trip was in Paris. We saw all the main attractions and fell in love with the city. My son, who was always good at running, discovered that the Paris Marathon was on when we were there, so he entered. He challenged himself and trained for months to be physically and mentally ready for the run. I was excited and nervous for him, but what was unexpected was the atmosphere of the event. Even as a spectator, it was incredible. Bands played music on street corners and locals stood with tourists cheering and clapping to encourage the runners. Parisiennes called out, "Bravo", and we joined in. It was emotional. I thought I was crying because my son was running in the Paris Marathon, but it wasn't just that. It was a whole community coming together, we all felt that we were a part of something very special. He completed the marathon, and we all celebrated his achievement. I was a very proud mother!

There are things that happen when you're travelling that just stay in your memory. Some of them seem quite insignificant, but memorable all the same. The lift at our accommodation in Paris could only take two people and could not be used for luggage. Very strange! We dare not risk breaking the rules as the sign warned that this would cause the lift to get stuck. What was worse than dragging seven suitcases up two flights of stairs? Getting stuck in a very old lift in a very old French building. It was tough getting the luggage up and down those stairs, but every time I think about it now, it makes me smile.

I remember also, the taxi ride from the Eurostar train station in Paris to our accommodation. The taxi driver was charming, but ripped us off. He charged us 110 euro for a 3km trip! What can you do? That's travelling.

We went to Disneyland Paris too; we loved it! We waited over an hour to meet Mickey Mouse, but nobody minded. My fondest memory there was when we were on my favourite ride, 'The Cups and Saucers'. (Don't ask!) Because there were so many of us, we were in two 'Cups'. I was with the older children. To be clear, this is one of the tamest rides in the park. Only minutes into the ride, it stopped, and the attendant marched over to my son, who was holding the baby. He was told in no uncertain terms that the baby had to be held on his lap or they had to get off. (It must be noted that the child was never in any danger.) We still laugh about the time that my 8-month-old grandson stopped the 'Cups and Saucers' ride at Paris Disney and almost got kicked off.

It's strange what you remember when you travel. Sure, you remember the amazing things you see, but what's extra special is how you feel. The people you were with and the funny and unusual things that happened. So, is my friend right? Can you see everything from your armchair on the TV. Probably, but you can't experience the world. You won't feel the exhilaration of the carousel horses going too fast, or the relief of just making it on the train before the doors close or experiencing a whole city come together for a marathon. No, you can't get that from your armchair, you have to travel for that, and I wouldn't want it any other way.

Sandra Ruddle

A Night in America

A storm.
Electric wasn't the word
Conceived when Thor
Took his forge
And struck the anvil
Of light
Evanescent
Upon the edges
Of Indiana.

Sheet upon sheet
Of lightning
Struck the earth
In violent
Accord with the
Strength of my anger
At this place.

Its thunderous smite
Reverberated
Upon every living thing
In one refrain:
Get out of here,
Get out of here now!

Mary Salter

Fabled Santorini

Dramatic rock faces
Furrowed, weathered bare,
Climb out of a navy sea.
Ancient volcanic rim
Circles darkly on a
Forever blue sky
While the curled shores
Spread like flared skirts
Hiding
A centre of fire.

Who knows when,
Upon what dictate
Of future fate will she
Burst upon the land-seascape
Once again.

Tumbling down
This ancient caldera,
White, azure, teal and gold hotels
Cling to the myriad pathways.
Steps and pebbled ways.
Vistas spread expansively
Upon this quirk
Of Atlantean myth
Dissembling an aura
Of harmonious quiet.

Almost impossible to conceive
The explosive tumult
Catapulting the island into
Its present incarnation.

Only a screed of black
Frilling the shores
Hints at
The white-hot origins
Of this holiday isle.

Mary Salter

Hong Kong Taxis

The drivers of HK taxis are a special breed. They work super-long hours in order to make ends meet. Maybe as a result of this, their cabs often become lounge rooms, decorated with numerous collections of toys. They are all over the dashboard and beyond: plastic farm animals, cartoon characters given away by McDonalds, framed photographs of sports stars glued to the backs of the seats and roof above, smiling cats, Chinese gods, bells hanging off the rear-vision mirror and even fresh flowers in vases adjacent to the air-con vents. Their cars are their homes, and may well have been decorated by their loving wives while the driver took a well-earned sleep.

Then there are the ones whose only focus is the job. No interior décor for them! Just a myriad of mobile phones in brackets, banked across the whole of the dash. Each one has its own ringtone and the driver answers each one with the briefest of responses to secure another fare for his growing group of drivers.

The scariest of all belonged to two groups. Those who used the red lights to take a nap and those who used the roads as a race track so they could get to the next job as soon as possible.

I remember getting into a cab with Eddy, my housemate, one Sunday lunchtime. We were going to lunch at our friend's house in Kowloon Tong. We lived in Shatin Heights, a mountainous area several hundred feet above the flats of Kowloon. As soon as we got into the car, Eddy said to me in a low voice,

"This is going to be the ride of our lives!"

"What do you mean?"

"I had this guy take me to the airport once. He drives like he's in a Formula One race."

Enabling the driver was the fact it was a Sunday morning, which is the only day of the week that the whole of Hong Kong sleeps. Hence, the roads are virtually empty. We were sliding around all over the bench seat as we descended through the numerous bends, bringing us down into Kowloon.

"PLEASE! Slow down," I squealed.

Thank goodness Eddy had a commanding voice, because the driver finally took heed of both of us ordering him to slow down and drive safely.

I must admit that, in recounting the journey to our friends, I did have a little sympathy for the driver being tempted by those rare, empty, open miles of Sunday morning roads in Hong Kong.

Mary Salter

Ramadan Bayram

(A 3-day holiday to celebrate the end of Ramadan.)

Higgledy-piggledy alleys are laden with tables so that barely a passageway exists between them. What resembles a way through is plied by vendors: The Mussel Man carries a huge old tin tray with high sides full of fresh mussels on ice and surrounded by cut lemons. The corn man is pushing a rickety wooden cart complete with coals and cobs of corn roasting on the glowing fire. The balloon man is carrying an impossibly high throng of pink, blue, purple and yellow balloons in one hand, whilst low in the other hand are children's animal-shaped figures. All of these compete (not forgetting, of course, the crowds of customers wending their way to this restaurant or that) with the waiters carrying sky-high trays of designer food to tables who knows where down which alley?

The stalwart managers, arms folded, shirts crisp and striped, beards trimmed to perfection are surveying their infinitesimal stretch of this convoluted space. The maestro, squat, square and shaven-haired, scalp glistening, wearing a waistcoat and jacket with brass-buttoned cuffs, muscles bulging, is slowly scoping his territory. A smile dares to appear briefly at the corners of his mouth as he calculates the evening's takings. Meanwhile, a group of short-sleeved waiters argue about where a basket of bread truly belongs, and yet another table gets laid with fresh white cloth, silver cutlery and shining glassware.

And I? I sit comfortably at the restaurant appropriately named "The Corner" with friends who've come to Istanbul from all over Europe. This is our last night and I'm glad I have my pashmina as the cool night air of early autumn settles on the alley. Finally, the couple who've sat on a table for four with one glass of red and one glass of water all evening, leave the table and wander away. We quickly join our table to theirs so the last two members of our group can have a seat. Let the festivities begin!

Mary Salter

The Stone Village, Crete

Based on the images of hot pink bougainvillea and rough-hewn stone buildings, I clicked on BOOK NOW with none of my usual references to descriptions, reviews and comments. I'd been to this seaside village in northern Crete before and had always stayed close to the beach.

I found out upon arrival, that this place was in the arid mountainous hinterland, a couple of kilometres' walk to the nearest beach, downhill on the way there, but quite uphill for the return.

I was apprehensive on my first day. There were too many kids playing around at the main pool, and the other pool, more for adults, seemed like a lonely affair, isolated from the main hub of the village.

I decided on a walk to explore my surroundings. I came across a lonely little taverna, with a limited menu, so I sat and ordered a simple Greek salad. Pondering what to do next, the local bus woke me from my reverie. I jumped on without thinking. Back to the beach; civilisation as I knew it! But the bar I jumped off at was already blaring electro-beat-dance-music in preparation for the early evening crowd.

On the walk back, a little voice kept telling me to just stay put at the Stone Village, to not worry about the beach. And, by the end of my stay I didn't want to leave!

Such peace, such silence, such proximity to nature, such privacy. The place was addictive!

I had my own house, handmade of earth, stone, and wood. I found out later that the owner had built the whole place himself over the years. Each building was separate from the others, and all around was nature. I had an ancient crooked olive tree that grew almost at right angles to my front verandah and door. I had to bend all the way around it to open it. Inside, there was no ceiling, just wooden beams holding up the terracotta tiled roof.

As day melded into night and day again, slowly, slowly I became stilled. All those fractured threads of myself were quietly joined back together again until my inner self took over and directed the minutiae of daily life: Lie down and rest, even if it is straight after breakfast. Get into bed and read, even if it is only 9 pm. Turn off the small lamp and sleep even if it is 9.40 pm. Do absolutely nothing except swim, read and eat. No movement apart from the triangle designated by the room, the pool and the restaurant.

I went to my room on the hottest day (37C) and lay on the bed after lunch; I didn't turn on the air-conditioning. The heat in the stone walls was strangely comforting, like a warm blanket softening the room, the air, myself. I was tuning into this world which was outside of me, all around me and I found myself becoming connected to it, a part of it again. The pleasure and satisfaction of this process were deeply nurturing to my soul, and I realised that no matter how magnificent the view of the Mediterranean, no matter how dramatic the backdrop of the Cretan mountains, nothing of this could replace the depth of reconnection to the earth that I was undergoing. No sheath of separation as provided by concrete or plastered walls, ceilings and floors, patios and outdoor living rooms "under the main roof" which today filled up that last remaining postage stamp of garden, could ever be a substitute for being surrounded by elemental earth.

I wondered before why people kept coming back to this place, for they all seemed to be friends of the owners. On my last day, I hugged the answer tightly and smiled in gratitude to the creator of this stone village, this place where the breakfast oranges are scarred and marred on the outside but gorgeously sweet and juicy on the inside. Where the ramshackle juicer is queued up for, as one by one, we scraped the pith away from the outflow juice into our glasses. Where the honey was of three kinds in vast containers (pine tree, thyme, wildflower) and ladled out over three types of creamy smooth Greek yoghurt (cow, sheep, goat) and the milk in three giant jugs came from the same sources as the yoghurt.

This place where healing and harmony work their magic through subtlety and generous bounty!

Mary Salter

June 1944

The memories of green fields, red flowers, yellow hay, family dinners, warm affection and the call of home were ever-present.

Leaving home to do his bit during World War II, he enlisted at 17 and registered his occupation as schoolboy, as did his friend and classmate. Both were assigned to a ship in the Royal Navy.

He wasn't tall, just over five feet four inches, and his appearance was inconspicuous. With his fair hair and grey eyes, he was just another young face in the multitude leaving for service overseas.

The ship was a minesweeper, and those on board became his new family. Fear, hard work, necessity, and duty bound them together until one day it didn't, and they were captured. The crew became separated, and he fell into the hands of the enemy as a prisoner of war.

He was taken to a place in Malaya where he met people like him, who would become his new family.

Surviving there for two years, he was identified as suitable for travel to work on the railway of death.

He boarded another ship. Crammed into tiny spaces in the ship's hold beneath deck they were desperate for air, water and food. Huddled together, squashed on top of each other, it was impossible for any air to reach them.

A few hours into the trip. a sound crashed into their world of misery, blasting their ears, and racking their bodies.

A torpedo hit the ship and split it in half.

He was in the half that sunk straight down to the bottom of the ocean.

He finally found a place where he could rest.

Stephanie Slanzi

The Train Trek

Travelling in a herd
Long march to destination
Train tracks beckon
Crowds stream across the station

Trooping along side-by-side
Ten abreast one-way traffic only
With so many people around
No train traveler could be lonely

Traipse up stair after stair
Sardine assembled, packed tight
Step by step by step by step
Is there no end in sight?

Footsteps find flat ground
Platform numbers disperse the troop
Trains scoop up the travelers
Who disappear like chickens to a coop

Stephanie Slanzi

Venice

View from the plane arriving at night
is of a dark gloomy place with little light
A patch of white glow here and there
nothing more can be seen from the air

The only way to reach our hotel
is by the water taxi visiting each port
Walking our bags twenty minutes to the water side
Thinking it would be easier if we had a car ride

Eventually, we realise in Venice there are no roads
only pedestrians and boats
Everything is transported this way
all is revealed by the light next day

Night time falls and we watch the boats land
tourists are delivered with bags in hand
Over cobblestones in the square they go
noisy visitors looking for their home

Moonlight shining to light their way
tomorrow they will know what we know today
Water surrounds us, gondoliers glide by
Venice is a fantasy place under the night sky

Stephanie Slanzi

“I go by sea; I go by land” *

The word journey comes from the French ‘le jour’ meaning day, and it meant ‘the distance one could travel in a day’. Before the time of good artificial lighting, that is, vehicle headlights or strong streetlights, most journeys needed to be completed by nightfall. The best journeys start at dawn or earlier. The lights are turned on and sleepily, one prepares for the day, an early breakfast and departure, dawn just breaking on the horizon, the sky gradually lightening and then sunrise. Sunrise is often spectacular depending on the arrangement of clouds. There can be a wonderful array of changing colours till finally the sun is fully risen and the day has begun.

In the early years of my life, my older sisters and I did a lot of travelling as our father’s occupation in the Indian Medical Service meant we moved between various places in north-west India. In the early 1930s, two positions became available, Quetta in what is now Pakistan, and Zabul in Persia, or Iran as it is now. Our father applied to both. We ended up travelling to Zabul on the eastern edge of Persia where the border juts into Afghanistan. Apart from being the Medical Officer for the area, our father was appointed to the position of vice-consul, too, so we lived on the grounds of the British Consulate there. I was too young to remember the train journey there, but my elder sister remembered that our nurse Nannie R. made mob caps for us to wear so our hair didn’t get dirty from the dust or the soot from the steam engine.

One of my earliest memories is the trip from Zabul to Meshed where our father's duties took him. We went by car, Father driving with Mother beside him and we three children in the back with our nurse, Nannie. The journey was completed in one day as there was no place to stay between where we lived and our destination. It would have been too dangerous to camp as there were "Brigands in the hills". We were accompanied by a lorry with some servants and our luggage. Two policemen also came along as guards. I do not remember much about the journey just barren countryside with hills in the distance where the brigands lived! It was a long journey not helped by the bad road; we were bogged in sand several times.

My mother tells the story of my elder sister, aged about six, stepping daintily out of the car saying, "I love travelling" and getting black looks from our father as he said, "Take those children out of earshot." We enjoyed the break as we could get out and make sandcastles while Father dug out the car again. We eventually arrived, but somehow the lorry with our luggage, which included our bedding rolls, had been delayed. I remember being wrapped in a curtain and put to bed on a camp stretcher.

During our time in Persia, we spent the hot weather in a hill station, Birjand. This was another long trip by car. Eventually, we returned to England, leaving Father to finish his term of office. Mother, Nannie and we three girls caught the ship from Karachi. This involved car and train travel to the port. I remember having a black arm band sewn onto my coat sleeve because the king, George V, had died.

We were stopped at the border going through to India and the customs people inspected our baggage. Silver was not allowed to be taken out of the country. Would they find the small silver pepper-pot hidden beneath the doll's clothes? I do remember one of the inspectors opening the drawer of the small chest where the doll's things were packed. I knew where the pepper pot was. I watched anxiously. Would they find it? They did not. My mother also had several other small pieces hidden somewhere in the baggage.

Other journeys followed this one. The next year, I returned to India with my parents. My sisters had been left behind at boarding school. Quetta (now in Bangladesh) was my father's next posting. Luckily, we had missed the big earthquake of 1936. The town was still recovering. The house we should have been allotted had been flattened and so our first house was just a temporary building. The baby, our brother Robert, was born there.

The hot weather was spent in the hill station of Ziarat, another long car journey. Father would come up when he could. It was there my mother started to teach me, using the Beacon Reading series of books, the very first … "I see a kitty." The words were in separate boxes then put together to eventually be read as a sentence – very boring. 'Look at that little cat' made more sense. I must have started to learn my tables, too, and my mother taught me geographical shapes using rice spread on a tray. "An island is a piece of land entirely surrounded by water." My grandmother sent the Child Education magazine from England which was useful.

When we returned to Quetta I started school. It was run by two Lutheran sisters in their house which had survived the earthquake. I was not there long. It was winter; a bad cold became bronchitis, and my brother Robert caught it, ending up with pneumonia. A worrying time: no penicillin, or sulpha drugs in those days. A steam tent was rigged up. He survived and we went down to Karachi to recuperate by the sea. Then a sudden promotion for Father sent us across India to Hyderabad, Deccan. Another train journey.

Train journeys tend to merge into each other. All I remember about that one was getting off at a station to have a meal in the dining room. The room was cooled by a punka system, (horizontal blinds hanging from the ceiling, attached to a cord that pulled them back and forth). Mother worried about Robert being left on the train with only the bearer to keep watch. I remember looking out of the dining room window to see, on the verandah roof below, a young Indian sitting there operating the Punka system by pulling the cord back and forth with his toes. Our bedding rolls, as usual, accompanied us, so we must have travelled overnight. When we arrived at the Hyderabad station, we were met by an official welcoming party and garlands placed round our necks. My mother complained that the garlands were always so wet. This was the first time I had been given one for myself and was thrilled. The flowers, the crinkly, coloured paper or fine tinfoil and the lovely smell, I thought they were beautiful.

Hyderabad was so different. We had a proper house which came with my father's new position. It was set in a large garden with a high wall with broken glass on top. There was a gate and a gatekeeper. Beside the gate was a small black box in which people could leave their calling cards. Soon after we arrived, I went with Mother to leave cards at various places. The house itself was big. It was a split-level one of white-washed stone with deep verandahs all round. It had a flat roof on which we could sleep in the hot weather. Under the upper level were go-downs that is, storage space. Across the road was the Residency. It was built like ours of whitewashed stone but much bigger and was more like a palace. The big iron gate was guarded by soldiers of the regiment attached there at the time.

When the new school year began, WWII had just started. I went to The Mahbubia, which was a school for Muslim girls, based on the English curriculum and ran by an English headmistress. It was situated in the enjoining city of Secunderabad. I was there till the hot weather started the next year, being taken there and back in a tonga (a horse drawn carriage seating two people with the driver in front). Mother had employed a nurse, Nanny W. to help with looking after my brother and me. When she left us, Mother then wrote to our previous nurse, Nannie R., asking if she were free and if she would like to come back. She willingly accepted the position. Not liking sea voyages, she did as much of the journey as she could overland just before the Italians entered the war. Mother was relieved to have her back and trusted her to take my brother and me to the hills in Kotagiri for the hot weather season (I went to St Mary's convent school there for the term). Mother could then stay with our father and continue her involvement with the Red Cross and the other organisations concerned with the war effort.

With WWII continuing, my parents wanted to unite the family, so arrangements were made for my sisters to join us in India. Then our mother would bring us down to Australia, where she had a cousin and family living. When my sisters arrived, they were almost strangers, and of course, they did not know our brother. We had six months together as a family and then were on the move again, leaving Father behind. We sailed from Calcutta (Kolkata) after a long train journey.

Once again, our journey continued through the night. Bedding rolls were brought out and laid on the seats. To keep the carriage cool, a large block of ice was set into a deep zinc-lined tray on the legs. The carriage fan stirred the air across this. We also had boiled water in a felt-covered canteen for drinking but used soda water for cleaning our teeth.

Being wartime (it was 1941), the date of the sailing had been kept secret. We spent about a week in Calcutta (Kolkata) and then boarded MV Tanda. The ship stayed on the river for a few more days before finally departing. At night, blacked out, only blue lights on the deck showed. There was no daily map or record of each day's sailing displayed. The passengers had to guess where we were when passing islands down the coast of the Malay peninsula. My passport shows we stopped at the Straits Settlement which must have been Singapore. We could go ashore but I only have a vague memory of it. One bazaar is like another. Then it was onwards till finally we reached Townsville where we went through immigration and had our passports stamped. We disembarked in Sydney and caught the train that evening for Melbourne where we stayed for a week. Mother went to look at schools and arranged accommodation in Geelong. Nannie took us sightseeing, catching trams and buses – a novel experience. It was winter and night came early. I was fascinated by the streetlights and bright neon signs. We settled in Geelong, attending new schools, C. of E. this time. When the war ended, Father rejoined us. A year later, the family moved to Tasmania. We started travelling by air as my sisters and I stayed at our respective places of education and flew back and forth for the main holidays.

Travelling was something my husband and I later enjoyed. Some trips were organised tours and others personal arrangements. With a daughter settled in the USA, there was a good reason to visit her after seeing cousins and family in the UK. As with sea travel, air travel has progressed over my lifetime, such as non-stop Perth to Heathrow now instead of six or more stops between the two.

Alison P. Smith

**The title comes from a children's prayer and seems appropriate*

Travelling East at Christmas time 1968

(With apologies to T.S. Eliot.)

A wearying time we had of it.
Just the worst time of the year
For a journey, and such a long journey.
The road rough and the weather hot
The very height of summer.
And the engine giving trouble.
There were times we regretted
Leaving our air-conditioned home.
The children in the back seat
Squabbling and grumbling.
The caravan parks crowded and charging high prices.
It was a difficult time.
We often travelled at night sleeping in snatches.
We said to ourselves 'this is ridiculous.'

We came to bitumen-sealed roads and travelled smoothly,
Through greener countryside.
Three silos against the blue sky.
A kangaroo bounded across in front of us.
We stopped at a service station,
It was a pleasant place.
Six hands on the shop counter pleading for ice creams.
We followed directions and so we continued.
Arriving at dusk not a moment too soon.
Finding the place (as you might say, satisfactory.)

All this was a long time ago I remember.
And we would do it again if it were possible.
But time moves on,
Circumstances change.
We returned from our journey.
Happy that we had been, but glad to be home.

Alison P. Smith

Darwin, Warm and Lush, 2023

Lucky me! I have just returned from a week spent in the warm weather of Darwin, in the company of eighteen other fantastic women and two men. We left on June 2nd and returned on June 9th. During that time, my family texted me about the appalling weather Perth was having: cold and wet. I must admit to feeling happy I was not there to experience such awful weather. However, that was the planning and reasoning behind our trip.

Our itinerary filled each day with an around-the-town tour, an on-and-off bus tour, a sunset cruise and dinner, and a trip to the Tiwi Islands, Kakadu, Litchfield, and Katherine Gorge. Not everybody did all these trips, we each chose those we wanted to do.

My purpose for visiting Darwin, besides the desire to leave the cold weather, was to go to the Tiwi Islands.

Together with Liz and Maisie, the three of us arrived at the ferry terminal, to wait for boarding along with several dozen others. We walked to the bag-checking table, where Maisie was greeted with, 'Hello, Nan.' Her grandson, one of the skippers who drive the ferry, had previously said he couldn't skipper her over as he had another shift, but he changed it to surprise her.

The two-hour crossing to Bathurst Island was calm and smooth. Once there, we split into two large groups, one to visit the art gallery and museum, the other to be welcomed with a smoking ceremony in which we took part, walking in a circle and being fanned with smoke. A talk about the history of settlement of Melville and Bathurst Islands, and emphasising the residents are Tiwis, not Aboriginal, gave us a good insight into the culture there. Damper, billy tea, and a sumptuous lunch completed the morning, after which we visited the art gallery, and were driven around the island, past homes, and the cemetery, the burial ritual explained carefully to us.

Storytelling Tiwi Islands

Arriving back in Darwin late that afternoon, we were pleased to pick up a taxi back to our hotel, where we showered, caught up with the others briefly before dropping into bed. It had been a twelve-hour day, and together with being on the water, we were ready to sleep the night away.

The next day we bussed to the Adelaide River to pick up our cruise upriver to see the jumping crocs. The guides explained that if the crocs chose to interact with us, they would be treated to some titbits, for which they stretch out of the water to take their treats. Several crocodiles entertained us for some time. We noticed the two crewmen kept whistling for what reason we didn't know, although we noticed a bird or two following us. After the croc's exhibition, our guides whistled to the birds, held out titbits in their hands, and within seconds the air filled with whistling kite birds, who swooped to take the food. Clever birds.

Feeding a jumping crocodile

Another long day by the time we returned to the hotel.

I didn't go to Kakadu, Litchfield, or Katherine Gorge, having been to those places several times in years gone. Those people who went thoroughly enjoyed themselves, although all remarked how tired they were, as each day was a twelve-hour day and Kakadu was a fourteen-hour day. Long journeys.

We visited the aircraft museum, where I managed to buy a key ring for my son featuring the F111 jet plane, which was what he worked on when stationed at Tindall Aircraft Base in Katherine, many years ago.

At the art gallery and museum, we saw the original graphic footage of the bombing of Darwin, which left me angry and sad at the same time. Also, in the same museum are photos and some relics of Cyclone Tracey. I didn't go into the art gallery, but others told me it was wonderful.

Like most visitors to Darwin, a trip to Mindal Markets is essential. Our group hired a taxi and arrived early, fortunately for us, as already at 4.30 it was busy. By 5.30, crowds packed each pathway and most stalls, particularly the food stalls, from which emanated the most aromatic flavours of spices, coffee, grills. Many people, food in hand, trudged through the sand hills to the beach to sit and watch the sunset, a tradition when visiting Darwin.

Melva and I found Charlie's of Darwin, a gin bar situated down a side street and up an alleyway; dingy, we thought. Yet, my doctor recommended it, I am sure for medicinal reasons. Funky and quirky, the gin bar turned out to be an adventure on its own. You enter Charlie's through a garage door, walk down a short way, past a bold and vivid wall mural to the lift, up one level to a myriad of passageways, passing along the way windows looking in the gin brewing rooms, and into the bar and restaurant. For somebody who has only tasted gin once in my life, I enjoyed the pink gin, tonic and slice of lime at Charlie's. My only other experience of gin and tonic was decades ago in England, when together with Stan we were visiting relatives. Tom handed me a gin and tonic, which was so awful that, when he left the room, I tipped it out onto the aspidistra. Oh, how that plant thrived, lush and green, I swear it tipped its leaves to me many times over the period we stayed with Tom and Pat.

Distilling room at Charlie's Gin Bar.

Again, with Melva, our final trip was to the Royal Flying Doctor exhibition, which included virtual reality of the bombing of Darwin Harbour; this time we were immersed in the fighting, quite anxiety filling. We didn't manage to see the footage of Dr John Flynn, the founder of the RFDS, as we were flying home that afternoon.

Inside war tunnels, Darwin.

Altogether this trip was thoroughly enjoyable. However, I won't go to Darwin again – there are many more places in Australia I would like to see.

I am fortunate to be able to travel with this group. Noleen and our travel agent, Tracey, organise great tours and trips. There are several of us who have been holidaying together since the inception of the group, while others have come to the end of their holidaying days. Each trip sees new faces and younger people. Now I have another trip planned for 2024 to Adelaide,

Kangaroo Island, three days up the Murray River, and Hahndorf. After that who knows? However, as my doctor said, 'Don't stop travelling!'

Lorraine Spring

My South Australia Holiday, 2024

With a whirr and a buzz, the chocks of the plane descended; rooftops and houses grew larger. As the runway loomed to meet us, I braced my hands on the seat in front of me, expecting the jolt of the wheels to thrust me forward, but a light bump or two showed we were on firm ground. Our travel group of ten women and two men was about to begin our holiday to Adelaide, Kangaroo Island, Hahndorf, and three days on the Murray Princess paddle-wheeler cruising the Murray River.

We checked in at two different hotels, due to the lack of available rooms for all twelve of us at our preferred hotel. After checking in, and as it was nearing six p.m., Noleen, Melva, Jan and I left to find somewhere for dinner. We found a burger restaurant around the corner – Grill'd. I chose flat bread instead of a roll, which gave me a juicy, very enjoyable beef burger without a lot of bread.

The following day, Tuesday, late afternoon, Jan, and I walked past Grill'd on the opposite side of the road. Outside, a line of people queued – I would estimate up to one hundred and fifty or more. We thought there must be an upstairs event. When we returned, the line had dwindled to a few, with a smattering of people seated inside. We asked a man what was on.

'Each Tuesday, this restaurant closes its doors to the public, and the city's homeless can come here for a free meal.' He told us that the same applies all over Australia – I am not aware of this either in Perth or Fremantle.

The next day, after breakfast, we left on our city coach tour up to Hahndorf. Adelaide is full of greenness, which frames heritage buildings and churches. In St Francis Xavier's cathedral we oohed and aahed over the magnificent timber framed and arched interior. We lunched in Hahndorf, a quaint touristy village with cafes and shops lining each side of the main street. After our meal, we had time to browse the shops before returning to our hotel. It was a full day. Noleen and I were more than happy to relax in our beds that night.

The next two days we spent on Kangaroo Island, a place of rugged and pristine terrain. Our bus took us to Seal Cove, where a community of seals live and breed. They are now protected from hunters. Centuries ago, when whalers and sealers arrived on Kangaroo Island, they killed seals for their pelts to send to fashion houses in Europe. I didn't walk the 900 metres and many steps down to the bay itself. I strode down the alternative walk to the viewing platform. From here, I could still glimpse some of these animals and listen to them calling to their pups.

At the Kangaroo and Koala Wildlife Park, the animals live in large, bush enclosures. Most of these animals arrive here from dead or injured mothers. They stay until they are well. The idea is to release them back into the wild, but there are some because of injuries that will never leave the park. In Western Australia, we have the Western Grey kangaroo. In South Australia, there are some Western Greys, but the main breed is a smaller, stockier kangaroo, deep grey, with thicker fur.

We drove to Flinders Chase National Park to the Remarkable Rocks. These are a group of rocks which, from a distance, look a little like marbles, but which, when close-up, look like a set of decayed teeth.

The next day, we boarded the bus at 9.30 am for our full day and evening tour of various parts of the island and industries. Near Pennington Bay, we visited the Raptor Park. Here, injured birds are brought in for nursing. Some can go back to the wild, but some, like the Wedge-tail eagle with one eye, will live in the park for life.

I enjoyed the Eucalyptus Distillery where we watched how they harvested and processed the leaves to make eucalyptus oils and creams. The eucalyptus fumes reminded me of the times when, as a child, I had a cold. My mother always gave me a handkerchief sprinkled with a few drops of eucalyptus oil to sniff and clear my head.

At the Honey Farm, we listened to the story of the bees on Kangaroo Island. Prior to 1880, Kangaroo Island was bee free. Importations of the Italian Lingurian bees occurred between 1880 to 1885, when the S.A. government proclaimed Kangaroo Island a bee sanctuary. The original idea was to provide queen bees for the mainland, to establish a honey industry there. I wanted to bring back a small pot of creamed honey, but it was against the law to bring honey into Western Australia.

We sipped wine and beer at False Cape Wines, (they didn't have gin, which I would have preferred).

The following three days we spent on the Murray Princess paddle-wheeler, the largest wheeler still operating on the Murray. Once aboard and cruising, I walked to the stern to watch the paddlewheel. The water whooshed up and flooded parts of the deck, and the stench of diesel caught in my throat. I soon learnt to avoid the stern when we were cruising.

The usually tranquil landscape buzzed with jet and boat skiers bumping their way along the river. Holiday houseboats lined the banks. I recalled that the Murray Darling is the largest waterway in Australia. The source of the Darling River is in Queensland, it joins the Murray River in New South Wales, and its mouth is southeast of Adelaide. It is beautiful. We moored at Murray Bridge, where my group caught the bus into town. Because I had done no exercise for days, I walked up the steep hill to join the others. At the top I leant against a wall, glad my lungs and heart held out:)

Our next mooring was at a small jetty further up the river. Here, some people enjoyed a brief tour downstream to learn about the various birds in the region. The rest of us stayed on shore. Some fished and caught carp. This predatory, imported species is impossible to eradicate. It causes much damage to the banks and to the native fish habitat. Once

caught, the deckhand kills and bins them. They may not return them to the waterways.

We formed teams to play Bocchi. Although our team won, it was not through my efforts. I blamed the weather for playing Bocchi in near forty-degree heat; it was overbearing.

After three days of cruising, we transferred to the Adelaide Airport Coach. We had finished our holiday in South Australia. Another three-and-a-half-hour flight and we landed at Perth airport.

Except for the continual air conditioning on our tour and on the plane, I enjoyed every minute of this trip. Although I wore masks and used hand sanitisers, I arrived home with an ear, nose, and throat infection. I tested negative for COVID-19. A few days later, I heard that three people in our group of twelve had come down with COVID-19. What an unfortunate end to a glorious trip!

I will have fond memories of this holiday. Adelaide, Kangaroo Island, and the mighty Murray River made this trip one to remember.

I am already curious about next year: where will our intrepid travellers' group journey too then?

Lorraine Spring

Ragondin and Noddy Boats

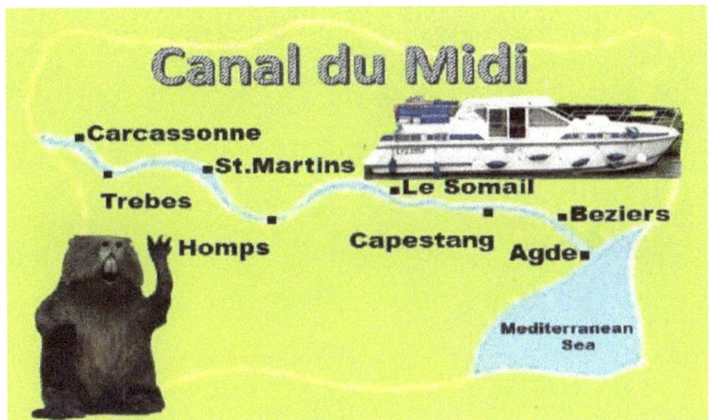

The flagpole hit the stone bridge with a thwack and we ducked. Frowns creased the brow of the hire-boat manager watching from the shore as he considered the potential damage to the 37-foot Tarpon, the self-drive boat we'd hired to travel down the Canal du Midi.

The amateur crew hauled the shattered pole on board (a newly purchased broom handle from Carcassonne) and disappeared beneath the bridge with reassuring waves.

On board, the three-novice crew breathed sighs of relief as their designated captain navigated the waters of the Canal De Midi. Jim, brother-in law of two, and husband of one of the three sisters was no stranger to boating – he'd always had his own sail boat. However, the locks proved a completely different challenge, one we were blissfully unaware of at that moment.

We had hired this self-drive canal boat to cruise down the length of the Canal de Midi from Carcassonne to Agde, a seven-day self-drive barge cruise through 120 kilometres of glorious French countryside and through 36 locks – what could be more relaxing?

The trip began in Carcassonne, where we bought the ill-fated broom handle, which was designated to hold up the Aussie flag at the stern of the boat.

Once we'd cleared the bridge, we looked at the shattered flag pole, snapped cleanly in two. Captain Jim, ever the optimist, re-seated it in its makeshift stand, then we were off, our flag shorter but still flapping around as we sped off at 4 kph – the top speed allowed on the canal. People pushed prams, and cycled along the towpath, overtaking us as we negotiated locks.

We had read about the locks – studied every Trip Advisor forum on them, but nothing prepared us for the sheer physical effort of jumping off the slow-moving boat, rope in hand, and running to the capstan to secure the boat before tons of water dropped off beneath us. The person who held the rope had to slowly feed it down the drop, and each one of us, when it was our turn, lived in fear of leaving the boat dangling in mid-air as water whooshed away in torrents below. It never happened – but for the entire seven days as we jumped on and off the boat, we expected it to. Jim, of course, stayed happily at the helm – not for him the nail-biting leap off the boat, then on again when it came out the other side of the lock. He was the only one who knew how to steer the darn thing, and we happily let him – who needs equality at times like this?

When we left Carcassonne on the first day of the trip, we had to negotiate the first 6 of the 36 locks – we thought it would get easier the more we went through – but it never did. However, that first day we thought it was great, this jumping off and on a moving boat, dodging the swinging rope, then turning the lever on the lock-gate.

The canal water was murky and full of rubbish, though we did see our first Ragondin, a huge rodent, climbing one of the banks. It had been an introduced species, imported from South America between the First and Second World Wars, for its fur. But it never took off – French women would not wear a rat fur coat – and they were released into the wild. They made for the canal and burrowed into the soil, causing untold damage to the canal banks. We actually learned this from the handyman who came to fix our leaking toilet.

We reached our first town, Trebes, at 7 pm that evening, and after mooring alongside several other hire-boats, rewarded ourselves with a few glasses of the remarkably cheap but exceptional wine from the supermarket at Carcassonne. Later, we strolled along the Canalside to a nearby restaurant to enjoy more wine and excellent food.

Having the toilet fixed slowed down our departure next day. After the handyman left, we walked into Trebes to stock up on supplies. Five bags of essentials later (baguettes, cheese, wine) we returned to the boat.

Rows of white 'Noddy Boats' lined the canal, the scathing name given by Rick Stein, whose French Odyssey down the Canal de Midi had inspired our own trip. From his 100-foot luxury hotel barge Anjodi, he gazed upon lesser mortals travelling in their white 37-foot hire-boats and pronounced them Noddy Boats. He and the French boat captain took a perverse delight in steering close by these hapless boats, causing a huge wash to push them into the bank. Later, we found to our cost this was nothing to laugh about.

At 3 pm we set off for our next stop, Homps. Several of the locks we passed through were 3-in-1, which meant after you entered the first one, you waited until the gate closed. Then water poured in, lifting the boat to the next level. After waiting for the gate to close, water lifted you again, then you waited for the third gate to close before exiting the locks. All this took longer than we realised, and after negotiating several more locks we knew we would not make Homps before 7 pm, when every lock closed. Our passage through the canal had not been made any easier by some of the bored and unhelpful lockkeepers who obviously had enough of tourists and were happy to let them get on with it by themselves. Several sat and smoked beside the lock gate, watching us throw ropes round the bollards, haul ropes back onto the deck, then run up to the gate to turn the lever to open it – which we had foolishly assumed was their one and only job.

Resuming our journey, we spotted a family of black swans bobbing alongside us. Having thought they were native to Western Australia, we later learned how they came to this part of France. Centuries ago in Europe, the black swan was regarded as a mythical animal, similar to a unicorn. In 1804, a French scientific expedition to Australia led by Nicolas Baudin brought the first living specimens to Europe. These became part of the Empress Josephine Bonaparte's Garden menagerie at the Château de Malmaison. The black swans roamed the gardens freely, and every black swan in Europe originated from this first pair.

The lock keeper at Fonfile phoned ahead to St Martin's, the lock before Homps, to make sure it stayed open. We reached it at 6.30 pm, and the lock keeper was not pleased at having to wait until we passed through before he could go home. He would not help at first, muttering a torrent of French, so Miv jumped off the boat at the first lock and tied up the ropes front and back. By the time we reached the next lock, he relented and helped attach my rope while Miv attached Pats. He even made a joke with Jim, calling out he must be Superman as he had three women. Lucky for him, we were passing through the gate by then – otherwise, he would have copped the death stares of three pairs of indignant female eyes. We had, however, learned a valuable lesson – in future, we must leave ourselves enough time to get to the next destination well before grumpy lock-keepers closed the gates.

Moored beside the bank, we spent a pleasant evening sampling platters of Gorgonzola and Roquefort cheeses, spicy sausages, and crackers, accompanied by glasses of wine. Rick Stein had, at this point in his trip, dined on garlic soup, rabbit and hazelnut pate, salads au chevre chaud, joint of roast kid with potato gratin and strawberries and Chantilly cream to finish. We doubted he enjoyed it as much as we enjoyed ours.

For the rest of the evening, we played Yams, the French version of Yahtzee. As we are all quite competitive, the clatter of six dice bouncing across the laminate table-top below deck resounded until late. Finally, we decided to call it a night – coinciding strangely, with the exact moment the wine ran out.

Next morning, knowing we had six locks to navigate we left at 9 am. It was hard going, especially as the weather had turned windy and whipped at our bare arms and legs. We jumped off the boat, secured lines, then jumped back on board as we fed the line out to decreasing levels of water in the lock. The Lockkeeper – who managed all six locks by driving between them – said we three women were a 'great team' – very satisfying!

We arrived at Le Somail at 1 pm, and had to moor just outside the village as most moorings were reserved for Nicols Boats – a posher rental firm than ours. As we walked past the canal to the village, we saw a wooden carving of the infamous Ragondin looking very much like a beaver crossed with a rat. Having only glimpsed the rear end of several of the rodents, it was fascinating to see the life-sized carving, bearing the humorous title 'The Beauty of Midi'.

Le Somail boasted several delights, according to Trip Advisor, so we made our way to the Hat Museum – to find it long since closed down! Another attraction, the Antique Library was open, a converted wine cellar that housed over 50,000 books. Of course, all the books were in French, and from the musty smell of the place had been there since the Revolution, so we didn't linger, and instead wandered round the village.

Many of its buildings dated back to when the canal was first constructed in 1681, by 17th century engineer Perre-Paul Riquetin. Built at the same time as the canal, Le Somail (Somail from the French word sleep) served as an overnight stop for the mail boats and passengers that passed along the waterway. In the late 1850s, with the advent of the railroad, much of this water traffic ceased.

We walked by a round yellow-stoned building, originally the ice-house for the village. Blocks of ice, carried down from the Montagne Noire by donkey then covered in straw all winter, helped preserve food throughout the long hot summers. Alongside the canal, barges served as colourful shops.

As we neared our boat, we found the mooring empty!

Further along the towpath, we saw a man pulling our boat by its towrope. Apparently, a passenger barge had passed, causing a huge wash (not funny, Rick Stein!) and lifted the metal mooring peg from the bank. Our boat then drifted into the middle of the canal. One of the harbour staff jumped on board another boat which took him out to our runaway. Grabbing the trailing rope, he hopped across another boat to the bank, pulling the rope along. Everyone ran to help, and between them, they secured the boat to another spike.

Enough drama for one day – we remained on board, afraid to leave the boat even for dinner. When we retired each of us secretly hoped the boat would not attempt to make a break for it while we slept!

Next morning, we set off for Capestang, passing beneath an archway of plane trees. Further on, many trees had been cut into logs and lay in piles alongside the banks. Later we learned that all the plane trees had been infected with a disease called Canker Stain. The Stain had been accidentally introduced in 1945 by Allied soldiers landing in Provence, with ammunition boxes made from American Sycamore already infected with the disease. The disease spread slowly throughout the south of France, before reaching the Canal du Midi. With no cure available, over 42,000 trees were burned on-site to stop the spread. It was a sobering sight to see the destruction of so many beautiful trees, but in many places, smaller trees had begun to sprout.

Today, with no locks to negotiate, we draped ourselves around the boat like self-indulgent movie stars while our captain steered around black swans, fluffy ducks and the odd Ragondin, scuttling beneath the banks.

In the distance, we glimpsed a huge chateau standing out above the vine-planted fields that covered both sides of the canal. Drifting pleasantly through the heart of the wine country, we couldn't wait to sample a glass or two when we reached the medieval town of Capestang.

Boats lined both sides of the canal as we approached our mooring, making it difficult to slide in and tie up. Jim and I decided to celebrate this excellent feat of boatmanship with a chilled glass of something French and unpronounceable, while Pat and Miv wandered into town.

Later, we all walked along the canal banks and dined at a La Bateliere, a restaurant overlooking the busy waterway

Back on board, we played Yams until the yawns drowned out the clack of the dice, settling in for another relaxing night's sleep.

Waking to a wet, grey day after heavy rain overnight, Pat and Miv sloshed through the puddles to ensure we did not miss out on our daily hit of fresh baguettes. Casting off straight after breakfast, we set off on what was to be our most tiring day on the canal.

First hurdle – the Malpas tunnel, which carries the Canal du Midi under the dËnserune hill in the Herault Province. Excavated in 1670, it was Europe's first navigable canal tunnel. This fact failed to impress us when, halfway beneath tons of earth, chugging along the narrow tunnel in the darkness, we discovered our horn didn't work. The rule was to sound the horn as you approached a bend to warn oncoming boats – so we all yelled at the top of our lungs instead. Fortunately for us, nothing approached from the other end of the 165-metre tunnel, and we emerged, unscathed into a much clearer day.

Over the next 11 kilometres, we tootled along happily, admiring the scenery both in and out of the canal. Families of ducks entertained us with their frantic herding of ducklings, swans bobbed by gracefully in our wake, and the towpaths on either side of us boasted healthy-looking Plane trees. This idyll, of course, could not last, and we finally approached the dreaded 'Staircase of Locks' at Fonserannes.

Seven locks, one after the other, carried boats down a drop of 21.5 metres – not exactly the Niagara Falls, but a massive feat all the same. People crowded the paths on each side of the locks to watch the spectacle, some cheering, but others offering to catch ropes and help the boats packed tightly into each lock. We entered the first lock, and the whooshing of water signalled the closing of the gate. Then we waited until the water dropped down a level, before the gate opened onto the next lock. The helpful spectators caught our ropes and secured them before the gates closed again and the water whooshed away. This continued until we had navigated all seven locks – a time-consuming exercise as we had to wait for each boat in our group to enter and secure itself. The 'bonjours' and waves from the spectators made it a pleasant trip, however.

We arrived in Villeneuve de Beziers at 4 pm that afternoon, our longest day on the canal so far. Despite our tiredness, the neat little town beckoned us, with its yellow stone buildings and flower beds everywhere.

Near the town centre, a large trompe l'oiel decorated the side of a house. We had seen these 'trick of the eye' paintings in several towns along the canal, but the ones here were stunning. A staircase appeared to go up the side of the building to an entrance shaded by trees. There was even a small dog watching from beneath another tree as two people walked down the staircase – we had to go up and touch the building to assure ourselves it was all painted on.

Nearing the centre of town, we heard music, which came from a large carousel, festooned with fairy lights. It spun slowly around, playing the kind of fairground music familiar in every country. Children clung on to garishly painted horses and trains, another sight we had encountered all over France. Apparently, the French had laid claim to inventing them, saying they derived from Louis XIV's jousting competitions, though we all failed to see the similarity.

We had originally intended to eat out in town, but tiredness got the better of us, and we returned to the boat to dine on a platter of whatever was in the fridge – a rich assortment of cheese, olives, sliced baguettes, and salad.

Instead of our usual cards or dice games, we lounged around reading a couple of English newspapers we'd picked up on our last shopping trip, and had an early night. We fell asleep to the faint sounds of the carousel tinkling in the distance.

We breakfasted on baguettes and croissants bought from the bakery in Villeneuve before setting off for our last town, Agde, on the shores of the Mediterranean Sea.

Today we had only one lock – and could not help feeling a bit nostalgic as we hauled ropes and jumped back on board for the last time. However, we were happy to bin the rubber gloves we used because of the slime and heaven knows what else clinging to the ropes from the murky canal water.

The trip today was also our shortest – three hours of gliding sedately down the waterway in no hurry to end our journey. Just before reaching Agde, Pat spotted one of the Ragondin swimming merrily towards the bank – it still reminded us of a giant rat.

Once moored, we snacked on a tray full of leftovers – the French version of which beat anything I could rustle up at home hands down – then we crossed the bridge into the pretty little seaside town of Agde.

In the centre of the old town stood the imposing Cathédrale Saint-Étienne d'Agde. Built in the twelfth century, it housed a magnificent pipe organ, and we were lucky enough to be there while the organist practised.

We stood in silence and listened as, in his skilful fingers, the air was forced through the pipes and the rich, warm music resounded around the vaulted ceilings of the cathedral. Beautiful!

Leaving the cathedral, we entered the town square, where more trompe lóeil decorated a few of the nearby buildings. After enjoying an ice-cold beer at one of the cafes, we took in the rest of the sights until dinner.

Tonight, we dined at Le Chapitre, a charming restaurant on a pontoon floating at the edge of the canal. The waiters and other guests were making a fuss over one of the other diners – who we learned was a famous T.V. actor, Coco. Not knowing exactly what he was famous for, we whiled away our meal imagining which TV soapies he starred in. The unanimous vote was for 'Desperate Housewives of Paree', which I sincerely hope is not a real show!

Back on board, we finished off the last of the wine and chatted about the trip, our captain finally hanging up his hat as his crew toasted an unforgettable journey.

Tomorrow we must take three trains to Barcelona to carry on with our European trip, but tonight, we sleep in our Noddy boat on the edge of one of the most amazing feats of engineering, the Canal du Midi.

Wendy Stackhouse

The Perfect Souvenir

Stowed in my suitcase were the usual Paris souvenirs, such as an Arc de Triomphe snow dome and key rings with images of the Eiffel Tower. But I hadn't found myself a holiday memento. I was contemplating what to buy as I walked to Montmartre Cemetery, a popular destination for history lovers. This hidden-away place is where many of the people who lived in this Left Bank precinct, and made it famous, have been laid to rest. It's a who's who of local artists, including painters Degas and Moreau and the ballet dancer Nijinsky. The singer Dalida's tomb, surrounded by flowers, is the most visited and Louise Weber, inventor of the French cancan and star of the Moulin Rouge, is buried there too. The cemetery became the mass grave for the bodies of those royals executed during the reign of terror, ironically sharing their resting place with their executioner.

The walk wasn't enjoyable. It was hot and the traffic noise made my head spin. I looked forward to crossing the metal bridge and looking down on the cool, tree-lined pathways of the cemetery with its glimpses of romantic statues and fountains; it is always a peaceful place for contemplation.

Then I spotted it. My souvenir. Passing a tiny nondescript street cafe besieged by road works, I saw a small tray holding a couple of used coffee cups on a grubby outside table. The picture on the tray depicted a gold-rimmed cup of coffee. Next to the cup's image a handful of coffee beans spilled onto a newspaper; the headline referred to an article about the French poet and filmmaker Jean Cocteau. How much more French could you get?

Inside the café, a couple of road workers sat silently over their coffees; the woman behind the counter looked tired. It took a while to make my request understood. She accepted the equivalent of a few dollars for the tray and I left triumphantly clutching my perfect souvenir. First, it accompanied me to Montmartre Cemetery, and now I enjoy using it daily back home.

Madeleine Tingey

Published in the Weekend Australian's "Follow the Reader" series.

the unwrapping

once   in second class
between *Torino* and *Monterosso*
near *Cinque Terre*   on the Salerno line
a man reached overhead

fumbled in his pack
pulled out a pear
of the most exquisite kind
peeled away its layers with a knife

turning it slightly to his lips
he held each slice
between thumb
& forefinger   as if to keep

each part of the body
close

as each slice disappeared
dipped in and out like the sea
the Mediterranean appeared between tunnels
rushed across the landscape in flight

in the darkness
he undresses her
devours every slice

Rose van Son

Published in Sandfire

Arrival: Warsaw

When I arrived, she said, I could see myself
in every store window
in the hollow neck or back
of every passer-by
in the turn of face of those
peering out from trains

When I arrived
my hair was not so yellow
my skin not so pale
my eyes not blurred nor dim
my ears could only hear
music of return
country of my mother
eyes that could not see

Suddenly
everyone who touched an arm
or wore a smile
looked
like
Me

Rose van Son

Published in Sandfire *Sunline Press.*

Hamelin Bay

We could not have chosen a better time. The weather was perfect. Although most mornings greeted us with complete cloud cover, even as we watched, a narrow slit on the horizon lifted gradually, like the lid of a box. Or a low cloud of fine mist was seen over the north side of the bay. But before mid-morning, without fail, an unbroken sky of radiant blue was reflected in the waters of the bay, stretching out towards the horizon. The only indication of another side to its character was the constant breaking of waves on the reefs, creating rhythmical explosions of contrasting white froth.

A pristine beach of white sand enhances the gentle curve of the shoreline, while just offshore to the south lies Hamelin Island, bearing the remains of an old lighthouse. Encompassed by the Leeuwin-Naturaliste National Park, cliffs and sand dunes covered in natural vegetation are protected as far as possible from the effects of growing numbers of enthusiastic tourists. Boardwalks prevent access to vulnerable limestone cliffs and provide information bays.

Early in the twentieth century, under very different weather conditions, this deceptively placid scene frequently became one of tragedy for ships. In good weather, four of these wrecks now attract snorkellers and scuba divers, while a reclining anchor from one of the ships marks the boat ramp and camping site. Another disaster, following a fire, resulted in the destruction of the jetty, built in 1892 for the prosperous timber industry of the area. The business ceased in the early 1900s, but the much-photographed and easily recognised remains have become an icon for the area.

At some time during the early hours of each morning, I was aware of waves gathering force and crashing up onto the beach time after time. Then vehicles towing trailers made their way to the boat ramp before daybreak, the men exchanging cheerful banter as they left the parking area. Shortly after, as I lay in partial oblivion, willing myself to stay awake and absorb the early morning sounds of this coastal environment, the throb of engines could be heard as the crayfishers left for their daily catch. On one occasion I also heard something scramble up the outside corner of the tent and looked up to witness the silhouette of a Brush-tailed Phascogale as it passed over the top.

My personal greatest joy on rising each morning was to sit on a bench above the beach, with a mug of tea in one hand, and view the early activity. Here, at Hamelin Bay, the boats are unobtrusive, designed only for a practical purpose, their presence in no way marring the tranquillity or idyllic holiday setting.

Although a short walk reveals the beauty of the surrounding vegetation, it is mainly peppermint scrub, which provides the natural shade and shelter for the camping area. Many small birds, including honey-eaters, could be spotted in the dense heath, but it was the more adaptable species that frequented the site. At the time we were there, Wattle-birds were the most vocal, but Willy-wagtails and Magpies also adapted readily to the influx of summer tourists. Each morning, we were serenaded by one Magpie in particular whose repertoire included the perfect rendition of a Willy-wagtail!

While my companions and I sat down to an outside breakfast on our prime site close to the beach, patrons from the camping area dotted the bay in skiffs and motorboats as they tried their luck. Others, having settled into a holiday routine, went about their tasks of washing dishes and sweeping out tents or caravans.

It was a companionable scene, with people stopping to chat as they passed by on their way to the beach.

Around lunchtime, as fishers cleaned their morning's catch at the site of the old jetty, stingrays turned up at the same time to wait patiently for the scraps. Just by wading into the shallows, we could feed these docile creatures by hand and, avoiding their tails, even stroke their velvet-like forms. Seagulls too, along with a small number of Pacific Gulls, bobbed around on the ripples for the opportunity of a feed. Not having experienced the totally unnatural lifestyle of 'urbanised' gulls, their manners were completely acceptable. This, together with so many other aspects, made Hamelin Bay in our south-west a delightful holiday destination.

Lyn White

On Visiting the Roman Baths

In the shadow of terraced figures,
flagstones, smoothed
by footsteps of ancient Romans,
define healing waters
of a sacred spring

Mossy growth echoes
obscure reflections in pools
Redeemed temple images
and the gilt head of Suris
symbolise a legendary past

Costumed characters depict
proletariat contribution,
when colonnaded splendour
arose from thermal energy
and a geological fault

Reclaimed for restoration
of former classic grandeur,
an amazing engineering feat
of plunge pools and aqueducts
remain a monument to mythology

Lyn White

Xi'an's Terracotta Army

My daughter, Ivana, and I, led by our tour guide, Susan Zhang, went straight to Qin Shi Huang's Mausoleum Site Museum in Xi'an, Shan Xi Province, China.

Susan presented her introduction: "This Mausoleum, with its whole area of 56,250 square metres, is so wondrous that it's been claimed as the Eighth Wonder of the World. It's also been listed as a UNESCO World Heritage Site since 1987."

"Susan, what has made it a wonder?" I wondered.

"My overall impression of this Emperor Qin's Mausoleum is that it's a grand necropolis, constructed as a microcosm of the Emperor's Imperial Palace, consisting of several offices, halls, stables, other structure and an imperial park, situated around the tomb mound.

"It's huge and magnificent. It's constructed in the period of 246 BC until 208 BC. It housed his 76-metre-tall earthen Mound. To the east of the tomb, there are four pits altogether with the total area of 25.380 square metres in this Mausoleum site. The amazing terracotta army was also produced then and placed in the pits. We can see the representation of Qin Dynasty's force, strength and wealth," Susan further elaborated.

"Wow, it's enormous," Ivana gaped.

Susan nodded: "In the three pits we are going to explore later, there are 600 trenches altogether, Wikipedia recorded there are 8000 figures of terracotta warriors, 130 wooden chariots, 520 horses, 150 cavalry horses, bronze weapons and the equipment for horses. Besides, there are other terracotta non-military figures being found, including officials, acrobats, strongmen and musicians."

"Unimaginable manual accomplishment in that era!" I gasped.

"However, they're found in fragments and pieces, and some were left with their faded colours. China's government prepared a reparation site for them to be repaired and reinstalled."

"So, mostly repaired?" I asked.

Susan nodded: "It's interesting to note that this famous Terracotta Army was accidentally found by a farmer who was trying to dig a well in 1975. There! The sign!" We were standing in the First Pit overlooking the rectangle rows of trenches.

"It's a spectacular view." I imagined the real, huge army.

Standing at the rail, Susan continued elaborating. "This First Pit is 230 metres long, and 62 metres wide. The whole area is 14,260 square metres. It simulated their military formation, consisting of chariots and infantry. They were a vanguard group of the front military formation, the rearguard infantry at the back of the formation, and the guard soldiers on both sides. Look! they are mostly facing the same direction: the east, the location of the former six kingdoms: Qi, Chu, Yan, Han, Zhao, and Wei. Just a few soldiers are facing each other."

"Wow! I can imagine how glorious and magnificent the real army was in 221 BC." Ivana stared at the awe-inspiring scene, open-mouthed.

"They're impressive!" I was staring at the rows of standing warriors with widened eyes.

Susan shifted her elaboration to the Second Pit: "From the eastern part of the First Pit, up in the north, the smaller Second Pit, sized 124 M long x 98 M wide x 5 M deep, was found in April of 1976. There are 1300 pieces of terracotta army and horses, consisting of four types of troops: infantry, cavalry, charioteers and archers or crossbenchers. They were stationed in the military formation to protect the main army."

"A duplicate of the types of the army in their time. Incredible!" Ivana exclaimed.

"In the Second Pit's exhibition area, we're going to look at the life-like warriors face-to-face, and the collection of the extraordinary artifacts. There's a lot of information provided in the museum. We can clearly observe the display of the actual size of the Terracotta Army: the general; the standing soldier; the kneeling one (half squatting and half kneeling soldier); the chariot and the charioteer; the terracotta soldier holding the chain tied to the horse; the terracotta chariot and the four horses, etc."

"You seem to be quite familiar with the display of the museum," I admired.

"It's my duty to know all of these," Susan smiled.

"You can go around with your eyes closed, I reckon," Ivana teased her.

Susan's face brightened. She described further: "In the western part of the First Pit, up on the north, the smallest Third Pit was found in May 1976. The First and Third Pits are complete, but the Second Pit is still in excavation. The Fourth Pit, located in the north part of the middle of the First Pit, was empty and left unfinished. Three years after Emperor Qin's demise, the Fourth Pit was stopped completely."

We arrived at the Third Pit before going to the Second Pit.

"What makes it more astonishing is that this Third Pit contains the military control centre. It imitates the headquarters of the military formation. It consists of four horses, one chariot, and 68 figures of terracotta warriors: charioteers, horse-riding soldiers, and infantry. Altogether they formed a mimicked military formation, such as geese's flight formation, or V-shape of military formation, which functioned as the rampart to protect the General or the Chief Commandant," Susan continued.

"A fascinating discovery!" Ivana gasped.

"As a brief overview of the whole pits, we can see their whole military formation design: the right army was in the First Pit, the left army was in the Second Pit, the control centre of the military and battle formation was situated in the Third Pit, while the unfinished Fourth Pit could be the middle army."

How amazing it was for me to imagine how Emperor Qin or his General in the middle surrounded and protected by their armies in the military formation! How marvellous the leader led the troops and won the battle triumphantly over the other six kingdoms in that age!

Reflecting on the history, I deduced that Emperor Qin must have mastered the strategy showed in this Third Pit as he was born after General Sun Tzu-544 BC - 496 BC, famous for the Art of War.

"Susan, I can vividly see that Emperor Qin must've been a great strategist," I commented.

"How brilliant their war strategy could have been!" Ivana remarked.

After looking around at the Second Pit, we entered the Exhibition Hall.

"Oh! This standing soldier looks so real!" Ivana exclaimed.

"Look! The clusters of hair were fastened in a knot. This one has a side top knot, his hair was parted in the centre," I said.

"There're top knots or side top knots. Different statues have different knots. Can you see them?" Susan pointed to the terracotta soldiers.

I observed and nodded.

"This one's got a little goatie beard," Ivana chuckled.

"Look, Ivana! The details of the individual hair look real. They were intricately plaited," I cried out to Ivana.

"There's the diversity of their hairstyles. They show different ranks. Each and every one has its unique face and features. Apart from different hairstyles, they also vary in height and uniform. Possibly it has to do with the different areas of China they came from. Moreover, originally, each one of them was painted in colours, such as purple, green, white, brown, pink, blue, red and black," Susan explained.

"If I consider the year around 200 BC the sculptures were produced, I would say their handmade sculptural troops are utterly marvellous!" I was amazed at the intricate details and the wonder of the craftsmanship.

"Unbelievable!" Ivana added.

"This Mausoleum represents the magnificence of Qin Dynasty. From the historical perspective, we can see that right after his father's demise, Qin Ying Zhen (259 BC - 210 BC) was enthroned as Qin's king at the age of 13. However, the incumbent Chancellor, Lü Bu Wei, a Confucianist, ruled as a regent who managed the kingdom effectively until the young king came of age."

"When did he order to start its construction?"

"In 246 BC."

"How absurd it could be for a teenager to prepare a tomb! Is it possible his father's early death had left a dark shadow over his mental state?"

Susan nodded: "Possible. He seemed to be obsessed with death. History recorded his quest for immortality. He sent out his physicians to look for the *elixir of life*, the medicine for eternal life."

"Obviously he was terrified with death."

"After he took over the reign from his regent, he used force and violence to kill ruthlessly to conquer the other six kingdoms."

"Full of blood! Deplorable cruelty," I commented.

"For him, it's a great achievement. Subsequently, he appointed himself as Qin Shi Huang Di – the First Emperor of Qin Dynasty, signifying he was the best, or august; divine ruler, since he was the only king who succeeded in defeating the other six kingdoms and unified the whole Qin or China," Susan said.

Ivana listened attentively.

"For the unification and standardisation of Qin Dynasty, he demanded to use one language for the whole of China, abolishing the other languages. He ordered to use the same currencies. He reformed the units of weights and measurements. He established a central government with its new system for the whole country. He used legalism – strict and cruel laws that imposed harsh punishment – he had little regard for Confucianism and Daoism." Susan showed her sound knowledge of Chinese history.

"He did leave the legacy of a united Chinese language," I nodded.

"To realise the legalism and sustain his power, he inflicted fear, terror and cruel punishment against his subjects."

"It's a social, economic and political reform. Surely, it's never been an easy task." I imagined the difficulties he must have faced.

"Sadly, he went to the extreme of 'burning the books and burying the scholars.' He killed lots of Confucianists and the intellectuals he regarded as a threat. He didn't allow different opinions. There was an abundance of repressed anger and hatred among the subjects against him. That's why there were many assassination attempts on his life," Susan continued.

"He must've been anxious, fearful and paranoid all the time. How could anybody with such a ruthless state of mind live peacefully?" I asked.

"Possible. He didn't even appoint a formal Empress. He had lots of concubines and fifty children, yet no empress tomb was built," Susan said.

"Has Emperor Qin's tomb been excavated yet?" I asked.

"No, it hasn't. A reliable historian, Si Ma Qian, recorded that for the prevention of theft or burglary, Emperor Qin set up a dire secret chamber inside the tomb, full of dangerous and fatal weapons.

"Hopefully by making use of advanced technology, the tomb will be open to the public.

"The earthen tomb mound by itself was located at the foot of Mount Li, a bit far off from these three pits. It's built in a truncated pyramidal shape. Its mound was just like the other common Chinese tombs. They imitated Confucius' way of burying his mother. I heard Confucius (551 BC – 479 BC) was the pioneer of a tomb mound. He also put up a sign to make sure he could find his mother's tomb after he returned from travelling."

"Oh, I see. That's how it originated. No wonder most Chinese tombs are all in the form of a small mound with a gravestone."

"He built the Mausoleum in such a magnificent manner. The whole terracotta army was the burial preparation to accompany him in his afterlife to assist him to combat enemies or conquer the spiritual world," Susan said.

"I have the impression he regarded the afterlife exactly the same as this world. He might've thought he needed to stay as emperor and fight enemies in his afterlife. It's so different from a Christian's view of eternal life with new heaven, new earth, new creation in the kingdom of God."

"From this Mausoleum, we can see how powerful and wealthy Emperor Qin was in China, yet how anxious, fearful, lonely and suspicious he was at the same time!"

I couldn't help but sigh.

"I have so much to digest. Still, it's worth visiting," Ivana exclaimed.

Chelsea Whitefield

My Trip to "Madhuban", India

I am flying to the Brahma Kumaris World Spiritual University in Rajasthan, northwest India.

We arrive at Delhi, where my first impressions are noise, dirt, more hi-rise than I expected, car horns beeping constantly for no apparent reason, pushbikes with 2 or 3 mounted, shops full of gorgeous materials and jewellery, and people everywhere. A twenty-four lifestyle where they live and trade on the streets and sleep wherever and whenever. I avert my eyes from the beggars who appear from nowhere, as I have been told if I give to one a hundred more will appear. Some of them have horrendous deformities that have been performed at birth so they will become professional beggars; this is a real lesson in detachment mentally. Crossing the road is hair-raising; there don't appear to be any road rules.

From Delhi to the university in Mt Abu is an 18-hour train trip, which is an experience in itself. If you leave your seat, it gets taken, and our suitcases are chained together. I fight my way over the sleeping bodies to the toilets with my roll in my bag. The Indians squat and wash. On the way back, I am offered some white powder by an Indian who isn't sleeping. I shake my head and smile.

With daylight, the poverty in the country seems worse. There are paddocks to live in, one for cremating the bodies and one is a toilet paddock. Lots of goats, pigs, cows and monkeys. I see women digging with shovels; the men watch.

We travel up the steep, narrow, winding road to Mt Abu; there is a holy man living in a cave in the mountains and I see eagles soaring. We arrive at "Madhuban", which means 'forest of honey'. There is an incredible vibration of peace, everyone smiling and welcoming. I settle in and go for a walk, watch the women in the village beat their washing on the rocks at the river's edge. They also bathe here. Back at the Ashram, I get used to using two buckets and a jug for washing and to the stand-up toilets [good for the thigh muscles.)

The day begins with meditation at 4.30 a.m. Later, I head for the kitchen to help chop vegetables. There are over 1,000 people here from many different countries; the food preparation goes amazingly well – everything is done with love. One kitchen is for making 'toli', a sweet confection the Indians love. I love the Indian tea 'chi', made by adding herbs like ginger, cardamon, cinnamon and nutmeg to the tea and sweetening with honey. Today, they are making ice cream for us all. There are mischievous monkeys here that steal almost anything and are so quick that one of the brothers has a full-time job chasing them away.

Today, a woman from Mauritius died; we had a cremation ceremony for her. We walk in a long procession up to the cremation grounds. The body is lovingly wrapped in white, sprinkled with ghee and flowers, and lifted on the pyre that has been made. Incense is lit, and as the fire burns, we meditate and send prayers and good wishes to the soul – a much nicer atmosphere than our funerals, more a farewell celebration.

I talk with the Indian brothers and sisters who have been meditating for a number of years. They are intoxicating, positive souls whose only interest is to serve humanity. They have opened hospitals and schools and are with the United Nations. Their religion is peace, they don't believe in violence, and they share their knowledge for free. They tell me this is my home and hope to see me again.

India is a land of such contrasts, from poverty to riches, yet there is an acceptance and spirituality that we have lost. The women are so colourful and graceful in their exotic costumes and a smile.

India is a land of festivals. Today is Holi, a Hindu celebration symbolising God colouring us with virtues. We have been warned that if we go to the village today, we may get coloured paint thrown over us. We have also been warned not to go walking after dark as bears and tigers prowl. We are up near the Himalayas. There is a gigantic rock where we meditate at sunset, feel the wind, hear the birds, and look down the valley – a magic place.

A last walk through the village where I stock up on the cheap oils and incense. In every street, a tailor sits at his sewing machine. I am approached from all sides by traders selling everything from jewellery to Bongo drums. The street's full of colourful people, beggars, cows, horses, camels and pigeons. I think to myself, if I was a beggar and had a choice between stealing or dying … well, there isn't much choice, is there?

The bus ride down the narrow mountain road, where I close my eyes around the hairpin bends. Driving here has to be seen to be believed, yet miraculously there are few accidents. Halfway down, we stop at the Brahma Kumaris Lotus flower complex where the fruit and vegetables are grown. They also make soap, vim and hand and body lotion and give us samples. On the overnight train to Delhi, we again chain our cases. I strap my money belt tight and manage to sleep quite well this time.

In one way, I'm a bit sad. It's like we're coming back into the dirt, yet the challenge is to keep this positivity I have gained and use it in interactions with others and in situations. I have gained inner strength and stability and realise meditation helps you to stay positive in this crazy world by getting control of your thoughts: it's an attitude of mind and choosing to be positive.

This has been a life changing experience, but I must admit I am looking forward to a nice, hot shower!

Sheila Williamson

Mind Travel

Only once have I visited India, but it doesn't take much for my mind to wander there, visualising the sights and sounds I remember so well. During the times when I was unable to travel, I found my photos and memories a valuable keepsake of all those precious moments I cherished. I am grateful, for not only did I get to see India, but I experienced the essence of life that is India. These thoughts have sustained me at times when I needed uplifting.

I look around my Perth living room and as I sit on my sofa, a mirrored cushion cover from Rajasthan slips to the floor, each tiny mirror a reflection of my many memories of India. All at once, I am high above the noisy, crazy world, on a rooftop in Delhi, a spectacular display of vibrancy and colour laid out in all its splendour. Kaleidoscopic mirrors, like souls, twinkling in the sunlight. Velvety soft textures and some that are dusty and dry. Enough cushion covers spread out to cover the clouds but not enough to block out the relentless smog that hangs over me, heavy and stifling. I wipe the sweat from my brow and look around. Everywhere, people are sitting, watching, waiting, a unique calmness among the ordered chaos.

The textiles I gathered on my journey, interwoven with the fabric of Indian life, have helped to create something of beauty in my own world. They are only part of my Indian legacy for it's not just about visiting India. It's about experiencing it every day as you get caught up in the rhythm of life.

I remember riding camels into the Thar Desert at sunset, sipping masala chai from a clay cup on the Ganges at dawn, zipping high above an ancient fort in Jodhpur, and risking my life in a tuk-tuk driving through busy Delhi streets. These memories form a montage of my journey of self-discovery, which took me 10,000 km around India.

Closing my eyes, I can still see the ever-changing images of bewitching gentle mothers with soulful brown eyes, bathing children who laugh and splash in the river. Unpredictable scenes, both unique and surreal, one moment an ancient ruin or vast towering fortress, the next a wandering cow or a cart pulled along by a camel. The tinkling of camel bells, the tooting of trucks and swerving tuk-tuks, the whistling of trains blend in with the gentle chanting of mantras. At temples, the smell of burning incense, camphor, and cow dung stimulates my senses, intensifying the memories.

Pink desert sunset skies and glimmering, shimmering moons on dark rippling water. Mesmerising turbans of red and saffron, saris of vivid pink and purple. I have no trouble remembering the relentless sounds, vibrant colours, and unforgettable spices that made my tastebuds sing. Exotic aromas and flavours of mango lassi, masala dosa, puri, parathas and poppadums. Today, wherever I find myself, smells of sun-ripened tomatoes, fresh coriander, ginger, and lemongrass will take me right back to a market stall in India, tantalising my tongue and captivating my senses.

Only once have I visited India, but my mind has been there many times.

Moira Yeldon

Other anthologies :

Footprints
The Silver Collection
Strand of Pearls
Wild Women of the West
A Gift of Jade
Life's Lessons Learnt
A Taste of Childhood
Telling Tales
Lest We Forget
Holidays and Holy Days
A Sense of Place
Cyberettes
The Ruby Collection
The Bronze Quill
Moments in Nature
Tapestry

About

The Society of Women Writers WA

The Society of Women Writers was first established in Australia in Sydney in September 1925, to bring together women writers and journalists in New South Wales. Their aims were to be a social body; to promote knowledge of literature; to encourage women writers; and to strengthen the ties of interest between Australian and visiting writers.

Until the 1970s, the Society was based in Sydney, using a postal critiquing system to keep in touch. During this decade, branches were established in other Australian states and the first Federal Constitution was adopted in 1978 with an agreement that Federal responsibility be transferred from state to state every two years. Twenty years later, the decision was made to decentralise, with each state forming its own Society.

The WA branch initially operated only through correspondence groups until the first President, Ethel Webb, was appointed in 1981 and members began to meet regularly. The Society of Women Writers WA was incorporated as an autonomous body on 25 February 2000.

Contact Details

The Society of Women Writers WA
PO Box 434
125 Stirling Street
Perth Business Centre
Western Australia 6849
Tel: 0415 840 031
Email: swwofwa@gmail.com
Web: www.swwofwa.com.au